Taking Sides

Taking Sides

A. V. Denham

ROBERT HALE · LONDON

© A. V. Denham 2008
First published in Great Britain 2008

ISBN 978-0-7090-8551-5

Robert Hale Limited
Clerkenwell House
Clerkenwell Green
London EC1R 0HT

www.halebooks.com

The right of A. V. Denham to be identified as
author of this work has been asserted by her
in accordance with the Copyright, Designs and
Patents Act 1988

2 4 6 8 10 9 7 5 3 1

Typeset in 11/14pt Palatino
by Derek Doyle & Associates, Shaw Heath
Printed and bound in Great Britain
by Biddles Limited, King's Lynn

ACKNOWLEDGEMENTS

Monmouth is an old town with a long history. The village of Otterhaven is imaginary and its villagers are purely fictitious.

My thanks go to the editorial team at Robert Hale for their helpful comments, to the staff of the Monmouth Bookshop, to Mary Newman and my supportive family. Thanks also to Carrie Hills who advised on a suitable sailing dinghy for a sixteen-year-old and who suggested the 'Flying Ant'; also to Rob and John Coles who told me about collectable Australian artists. (Margaret Olley's interiors are highly covetable and she is now an Australian National Treasure.) Thanks also to Joy Perrott, whose memories of leg injuries are still vivid.

Thanks especially to Janice Williams, whose admiring gold-work student I am, and who not only suggested the stitches for the church cushions but at the time of writing was tutoring another student in the design and making up of a stole not too dissimilar to the purple one I describe.

CHAPTER ONE

'They gave old Bert Wilson a good send-off, then.'

'Half of Otterhaven must have been there.'

'Lived in the village all his life, they do say.'

A group of villagers was gossiping in the general store in Otterhaven's St Bride's Street, waiting for Mr Powell, who was out at the back ferreting for plastic bags.

'Young Suzie came up trumps in the end. It were a good do.'

'Them ham sandwiches were a bit curled up at the edges, mind.'

As if she could contain her ire no longer, Mrs Powell, who ran the post-office counter, observed indignantly: 'They had the For Sale notice for the cottage up no more than an hour after we'd left the wake. Bert wasn't even cold in his grave.'

'Scandalous, I call it, what they're asking for that place.'

'Such a pity,' sighed Vera Crawford, who owned the gallery.'If my Jolyon could only afford to buy a house in Otterhaven I'm sure he'd marry Helen tomorrow.'

As Jolyon Crawford's reputation for philandering was second only to his love of fast cars, this sentiment was greeted in silence. All the same, the price of village houses and the difficulty of the village young to find anywhere affordable was an everpresent problem.

'I suppose some wealthy incomer will snap it up,' commented Linda Griffiths, an established villager of advancing years.

'They'll need plenty of cash. Bert Wilson neglected it something awful.'

'It was only after his wife died. When he went . . . you know.'

There was a reflective pause following this as each person present contemplated the effects of advanced senility.

'Incomers,' snorted Vera. 'They needn't think I'll bend over backwards to be friendly.'

'Silly old bat,' said Mr Powell, when all their customers had gone. 'Of course Vera'll be friendly, if an incomer uses her gallery. Stands to reason. Just as we will, won't we, my love?'

'I repeat, I am not coming with you to Canberra,' Marnie Edgerton, her body tense with determination, said vehemently a few days later on the other side of the world.

Dr Jack Edgerton, sitting at the head of the table, snorted and turned the page of his newspaper with an impatient snap.

Gemma Edgerton, Jack's wife of twelve years, suppressed a smile as she continued to spread Vegemite on a piece of toast. It would be amusing, this role reversal – stroppy parent, disapproving son – if the consequences were not going to be quite so dire.

'Why aren't you coming with us, Granny?' There was a wobble in six-year-old Felicity's little-girl voice.

A glimmer of a smile lit Marnie's eyes as she replied, 'So that I can buy Marmite. I can't get it in Perth.'

'You can't buy Marmite anywhere in Australia, Granny,' Josh pointed out with the reasoned logic of his eight years. 'Can I have another Weetbix, Mum?'

'May I,' prompted his father.

'Do stop splashing your juice on the table, Fel,' said Gemma. 'Marnie, I still don't think this scheme of yours is necessary.'

'And who will read to me at bedtime if you stay here?' Large blue eyes with a sheen of tears in them gazed at Marnie without blinking.

Marnie steeled her resolve in the face of overtly underhand tactics. 'I read to your father and to Auntie Chloë every night until they were about eleven,' she said to them. 'Don't you think it would be a good thing if your mum or your dad read to you from now on?'

At the mention of his sister's name, Jack put down his newspaper to address his parent. 'Are you telling me that the real reason you are going to England is to find Chloë, Mother?'

'And if it were?' Marnie countered defensively.

Jack snorted again as he opened his paper. 'Fortunately we don't know where she is. So I doubt if you'd succeed.' His tone suggested it would be just as well if his sister did remain out of contact with her family.

'Did Auntie Chloë like being read to?' asked Felicity.

'Yes, she did, when she was your age,' Marnie replied. There was a thickening in her voice that she tried to conceal by drinking her coffee.

'I like being read to and I'm twelve,' interrupted Ellie, the oldest of the Edgerton children. The children knew that their aunt's name was rarely mentioned, but not why. Ellie thought it was a pity to miss the opportunity to unravel a family mystery but she had other things on her mind. 'Gotta go, Mum. Izzie's dad's picking me up.'

'You'll be ever so lonely in Perth when we're in Canberra, Granny,' Felicity persisted.

'I thought you understood, Felicity dear. I'm not staying in Perth. I'm going Home. I'm going back to the UK.' Like so many new-Australians of British extraction, Marnie capitalized the Home she had not seen since she left it many years before.

'You've lived in Australia for twenty years. I thought your home was with us, your family.' Jack folded his newspaper meticulously, smoothing it along its creases. There was a pugnacious lift to his chin and his tone was aggrieved. 'How can you even contemplate returning to constant drizzle and grey skies?'

'The sun does shine sometimes, you know. It's in the order of things. My dears, I'm not abandoning you, any of you,' she said.'I just want to . . .'

'Find Chloë,' observed Jack drily.

'Oh, let's leave this for now or we'll all be late,' said Gemma impatiently.'Come on, Josh. Where did you put your shoes? Don't forget your packed lunch, Fel. School bag, Josh . . .'

Once they had all gone, Marnie ruefully surveyed the kitchen debris the family had left behind. Retirement had not brought with it unalloyed joy. She sat down with the discarded newspaper in a cushioned chair in the small garden that had always been her province. When they moved to Perth from Sydney the garden had contained wilting bedding plants and a tired herbaceous border over which its English growers had struggled with little success, their landscaping reminiscent of what they had left behind. Marnie had ruthlessly uprooted everything foreign and had restocked the garden with indigenous plants; eucalyptus and a red flowering gum, banksias and a dryandra, so that it was a shady, trouble-free haven for the Australian family, a flock of cockatoos, a noisy kookaburra, gorgeous butterflies and various nocturnal creatures.

Her declaration that she was to return to the UK instead of moving with them to Canberra had astounded and dismayed everyone.

'You love Australia and you've always said you like living with us, particularly since that business with Ellie's operations and then Father,' said Jack, when his mother first told them of her unexpected plans. 'You came to Perth. Why won't you come with us now?'

'That's the whole point, Jack. I followed your father. I moved with you to Perth. Am I being so very selfish? This time I want to do something for me.' There was something else which Marnie would not admit to her family: she also felt an urgent need to learn to live on her own.

Marnie Lucas was born in Chepstow in Monmouthshire in 1946, in a street overlooking the Severn estuary. Marnie was not particularly academic. She was, though, reasonably intelligent and very hard-working. She obtained a secretarial qualification with little difficulty, got a job in local government in the planning department and, being the age she was, continued to live happily at home. It was through this job that she met Felix Edgerton.

Felix, seventeen years Marnie's senior, was into property development in Bristol when he encountered Marnie. This was the late sixties, a time when building was booming.

Felix was a large man. Of somewhat more than medium height, he carried himself well, which gave most people – women especially – the impression that he was even bigger and taller than he was. He spent money on his clothes, which were expensively understated, and there was always about him an impression of strength and competence.

What was it that such a man found so attractive in Marnie? Maybe it was because she was almost as tall as he was, but willowy, with fair skin and intensely blue eyes. Maybe it was her essential goodness, a commodity with which Felix was not too familiar. Marnie was loving and considerate. She believed the sun shone from her husband. Marnie gave him first a son, Jack, then a daughter, Chloë. It was the advent of this daughter that persuaded Felix that reprehensible practices in the building trade might not always be shrewd. So, having by then also made a tidy sum, he decided to emigrate.

'Australia is thousands of miles away. I'll never see my family again!' his aghast wife wailed.

'Think of the excitement of a new country. Think of the weather in Sydney. You can fly home to see them all once I've made my million.' It was a promise that Felix truly intended keeping.

On their arrival in Sydney, he set about buying a modest house with a view of Middle Harbour; a few years later moving to a bigger house with a pool and the same harbour view. Within a few years he was a wealthy man, by anyone's standards, the family home increasing in size and value every five years or so.

Jack was sixteen when they arrived in Australia, Chloë was only nine. Volatile as she was, it was Chloë who made the most fuss about leaving her friends and the ghastliness of her new school. Paradoxically it was Chloë who settled very quickly and maintained that never, ever, would she leave.

From the first, Jack found it hard to make friends. Much to his parents' amazement he was drawn to academic life, putting his schoolwork first. He was not the least bit interested in football and cricket bored him to tears. But when Felix bought Jack his

11

first boat, a Flying Ant which he called *Scimitar*, the teenager was jubilant. He once told his mother that to watch his red sails swell with a fine breeze off the Tasman Sea, to feel his craft scudding over the water under a blue, blue sky was to be in paradise.

Marnie was convinced that it was *Scimitar* which prevented Jack from going to pieces, maybe taking the drugs that were as freely available in Sydney as ever they had been in the less salubrious parts of Bristol. The results of Jack's Year Twelve exams were among the top ten per cent of the country, which meant that he was able to go to the university of his choice, Sydney. Jack had Sydney and sailing, and soon, Gemma.

'You do know how much Jack'll miss you, don't you, Marnie?' That evening Gemma tackled her mother-in-law.'It may sound over dramatic, but I think that Jack feels he is being abandoned by a second parent.'

Jack's mother said softly, 'Dear, the very idea is absurd. You know that wherever I am I'd never abandon any of you. Unlike Felix,' she added woodenly. Marnie also knew that Jack, a sensitive soul, had deeply resented what he saw as his mother's newfound obsession with his disturbed sister; had never come to terms with his own feelings for Chloë whom he still considered purely manipulative. 'But Jack must also understand that I have an enormous feeling of loss because my daughter is estranged from her family.'

'You don't actually have to go back to the UK to contact her,' objected Gemma. 'Besides, Canberra is a great place.'

'No, it isn't,' retorted Marnie.'It may be the capital, but it's full of people who can't wait to get away. Do you imagine that Jack will stay in Canberra every weekend? Of course he won't,' she answered her own question. 'He'll be in Sydney for the sailing, as often as he can. You all will. Your parents will be only too delighted to see you.'

'You also,' said Gemma diplomatically, who agreed with every word her mother-in-law was saying, though she was not quite so sure how much her own mother would appreciate Marnie's participation in their social life.

'Gemma, dear, I know very well that this is a splendid oppor-

12

tunity for Jack.' It had been Jack's ambition for as long as Marnie could remember to end up with a good professorship. The University of Western Australia had been only a beginning. When, in 2000, Jack was appointed a lecturer in Perth, they had all moved there very happily. He had recently been awarded his doctorate, his subject gene therapy. Now the next step in Jack's scheme of things, a senior lectureship, was imminent.

'Jack won't want to stay in Canberra for ever,' said Gemma.

'Oh, I know that,' said Marnie.'He wants to end up in either Melbourne or Sydney. That'll mean another move in a few years. I'm sixty-one. I've enjoyed living in Perth. I daresay I might enjoy living in Canberra but I really don't want to put out tentative roots at my age only to have them wrenched up time and again. No, it's time I went Home and rediscovered my roots there. Once I have sorted out my finances I shall have more than sufficient to buy something to my taste, and exactly where I decide I should like to live.'

'Buy?' She and Jack had not expected that, so drastic an action on Marnie's part. 'And where will that be?'

Marnie shrugged.'I've not yet decided.'

CHAPTER TWO

By 1995 Felix Edgerton had seemed to be happily settled in his new life in Australia. His wife was content, working three mornings a week for a small transport firm. Jack was on course for a first-class honours degree with the best of all possible worlds, home comforts, Sydney and sailing. Felix's cherished seventeen-year-old Chloë, whom even he had to admit could be a truculent teenager, was in Year Eleven at an exclusive Sydney girls' school.

From the moment she turned thirteen, Chloë's relationship with her mother had altered catastrophically. From the loving little girl whom Marnie still remembered with bitter nostalgia, overnight she became argumentative, rebellious, hurtful. By the time she was seventeen she only addressed her mother to abuse her. Felix never heard any of this. Chloë continued to adore her father and when he was about she immediately reverted to being Daddy's little girl, totally beguiling him. He just would not believe that there were any problems between Chloë and Marnie that could not be sorted out. Moreover, if there were problems, these were entirely Marnie's fault.

It was while Jack was sailing that he met Gemma, the daughter of a boat builder. What might have happened to this relationship no one knew, but Jack, by then working as a not very well paid research assistant, got Gemma pregnant.

'We love each other,' Gemma declared.

'We want to get married,' said Jack defiantly.

Both sets of parents expressed varying degrees of shock, astonishment, and guarded pleasure. In the end there was a civil

with no harbour view, and a moderate settlement. He took with
him Bella, his nubile secretary, the last of a long line of attractive
women who had worked for him, and he took his equally nubile
eighteen-year-old daughter, Chloë, who was only five years
younger than Bella. Both women were convinced their future life
was safe in Felix's hands.

Three years later Felix had a massive heart attack and died.

From the day he left her, the only correspondence Marnie had
with her husband was through his lawyers. Felix sent infrequent
letters to his son, and signed his cards From Dad and Chloë. But
what had happened to Chloë once Felix was no longer there no
one really knew, for Jack flatly refused to attend the funeral.

Marnie could not bring herself to communicate with Bella to
discover exactly what was happening. Felix's death also coin-
cided with one of Ellie's operations and subsequent convalescence. The immediate concerns seemed to Marnie more important than the lack of communication with a difficult daughter.

Chloë continued to send e-mails at irregular intervals, though
she told her mother very little about what she was doing. Now,
a Christmas card had arrived only a few days before. It
convinced Marnie that maybe Chloë was not entirely lost to
them after all.

Jack was not impressed with the Christmas card, as he told his
mother over a sandwich lunch the day it arrived.

Marnie protested to him: 'Jack, dear, don't you think there is
the possibility that Chloë might have changed in seven years?'

'I've always known you preferred Chloë to me. Just like
Father.'

'That is utter nonsense. You should know from your own children that it doesn't work that way. It was Chloë who made the
decision to live with her father. It was Felix who took her away
from us. I've never forgiven him for that. But that doesn't mean
I abandoned Chloë in my heart.'

'So you are going back on her account.'

'She needed to learn how to cope on her own and there was
always Bella. But who knows how Bella treated her stepdaugh-

17

ter once Felix died? You know, if it hadn't been for Ellie's last operation taking place so soon after Felix died, I should have been on a plane then, just to satisfy myself that Chloë was all right. But I didn't go, so now I do have these feelings of guilt towards her. I need to make my peace with her. If any of that angers you, I'm afraid that is a problem you have to deal with yourself.'

Watching her son as he left her to return to the lab, affront in every line of his back, Marnie wondered with anguish if she were not about to try to regain the trust of a long-lost daughter at the expense of the love of a son. How complicated her family relations were, and how could she have let this happen?

In the end, Marnie did go to Canberra, to join the family as they received the keys for their new home. But she stayed only long enough for the largest of the boxes to be unpacked and for her to claim one of the five bedrooms that had its own *en suite* bathroom. 'For when I visit you all to prove that I am not abandoning you.'

So a few favourite pieces of furniture were in that room in Canberra, along with personal possessions like her sewing machine, her books and a picture, a vibrant kitchen interior by Margaret Olley, which Marnie had always loved and couldn't bear to part with now, though Felix had always thought it sentimental. Over the years, Felix had bought a number of pictures, acquiring among others a Betty Kutunga Munti and a Paddy Kunmanarra, when Aboriginal art could be bought for a song. Now these were valuable assets that Marnie was selling to obtain funds to help her with her move.

Marnie's delayed departure meant that it was the end of February before she arrived at Heathrow. Spring, she had thought. How delightful it would be to arrive in the UK in time for the daffodils, to walk with her newfound daughter under a pale-washed sky among the primroses and early blossom.

What had she done! Marnie emerged from the airport building into a howling gale; to a grey sky with darker storm clouds scudding overhead, and almost horizontal rain. And it was freezing. Of Chloë, whom Marnie had e-mailed hoping to be met by her, there was no sign, nor message. Marnie was on her own.

To Marnie's intense delight, when she returned to the hotel the following morning after a foray into Bath, where she was staying to attend to financial matters, she walked back into the foyer to discover her daughter sitting there waiting for her.

Chloë saw Marnie first and sprang to her feet.

'Mum!' she exclaimed, and threw her arms round her mother.'Wow, you do look well. God, this is totally amazing. I never expected to see you here, in Bath.'

'Chloë,' said Marnie faintly. Then she hugged her daughter, hard. Whatever she had expected, it was not this exuberance; such a display of high spirits.

'I am so, so sorry about yesterday. There was an accident on the motorway and I was stuck in a tailback for hours. Then, when I finally arrived at the airport, you'd gone.'

'I hung around for a bit. I wasn't sure you'd be meeting me.'

'Not meet you! Of course I intended meeting you.'

'Well, never mind. It's good to see you now. Um – where have you come from?'

'Usk.' Chloë grinned a little sheepishly, naming a village in Monmouthshire. 'I guess I've a lot to tell you.'

She still had that Australian inflexion in her voice, Marnie thought, even after seven years. The one that ended sentences, whatever their content, with a question mark.

'Will you have dinner with me? Do you have to get back tonight?'

Chloë was looking good. Beautiful. Her skin glowed. She was wearing her thick, glossy, fair hair loose and it hung just below her shoulders. Her blue eyes were clear and she was actually regarding her mother with affection. She was trim, in well-cut jeans with leather boots and a leather jacket. Whatever Marnie had dreaded to find, that fear was confounded. Her heart lifted.

'You look wonderful.'

'Thanks, Mum. Dinner would be really great.'

There had been such pain in losing Chloë, Marnie thought. It was almost an anti-climax, finding her like this. To lose a child – at whatever age – was unnatural. You bring them up to become an adult and move on. If a child dies young, for whatever reason, it is harrowing. If that child rejects its family, what feelings of pain, grief and guilt there are.

Marnie felt utterly bewildered by events. Here was Chloë, cheerful, happy, optimistic and quite without the resentment that, at seventeen, had been her habitual mood. It appeared that Chloë had moved on in the best of all possible ways. Then Marnie reflected sensibly that any moving on would probably bring its own complications.

CHAPTER THREE

So there was a lot of catching up to do. At a quiet corner table in a small Italian restaurant, Marnie sipped at a glass of red wine and listened to her daughter.

Chloë was at college in Usk, in Monmouthshire, part of Coleg Gwent, she said, laughing with satisfaction. She was doing a BTEC National Diploma in horticulture. 'I bet that surprises you, but I want to run a garden centre eventually.'

'I can't imagine where that comes from,' commented Marnie dazedly, for Chloë had never shown the slightest interest in any form of gardening, or plants. 'Could it be from my side of the family?'

'I guess it's a throwback from some hoary ancestor.'

'When did all this begin?'

After their arrival, once Felix had bought a house, Chloë had spent the best part of two months in Brighton doing very little but partying and sleeping late, she told her mother.

'But I soon got bored with the club scene. It was all so predictable, you know, drugs and sex and things.'

Marnie shuddered inwardly and tried not to look shocked.

'Don't look so shocked,' Chloë continued cheerfully. 'I was well out of the drugs scene and by then the whole sex business seemed so pointless.'

Marnie also registered the 'out of the drugs scene'. Wisely she decided not to pick up on it. That could come at another time.

'Bella was horrible to me, too. Though I suppose it was

mutual. I mean, I didn't do much in the house. She resented me and showed it. There were constant rows with Dad, about me, but Dad always took Bella's side. That jolted me, if you want to know,' the girl said, with the defiant lift of her chin that Marnie instantly recognized from all those years ago. 'Dad threatened to kick me out unless I got a job or went into higher education.'

'Which did you do?' Marnie asked. Chloë had not finished her Year Twelve in Sydney and while Jack had spent several vacations as a lifeguard, Chloë had said serenely that she didn't see the point in exhausting herself unnecessarily when all she had to do was ask for whatever she wanted.

'The problem was, there was no way I could get into a degree course. Dad paid for home tuition and I sat A levels and did well enough to get to college, where I started a course in business management, which seemed to please him. Anyway, he agreed to pay the fees and to set me up in a flat. But then he died.'

'Oh, Chloë. I should have come over. Or I should have insisted you came back home,' said Marnie helplessly.

'I hoped you would come over. When you didn't I just got on with things. There was a series of horrendous jobs.' Her tone of voice had altered perceptibly. 'God. Is that the time? Can't stay, Mum. I'll call you.' She got up clumsily, scraping the chair against the floor.

Marnie had the sense to realize that, for the moment, these were all the confidences she would get from her daughter and that there was no point in pushing her further. There were no more embraces. Chloë left hurriedly.

Marnie did not settle the bill immediately. Coffee was never going to be a good idea, as she'd certainly pay for it in the night. Instead, as Chloë left the restaurant, she expelled her breath forcibly and sat down again. When the waiter hurried across, she asked for another glass of wine. So that was the first hurdle over.

Marnie sipped her wine slowly. How difficult the teenage years could be, for everyone – these issues that none of them had recognized at the time. Drugs? Why hadn't her mother considered that? Marnie knew that drugs had always been available. For some reason she'd never imagined they could affect her daughter. Sex? Boyfriends? Marnie began to wish fervently that she and Felix had insisted on meeting boyfriends. But Chloë had been so adept at playing one parent off against the other.

Marnie also acknowledged that during Chloë's difficult teenage years her parents had gradually stopped talking to each other. You had to have an agreed attitude for parental discipline to work. Marnie sighed. So many mistakes. None of them made deliberately but with disastrous consequences. She paid the bill and left.

Later that night, staying up with fortitude when her body craved sleep, Marnie telephoned Jack.

'So you did manage to track down my elusive sister,' Jack said drily, but he sounded indifferent and he then spent some minutes telling her about Josh's latest sporting exploits and how well Ellie had settled into her new school.

In truth, Marnie was aching to hear about her grandchildren. 'I miss them so much,' she said. 'Is anyone there to talk to me?'

'Mother, they are far too busy. It is a school day, you know.'

Was he punishing her for what he saw as her defection? Of course he was. Then Marnie remembered that Jack and Gemma had given Ellie an e-mail address when she left her Perth school so that she might keep in touch with her friends. Despite objections, Ellie had insisted on being 'thegirlwiththesilverflute'. Now there was nothing to stop Marnie from sending Ellie an e-mail herself.

'I must phone at the weekend next time. Do give them all hugs and kisses from me, won't you, Jack?'

'Yes. Of course.' He sounded warmer. 'But aren't you coming home straight away? I mean, now that you've seen Chloë there's not much point in staying, is there?'

Marnie suppressed a sigh, telling her son that she most certainly was going to continue with her plans to find somewhere to settle.

23

'I think I might give myself a holiday next winter. There is a lot to be said for the Australian sun at this time of the year.'

'Finding it cold, are you?'

She gritted her teeth at the satisfaction she heard clearly. 'The chill goes right through you,' she replied cheerfully. 'But, hey, I'll join you for Australia Day next January.'

'Have you really decided to live here, in Chepstow?' Chloë asked. She was visiting her mother in the B&B to which Marnie had moved.

Marnie sighed. 'If you want to know the truth, I'm a bit disappointed in Chepstow. It's grown out of all recognition.'

'Mum! How many years ago was it you lived here?'

'Far too many. There isn't a soul left I remember, or who remembers me.' She had lost touch with so many friends years ago. That was something that had happened very soon after she had married Felix. He was scathing about her friends. As the girls married, one by one, he very soon showed contempt for their choice of husband. Gradually the mutual visits became scrappy letters. The scrappy letters became annual Christmas cards. With some, these ceased after a few more years, even before the Edgertons went to Australia.

'Well, there it is,' sighed Marnie.'I shall just have to find new friends.' Not so easy at her age, she thought dismally.

'I don't remember you having all that many friends in Sydney. Dad didn't really do friends, did he?' Chloë observed.

'I think the way he did business meant he wasn't the type of man to confide easily.'

'Just like Jack, then. Mum, you know you were saying that you wished you'd come over when Dad died? Well, I always knew you wouldn't, because of Jack. And I didn't blame you, honestly I didn't, but I certainly couldn't have gone back to Sydney. I'd left too much baggage behind.'

'Are you trying to tell me you were jealous of your brother?' In the same way that Jack was so obviously jealous of Chloë?

'God, no. Jack's a prat, and I never did care for Gemma, but I did understand that Ellie was very important to you and everyone knew how much work there was involved with her heart condition.'

'I did it gladly,' Marnie said defensively.

'Of course you did, but then the other babies came and obviously you were even more wrapped up in Jack's family. But it wasn't only that. I just knew that the moment I got back to Sydney the old crowd would suck me in again. You know.'

'I don't think I do. But I think I was very unperceptive. I take it you are referring to what you called the drugs scene the other day?'

'Why do you think I was so impossible when I hit thirteen?'

'Were you impossible?'

'Mum . . .' Chloë looked at her mother, discovered a small smile, saw the sheen of tears.'You were the one person I thought would see what was happening. When you didn't I just hated you.'

'Oh, Chloë, come here!' Marnie held out her arms to her daughter. Chloë came into them reluctantly but after a moment her body seemed to relax. It was only a brief hug, but it was a real embrace. 'I knew you disliked the restrictions I tried to impose. You know how unsuccessful I was. I hoped you didn't actually hate me. I thought it was just teenage angst . . .'

'I started smoking when I was twelve. The drugs began two years later.' She stated it baldly, as though it were of no moment. 'We, the crowd, met on the beach. You remember?'

'I thought you went there to swim.'

'Mum . . . Anyway, it wasn't serious, at first. But by the time I was seventeen there were two of the boys into heroin. I stopped very much short of that. But I knew perfectly well what would happen if I went back to Sydney. Coming over here had given me the chance to break the habit. I mean, it was go out, find a new supplier or quit. I tried the club scene for a while, but didn't much like what I saw. The girls were daggy, the boys were either pimply or just plain horrible. So when Dad gave me his ultimatum I took that as a sort of message. And, to tell the truth, I was afraid I was in danger of frying my brains so it wasn't all that hard to stop. Then Dad died.'

'Did your father know any of this?' Cold anger was beginning to seep into Marnie's veins. Anger at both herself and Felix. She'd been at fault, but Felix was no less culpable. Or was she being unfair? How much was ill health already dragging him down? Was issuing an ultimatum Felix's method of coping with his wayward daughter?

'Dad hadn't a clue. I think he thought that if you were taking drugs you needed an aspirin, or possibly an antibiotic. Bella might have known otherwise. But, as I told you, we didn't get on. So, if you don't like Chepstow, where are you going to look next?'

The abrupt change of subject had Marnie reeling. There was so much more she wanted to know: like just how hard had it been for Chloë to stop the drugs and how difficult had she found it to return to studying? She wanted to tell her how very proud of her she was to have achieved what she had. All of it needed to be said, soon.

'A sheaf of particulars came in the post this morning,' Marnie replied, only a little unsteadily.'I've just had time to separate them into the obviously unsuitable and those worth considering. You know, you ask for a small town house or cottage and they send you details of a five-bedroomed family house in a new estate. I ask you.'

'We'll spend the afternoon driving round to see the outside of a few of them,' said Chloë, also offering to do the driving. 'It will give you a better opportunity to look at the countryside.'

There wasn't much that tempted Marnie to arrange to look over the following week but, as Chloë pointed out, there were other agents to visit and other areas to consider. Chloë said that if her mother liked the look of a house in the rain, it would look even better when the sun shone.

'I'm so proud of you. You do know that, don't you?' Marnie said, as she hugged Chloë goodbye.'I think you're amazing. I am so appalled that you had to go through all this on your own and I am so sorry I wasn't there for you.'

Chloë shrugged as she moved away. All the same, Marnie could see that the praise had touched her. 'It's all right, Mum. It was partly my own fault as well as circumstances.'

'Well, I am here for you now, if you need me, and thank you so very much for looking after me today.'

In the middle of the following week, Marnie found Otterhaven. She hadn't exactly found it, for she vaguely remembered its existence from her childhood but she didn't think she had ever done more than pass through it in a car. Otterhaven was a largish village not far from Monmouth, in the Wye valley. She loved Otterhaven from the moment she entered it, saw the small row of useful shops, the old terraced houses mainly of pink Monmouthshire stone (sadly none for sale), the village pond and the green beside it.

A Monmouth estate agent had sent her to view two properties, a small terraced house in Otterhaven's new development and 2 Church Lane. The first was sensible. It was semi-detached, exactly the right size, with two good-sized bedrooms and a tiny one where she could store things or use as a study. It had a bathroom and a downstairs shower room. It also had a garage and a small garden. It was the right price. It was also boring.

The terraced house in Church Lane was structurally sound. Its bathroom made Marnie's eyes (accustomed to Australian ideals of space and modern living) widen in horror. Its kitchen was so elderly it was positively retro. The garden was a wilderness, though Marnie suspected there were some lovely old roses and interesting shrubs hidden in its depths. The house had belonged to an elderly widower who had lived there all his life and whose heirs wanted a quick sale. Doing it up, if she bought it, would occupy Marnie for months.

'It would probably be a good investment,' said Chloë thoughtfully.

'I am amazed,' said Marnie. 'I was sure you'd advise me to buy the new house. But I do have to make a quick decision. The agent says that there has already been an offer, but a very low one and by someone in a chain.'

'You haven't actually got your money from the auction yet,' pointed out Chloë cautiously.

Marnie laughed. 'Your father would have said go for it.'

'No, he wouldn't. Dad would have taken one look at its decrepitude and walked away.'

'I shall buy it,' declared Marnie Edgerton.

CHAPTER FOUR

Marnie had bought herself a laptop and organized broadband. If she had learnt her lesson the hard way over Chloë, she knew she must not make the same mistake over Ellie and she knew she must keep in regular contact with Jack. How very much easier it was, she thought cravenly, to tell her son about the cottage at one remove.

For Jack, in Canberra, reading his mother's latest e-mail out loud to Gemma, exploded.'I cannot believe what she has done,' he said, aghast.'I suppose that idiot sister of mine talked her into it because it was cheap.'

'Surely even Marnie wouldn't do anything to jeopardize her future, even if Chloë was stupid enough to talk her into it. You'll have to speak to her, Jack, or go and see for yourself what's going on.'

'And when do you imagine I'd have the time to do that?'

'It's one or the other. You don't want your mother coming back absolutely penniless, do you?'

So Jack found time to phone his mother.

'I am not being stupid,' Marnie told him forcefully.'And your sister has had nothing to do with my decision. Chloë set out the pros and cons very clearly. But I love this place. It's so quaint.'

'Quaint, Mother? I suppose you mean that it's falling down?'

She described the cottage to him in detail.'Structurally it's sound. It just needs lots of TLC.'

He said grudgingly: 'I suppose you could make a bit of a

profit, when you come to sell. And at least it's something for you to do.'

'Quite. Jack, is Ellie there?'

Apparently Ellie was hanging on to her father's arm.'Granny. Granny. I got your e-mail to me. Awesome. My friends think you're ever so cool e-mailing me from the other side of the world.'

Feeling very technologically with it, Marnie asked about the orchestra and her friends.'Please e-mail me back occasionally,' she begged Ellie, as one grandchild was about to pass her on to the next. Both Felicity and Josh said a few words (Josh said a very few) then he gave the instrument back to his father.

'Do you have a good lawyer, Mother? That's very important.'

'I think you'll find that the searches and so on will be done competently, Jack. Yes, Chloë suggested I use a Monmouth firm called Firmer & Jenkins. I'm seeing a very competent young woman called Ms Firmer. I'm sure you'd approve.'

Marnie had almost decided to put names of local solicitors in a bowl and just pick one randomly. Then Chloë had mentioned that she knew one of them, a Polly Firmer. 'I don't exactly know her, but some of the local students belong to the Young Farmers' Club and occasionally Simon Hunter lets us use his land for events. I should have explained. Polly Firmer is married to Simon Hunter. She just uses her maiden name for her professional work.'

'That's interesting. I went to school with an Alison Evans who married a Firmer. We continued to write to each other when we were married but didn't meet again. And I never met her husband at all. It's difficult to maintain relationships at a long distance, though I think we stopped exchanging Christmas cards only a few years before Felix left me. I'll get in touch with Firmer and Jenkins and ask to see this Polly.'

The solicitors, Firmer & Jenkins, occupied one of the Georgian town houses in the centre of Monmouth. Polly Firmer was a small, dynamic woman of an age Marnie found difficult to estimate. Dark, poised and elegantly dressed, Polly inspired confidence the moment she came into the reception to meet Marnie, her hand outstretched and with a warm smile on her face.

'My office is on the first floor. It has a lovely view, but if you would prefer not to use the stairs we have a room available on the ground floor.' When Marnie assured her gravely that she was perfectly able to climb stairs, Polly went on, 'I thought you looked very fit. Please don't be offended, but we have to make sure about that nowadays.'

Marnie did so hope that the villagers of Otterhaven had not already formed the opinion that a decrepit geriatric was coming to live among them.

The interview proceeded along expected lines. By the end of it, Marnie was reassured that she had made sound choices, both of her future abode and of her new solicitor. As she gathered her things together at the end of the interview, she hesitated. Then she said, as she had said to Chloë:

'I was at school with an Alison Evans who later married a Luke Firmer. We were part of a group of friends and Alison and I corresponded for many years. But you know . . .' Marnie shrugged. 'Gradually the letters became the Christmas round robin and just before my divorce the cards stopped altogether. I suppose you wouldn't be any relation?'

'Goodness!' As Marnie rose from her chair, Polly said with an enigmatic expression on her face: 'I'm their daughter.'

'How splendid. I did wonder because you have a certain look about your mouth that reminds me very strongly of your mother. Then you'll be able to confirm that I have the correct address. I must get in touch. There aren't any of my old friends living locally, as far as I can discover, and I should so like to see Alison again.'

'I can do better than just give you their address. Why don't you come to tea on Saturday? Then I can fill in all the family details.'

'That's extremely kind. But . . .'

'Perhaps you are spending the day with your daughter?'

'Chloë took time off last week while I was house-hunting so she tells me she has college work to do this weekend. That would be so kind of you, if it isn't a bore.'

'Not at all. I gather you know I'm married to Simon Hunter.' Polly was drawing a quick sketch map of Otterhaven's environs as she spoke. 'Just continue on this road for about a mile and you'll find our driveway on the left. You can't miss it. It's still called Hunter's Farm and it's been in the family for generations. Shall we say threeish?'

Marnie had spent two mornings in Bath buying clothes for her new life: tweed trousers, a long wool skirt, sweaters, a fleece jacket and a waterproof anorak, and leather boots, along with various necessary items of thermal underwear. At the end of her shopping spree she made an impulse buy of a very elegant (and expensive) tweed coat which was still in the sales. On this Saturday, she looked at the lowering sky and walked into Chepstow to buy Wellingtons.

She found Hunter's Farm without any difficulty. There were wrought iron gates, opened wide against a hedge that seemed to be mainly bramble and beyond the gates a cattle grid. She did notice that the wrought iron was rusty and one of the gates sagged and the unmade-up driveway was full of weeds. But when she reached the farm she found modern, purpose-built barns and cattle sheds. Beyond the farm buildings was the farmhouse, a Welsh longhouse built of stone. Marnie thought it was beautiful, clad in wisteria and an ancient climbing rose. It had a small garden in front that was covered with a few late snowdrops and masses of daffodils, and from the kitchen window, where it appeared Polly and Simon spent much of their time, there was a long view towards the Black Mountains.

'You can see the Skirrid on a clear day,' said Polly. 'A view is a dreadful time waster, but I do so love it. If I have urgent work to do I use a desk in the living-room that has no distractions at all. This part of the house dates back to the early years of the eighteenth century, but recently Simon came across a well that seems to be even older.'

Simon Hunter, who joined them for a quick cup of tea, was a tall man with hair already showing more than a sprinkling of grey. His eyes crinkled at the corners and his skin was weather-beaten. His manner was calm and quiet, his smile beguiling.

He told Marnie that some years previously he had been able to buy farmland on which fertilizers had not been used for twenty years. 'I have two meadows that are just a mass of wild flowers in June: spotted and greater butterfly orchids, birds-foot trefoil, knapweed, ox-eye daisies, and hay rattle. When the hay rattle turns golden and you can hear a rattling sound you know it's time to cut.'

'I'd forgotten that, if I ever knew it,' said Marnie.

'You should just come and see our butterflies.'

'Simon cuts the sward after the flower seeds have fallen and afterwards brings in young stock to graze so that a soil-enriching mulch cannot fertilise the meadow and prevent spring germination,' Polly said, her pride in her husband evident.

'So we gain, as do our neighbours who need additional grazing. I'd like to think our old meadows might become flower-rich grasslands, but it'll take time. I mean it, that you should come and see us when our meadows are at their most beautiful. You see, we open for visitors and give the proceeds to charity. It's good to have new blood in the village,' Simon ended.

Marnie laughed at that. 'New, but not very young blood.'

'But you have a daughter. Maybe she'll settle in the area. It's when the young leave we have problems.'

They talked a little more about village affairs and then he left them, saying he had work to do. Marnie said to Polly: 'Does your Simon have a younger brother?'

Polly spluttered over her tea with amusement. 'Actually, he does,' she said soberly, 'but Nicholas fell out with his father and even though the old man died four years ago, Nicholas and Simon still barely acknowledge each other if they happen to meet.'

'How sad.'

'Families do the weirdest things. More tea?' When Marnie declined, Polly said: 'I'm sure you were wondering why I didn't just give you my parents' address. It was partly because I had another appointment, mostly because I needed time to explain about their circumstances. It's just that my mother isn't very well. You see . . .' Again she hesitated.'Oh, for goodness' sake, there is no need for me to be so secretive. The fact is, my mother has Alzheimer's.'

Slowly, hesitantly, almost as if she were ashamed of the very fact of senile dementia, Polly told Marnie about her mother. Over the years, Alison had acquired a reputation in the village for being something of a recluse, one who was rarely seen at social gatherings, preferring to spend her time in her own home.

'When we were small I remember it being so different. I mean, we would go to children's parties and Mum would take us and she always had plenty to say to the other mothers.'

Marnie thought back to their schooldays. She and Alison had first met at the girls' school in Monmouth when they were eleven. But Alison lived in a village on the far side of Monmouth and, like Marnie, she came to school by bus. There were not very many opportunities for the girls to meet at the weekends – which, in any case, were taken over by homework and family matters. They rarely saw each other in the school holidays, but when each new term began their friendship was renewed on the old, familiar pattern.

'Mum had a wonderful garden. So productive. She'd loathe this, wild and very often unkempt.' Polly gestured towards her own garden as she explained that Alison grew soft fruit, and with it in the summer she made jams and conserves and later on in the autumn she made chutneys and marmalades, selling her products at the Women's Institute stall in Monmouth's market. 'The locals accepted her for what she was and no one appeared too concerned when she became a little vague. I mean, we all thought it was Mum being Mum.

'Although we didn't recognize it at the time, that was the start of it,' Polly continued. 'My father took Mum's illness so hard. He simply refused to accept that there was anything wrong at all that couldn't be put right in some way. He was very much into vitamins and exercise, which was the sort of regime Mum liked, too. Then, about five years ago, what had been vagueness became a more serious memory loss. Dad did try to get medical help for Mum. The doctors said at first that her illness wasn't serious. Then they said it wasn't serious enough to warrant drugs.'

'That seems a little hard,' said Marnie.

'It totally bewildered Dad. It was then that he took early retirement – yes, of course, he was the original Firmer – saying that the work was becoming too much for him. I'd recently come back to Monmouth and joined the firm, so there was still to be a Firmer practising law.'

'I expect that pleased him enormously.'

'Yes, it did,' said Polly, sounding complacent.'It was what I had always wanted, too. Anyway, with Dad at home, Mum seemed to be able to manage.'

'So your father is looking after your mother. How very caring.'

'Yes, and no,' replied Polly. 'Maybe if he had sought alternative medical advice sooner, they might have started her on the drugs and controlled the whole thing better. I don't know. Nowadays all you hear about are the cutbacks in the NHS and the difficulty of being prescribed the best drugs for whichever condition it is you have. Anyway, Mum is still living at home.'

'But Alison doesn't care for visitors?' suggested Marnie carefully.

'Mostly she seems quite normal. Then her brain does a flip, or whatever happens to it, and she has to be watched all the time, mainly in case she manages to hurt herself.'

'That must be so wearing, not being sure how she is.'

'It is,' agreed Polly fervently.'My father won't hear of me taking time off work but a couple of times a week I spend the night with him to take the responsibility off his shoulders for a while.'

'It must be incredibly difficult for you all. I had no idea. You must say if you think it would be better for me not to visit at all.'

Polly thought for a moment. 'You know, I believe it might be a good idea for you to visit. It would have to be when Mum's not having a bad day but it might stimulate her. I'll definitely talk to Dad.'

'As long as my visit wouldn't cause Alison any anxiety,' said Marnie. 'Don't people who suffer from Alzheimer's become upset if they see something as a challenge too far?'

'I'll see what Dad says.'

CHAPTER FIVE

The money from the sale of her aboriginal art became available at just the right time for Marnie to buy 2 Church Lane without a bridging loan. Thanks to Polly's recommendation, she also found herself a local builder, with a plumber, who was willing to move into the cottage the moment the deeds were signed to put in a new bathroom and the central heating. Marnie had decided that with a considerable amount of scrubbing she could manage with the kitchen as it was. But with her blood thinned by the Australian sun, the lack of heating and the appalling bathroom was another matter.

Chloë was very amused and teased her mother relentlessly. 'There you go,' she said. 'You'll be giving Aussies a bad name if people start thinking we can't cope with the odd cockroach. Besides you know everyone believes we keep snakes in the dunny.'

'I thought it was spiders.'

Chloë shuddered. 'Remember that time in the park when no one dared use the dunnies because of the Redback spiders up in the rafters? Do you remember how their creepy, dangling threads enveloped the cisterns like a shroud?'

Marnie smiled, thinking back to that day, not long after they'd arrived in Australia, when the family had gone into the Blue Mountains for a barbie. She'd mentioned the spiders casually, describing black ones with a distinctive red spot. Their friends had been horrified, for Marnie had given a vivid description of one of Australia's most feared arachnids.

'Bella is Aussie-born, isn't she?' asked Chloë now.

'Whatever made you think of Bella? Ah, the Black Widow, I suppose, the other name for the Redback. I don't imagine she was really quite as bad as that.'

Chloë gave her mother an old-fashioned look. 'What is it you want to know, Mother?'

'I just wondered how you got on with her.'

'I thought I told you. We didn't get on. Though I'm willing to admit that was partly my fault.'

'What did happen to her once your father died?'

'She married again, pretty quickly, as a matter of fact.'

'You're not suggesting . . .'

'I shouldn't think so, Mum. Dad was an astute man. I think he'd have known if Bella was having it off with anyone else. Of course, she did have a temper and he didn't have everything his own way.'

'How very different from our own dear home,' said Marnie drily.

Again Chloë gave her mother a quizzical look. 'Yes, well, Bella did very nicely out of the will. Not as nicely as she would have done if they'd had a child.'

'Did your father want more children?'

'Probably not. But apparently he'd made a will giving half his estate to Bella, if there was a child, the other half to be shared between Jack and me. Since there was no child, Jack, Bella and I shared Dad's estate. After all those years with him you didn't come out if it very well, did you, Mum?'

'I did well enough,' said Marnie defensively. 'Your father made sure I would have a comfortable pension long before there was any suggestion of the divorce. And everything I earned myself, I kept separate. I'm by no means wealthy but I have enough. Are you still in touch with Bella?'

'God, no. I can't imagine why I would want to be.'

'I think I feel, well, not quite responsible . . .'

'What rot! I thought you hated Bella. I did,' said Chloë feelingly.

'I disliked her very much, at the time. Though it was for what she had done rather than the woman she was. Of all Felix's secretaries – and he got through a lot in his time because he was so intolerant of mistakes – Bella was the one I never really knew. I suppose that was significant. Anyway, I never truly hated her, any more than you hated me when you were a teenager. And if she's remarried there is obviously nothing to concern myself about.'

'I think the man she married is something in the City. I heard she certainly did well enough for herself. Mum . . . Did Dad have, you know, affairs?'

'Why do you ask?'

'I just wondered if Bella had been the first.'

Marnie sighed. 'She wasn't the first. Oh, Felix was very discreet. But there were certain signs . . . He'd buy new clothes, new toiletries. He'd have a reason why he had to be away for a long weekend. Oddly enough, whatever was going on stopped very soon after the long weekend.'

'Didn't you ever say anything?'

'What was there to say? They didn't last. They didn't take anything from us, as a family, I mean. I let it go.'

'Until Bella.'

'No, it was your father who decided to leave me. I'd had my suspicions but I thought she was just another fling. How wrong I was. Still, there it is. Anyway it would seem she's unlikely to want to return to Sydney.'

'I shouldn't think so.'

'I'm glad I asked, though,' said Marnie Edgerton.

It was going to be several weeks before Marnie was able to move into 2 Church Lane, despite her determination to settle herself into Otterhaven at the earliest possible moment. Inevitably problems manifested themselves. The wiring was found to be hopelessly inadequate. There was damp in the bedroom Marnie wanted to use herself, caused by a broken gutter and leaking down pipe. There was blown plaster in both the kitchen and the sitting-room because there was no damp-proof course. Marnie moved out of the B&B in Chepstow and into a small B&B on the edge of the new development in Otterhaven, and gave the cottage over to the builders. She also allowed herself to be persuaded into installing a shower and downstairs loo in the little room she had thought to use as a study.

'Another selling point?' asked Chloë.

'Exactly so,' replied Marnie.

So Marnie was able to spend the days that were not wet or frosty in her new garden. Not that this work involved much more than hacking back some of the worst brambles. She discovered drifts of bulbs that would have to be left until their leaves died back. There was a huge old buddleia that she was able to prune severely, also several old roses. She cleared undergrowth round a lilac that looked as though it was going to flower prolifically and round a flowering currant just coming into full bloom. Chloë was good at identification, which greatly impressed her mother, but she insisted that Marnie would just have to wait until she discovered exactly what there was in her garden before she did anything too radical.

It was late April with blossom everywhere in Otterhaven, a week before her move into 2 Church Lane, when Marnie received a call from Polly Firmer suggesting that she might like to visit Alison and Luke for a cup of tea that afternoon.

'I hope you didn't think I'd forgotten about you,' Polly said apologetically. 'But Mum had a few bad weeks and it's only now that Dad thinks it would be all right for you to call.'

'Are you sure it'll be all right?' Marnie asked anxiously. 'I really wouldn't want to distress Alison.'

'Dad is so looking forward to meeting you at last.'

'Me, too. Will you be there?'

'I'm working. They're expecting you at 3.45, unless it's terribly inconvenient. See you sometime soon, though? I do hope you're not too busy with your move?'

'It's fine. The builders haven't quite finished in the sitting-room and I am going to redecorate that myself, but they actually managed to find me a reconditioned Aga, which they've already installed, so I shall be able to sit in the kitchen in the evenings and be as warm as toast. The new curtains arrive next week. I was only going to do a little more work in the garden this afternoon, so this will be a real treat.'

Luke and Alison Firmer lived at The Dingle, on the old road out of Otterhaven, just before the turning to Ottergate Castle where the ground dipped and a small stream flowing from the hill on which the castle stood entered the village. This stream, with overgrown banks and what looked like ancient stepping stones that must have been the original ford, was crossed by an old stone bridge. Marnie, who was wearing her long wool skirt and black leather boots with the heathery tweed coat she had found at the end of the sales, had decided she would do best to drive there.

What Marnie took to be The Dingle was surrounded by a high stone wall behind which were tall shrubs and a few deciduous trees, making the garden completely private. But there was no name on the gate – which was open – that Marnie could see. She drew in to the entrance and let the car's engine idle while she looked for her instructions in her bag.

A dirty Land Rover pulled in behind her and a scruffily dressed man with filthy boots got out. At the sight of him, Marnie hastily closed her window and checked that her doors were locked.

The man asked cheerfully: 'Are you lost? May I help you?'

Scruffy but probably not dangerous, nor a mere farm labourer, the city streetwise Marnie thought, and wound down her window.

'I'm looking for The Dingle,' she said. 'There isn't a name on the gate so I thought I'd better check my instructions.'

'It's right here. Er ... do you know the Firmers? It's all right, I'm Ian Beresford, not a desperado. We live at Ottergate Castle. You know, the turning just ahead of you, by the bridge.'

'I'm Marnie Edgerton and I've just bought a cottage in Church Lane. I was at school with Alison but I've been living in Australia so I've never met Luke.'

'Number two? Then welcome to Otterhaven, Marnie Edgerton.' He seemed about to put his rather grubby hand through the window, then he grinned ruefully and gave her a

41

friendly wave instead. 'You must come and visit. I'll get my wife to phone.' He hesitated. 'I hope you find the Firmers well.'

The driveway to the house was gloomy from the trees and overgrown rhododendrons that Marnie had seen from the road. On its open side there was a wide bed of heathers interspersed with dwarf conifers and beyond the heathers there was a lawn and several rose beds, all dug and neatly mulched with manure. She guessed that behind the house was the sunny garden where Alison spent her time with her soft fruit.

The Dingle was early Edwardian, a double fronted and substantial red-brick house with an ornate wrought-iron veranda that needed painting. Marnie left the car near the garage and went to the front door and rang the bell. It was an old-fashioned brass bell pull and it clanged satisfactorily somewhere deep inside the house. After a moment, the door was opened and a man whom Marnie presumed must be Luke Firmer stood on the doorstep to welcome her.

'Hello,' he said.

His voice was low, gravelly. Marnie wondered if he'd been a smoker in the past. He was a tall man who held himself erect, making him look taller still. Dressed conservatively in cavalry twill trousers and a greenish tweed jacket with a check shirt underneath, he was even wearing a tie. Marnie wasn't sure what she had expected. She thought she had probably become too used to the informality of the Australians and she was enchanted.

'You must be Marnie. Do come in.'

Luke Firmer would have been devastatingly good-looking in his youth, she thought dreamily. He had what used to be called craggy good looks, with a cleft chin, and his hair, though quite grey, was still abundant. But it was his eyes that mesmerized her. They were very dark; impenetrable as they held her gaze. Absurdly, and in a snap judgement that was unlike her, Marnie thought there was an aura of sadness about his face, the way those eyes ought to be etched with laughter lines but instead betrayed wariness.

'Marnie Edgerton?' He held out his hand and Marnie took it.

Marnie blinked, realizing she had yet to greet her host. She let go of his hand quickly, thinking how extremely absurd it was to be found wanting in the social graces – as though she were nothing more than a colonial bumpkin. 'I do hope my visit really is convenient.'

'Come in, please come in. There's too cold a wind outside today to stand here talking.' He moved away from the front step, holding the door open for Marnie to enter.

Feeling as though she was entering a veritable lion's den, Marnie followed him into the hall.

CHAPTER SIX

Marnie had pulled herself together by the time she had crossed the threshold of The Dingle. 'I've been so looking forward to meeting you, and seeing Alison again,' she told her host, only to find that Luke Firmer was regarding her now with a tinge of amusement, as though he were only too well aware of the effect he was having on her. She gritted her teeth in annoyance.

'We really wouldn't have asked you for tea if Alison were not having one of her good days,' Luke assured her.

'Of course not.' Glad that she had dressed up for tea, and disconcerted by the suspicion that he was laughing at her, Marnie handed Luke a small branch of cherry blossom, the bottom of which she had carefully wrapped in damp tissue and covered with a plastic bag. 'I'm sure this is coals to Newcastle but there is so much blossom in my new garden and I thought Alison might not want to pick any of hers for the house.'

'That's a kind thought. Come into the drawing-room,' Luke said, putting the blossom on a table where a telephone also stood, taking her coat and, after he'd hung it up somewhere, leading the way across the hall to a door on the far side.

His tone of voice was so warm that Marnie decided she was being overly sensitive. Giving herself another mental shake, she followed Luke. Used to the spaciousness of the average Australian living-rooms in newly built houses, Marnie was still aware of the subtle differences between English drawing and sitting-rooms. This sunny drawing-room was large, with floor-to-ceiling windows. There were beautifully draped curtains, comfortable chairs upholstered in chintz and occasional tables on which were displayed pieces of silver and a few china figurines, mainly of shepherds and shepherdesses. The floor was polished wood and on the floor lay several silk Persian rugs, subtly coloured by vegetable dyes. Standing by the window gazing into the garden was a woman. Her hair had been styled recently and she was wearing a long purple skirt and a purple jumper and a thick, long purple and black cardigan.

'Alison.' Marnie spoke her name quietly. The woman turned. 'You've not changed a bit. I would have recognized you anywhere.'

'Hello, Marnie. Do sit down.'

Marnie hesitated. Her instinct had been to embrace an old friend but Alison Firmer moved away from the window, gesturing towards an easy chair and sitting down herself, so the moment passed.

'I think I'll fetch the tea,' Luke said.

It was a subtle hint that the afternoon visit was not going to be prolonged, Marnie realized. Perhaps Alison's day was not such a good one after all. But it appeared she was wrong.

'I would have known you, too. Such a pity we lost touch,' said Alison warmly. 'But there, it happens. I know you've met Polly. Our son, Rupert, doesn't live round here, unfortunately. He's married now, did you know that? He and Lisa live in Canterbury so we don't see very much of them. No children, yet, so I don't have any grandchildren, more's the pity. I'd love to see grandchildren running round the garden.'

'No, you wouldn't,' said Luke, coming back into the room pushing a trolley on which was a silver tea service, some fine bone china and several plates of sandwiches, biscuits and a sponge cake. 'You'd be afraid they would kick balls into your borders. How many grandchildren do you have, Marnie?'

They discussed grandchildren while Luke offered tea – 'Milk or lemon?' – and passed the plate of sandwiches.

'Cucumber sandwiches! Delicious.' Marnie put her plate

down and opened her handbag for the photographs of Ellie, Josh and Felicity, which she kept there in a small leather folder. As Alison took the folder, Marnie observed a fading bruise on her wrist.

After she'd admired the photos, Alison wanted to know why Marnie had chosen Otterhaven to live in and Marnie reminded her about Chepstow. That led to reminiscences of their schooldays, during which Alison, laughing animatedly, recalled several incidents that Marnie had totally forgotten. Marnie did remember, though, how much she had liked Alison then and how much she had enjoyed her company. Why had she allowed herself to lose touch? It was so unnecessary with all the modern methods of communication.

But the hunch that this first visit to the Firmers' shouldn't be extended for too long persisted. When she had finished her tea, Marnie rose to her feet.'It has been such a pleasure, seeing you again after all these years, Alison,' she said warmly.'I wondered if there would be any of my old friends left in the vicinity and I'm so delighted to have found you.'

'I don't think there is anyone else living nearby, is there, dear?' Luke said.'Let me get your coat, Marnie. You must come again.'

'Yes. That would be good,' said Alison.'Come to tea next week.' She sounded as though she meant her invitation.

'I should like that.' Marnie followed Luke into the hall, where he helped her on with her coat. 'Thank you for tea,' she said.

'Thank you for coming. We don't see too many visitors.' He opened the front door for her and went outside with her to her car. 'Alison isn't . . .'

'Yes. Polly did tell me,' Marnie said hurriedly, not wanting the man to have to spell out the nature of his wife's ill-health. 'But I would like to come again. If I'm invited.'

'Oh, you will be.' Luke smiled, his smile crinkling his face around his eyes. 'But it might be better if I rang to confirm in the morning. Today week? Just another short visit, you understand?'

'Not a problem,' said Marnie cheerfully, aware once more

what an attractive man he was behind the concern he had for his wife.

Concern for his wife made the man attractive, of course, she thought ruefully as she drove out of The Dingle. Concern for his wife's welfare was something that Felix had not exhibited for quite some time before he left her.

The following week was taken over with preparations for Marnie's move into Church Lane. There had been a problem with curtains. Fortunately Marnie, needing a small sample of curtain fabric to match lampshades, decided to call into the shop where the curtains were being made.

'Excellent timing,' said the assistant.'Your curtains were delivered late yesterday afternoon. I tried to telephone you this morning but there was no reply. Would you like to see them?'

'Yes, please,' said Marnie.'I came in for a sample of the fabric.'

'I'll cut you off a piece. This is one set,' she said, throwing a curtain across the counter. 'The others are in that parcel.'

Marnie looked at them critically. They were exactly what she wanted, and they looked well made. She picked one of them up. Then she frowned.

'Are you sure these are mine?' she asked.

'Certainly, madam.'

'Only this curtain is very short. Far too short for the French window in my sitting-room.'

'Surely not . . .' The assistant saw Marnie's face. 'Perhaps we'd better check the measurements . . .'

Marnie had insisted on the shop sending someone to measure her windows. The measurements were correct, the instructions as she intended. The curtains had been made up incorrectly.

'You're a bit short of time now, aren't you?' Marnie was commendably smooth-tempered. 'I do hope you'll have my order finished before I move. In five days . . .'

It was a week to the day when Luke Firmer rang her as he had promised.'Alison and I would be so glad if you could spare the time for a cup of tea . . .'

Once again Marnie dressed herself in her wool skirt and drove out to The Dingle. Once again Luke welcomed her at the door. As before, he was wearing a jacket and tie.

Alert to possible signs of a preoccupied mind, Marnie was reassured by Alison's welcome and they sat down in the drawing-room while Luke went to fetch the tea trolley.

'Did you bring photographs of your family with you?' asked Alison. 'I should so love to see them.' Her fingers were plucking at the wool of her purple sweater, similar to the cardigan she had worn before.

'But . . . Why, yes, I have a few with me,' said Marnie. Having photos of Ellie and Josh and Felicity with her made it seem as though they were not so very far away, after all. She produced the leather folder and showed them to Alison as though for the first time.'Ellie is going to be so pretty.'

'I think she's lovely already,' said Alison, handing the photographs back. The bruise on her wrist, which Marnie had seen on her first visit, was almost gone, but just above the old one was another, blue-black and tinged an angry yellow.

'Ellie is pretty,' Luke said, his eyes on his wife's face as he passed her the plate of sandwiches.

Marnie almost commented on the bruises, but she thought that maybe Alison had reached the age when she bruised easily and that she wouldn't care to be reminded of it.

'You know, we were all devastated when Felix took you to Australia,' Alison said, leaning forward and patting Marnie on the knee. 'We all thought he was far too old for you, anyway.'

'Marnie obviously didn't agree,' commented Luke, sitting back in his chair.

'We had many happy years,' said Marnie, defending her marriage.

'Happiness is indefinable, isn't it?' Alison turned her face away from Marnie to look out of the window.

Marnie was aware of a sudden tension.'Are you well enough to garden nowadays? It looks so beautiful out there,' she commented.

'You must come in the summer and we'll show you round it,'

said Luke. 'The last project Alison had was a pergola with wisteria growing up, intertwined with clematis.'

'It sounds lovely.'

'It is. I chose varieties to flower throughout the summer and autumn. Such beautiful colours,' said Alison.

She warmed to her subject and insisted that Marnie should make sure she had clematis in her garden. She even went to a small bookcase and produced a book on clematis that she positively insisted that Marnie should borrow. By this time Marnie was struck by the thought that Alison had not worn well at all, for the woman was stick thin rather than slim and her bones looked as if they were brittle. Her face was smooth and her hair was newly washed but her hands, which were restless, looked papery. Those bruises must have come from knocking herself against furniture in the house, she thought, and Marnie wondered just how long ago it was since Alison had tended her garden herself, even though it appeared well cared for at a distance. She supposed they might employ a gardener for the rough digging.

There was the sound of the telephone in the hall. 'Excuse me. I'd better answer that,' said Luke, getting up and leaving the room, closing the door behind him.

'So inconsiderate, ringing at this time,' said Alison crossly. She also got up, but she went to stand in front of the window where, as before, she had been when Marnie arrived.

'I believe you also grow lots of soft fruit,' said Marnie. 'Do you have a fruit cage?'

There was no reply from Alison. Marnie repeated her question. 'Do you have a fruit cage?'

'The birds have the fruit now,' said Alison vaguely. 'I like watching them. At least, I think I like watching them. Perhaps I prefer knowing that they aren't going hungry.'

'Quite,' said Marnie inadequately. She sat silently, feeling a little on edge and not sure where the conversation should go now. The conviction that it was time for her to leave was strong.

The door opened and Luke returned. 'That was Lisa,' he said. 'She and Rupert want to come and visit at the weekend. I said we'd love to see them.'

'That's nice for you,' said Marnie. She rose from her chair. 'I think it's time for me to go home,' she said. 'I'm so pleased to have been invited again, Luke. It is really splendid catching up with Alison. Thank you so much for inviting me, both of you.'

'Luke! Who is this woman?' Alison had turned back from the window. She was glaring at Marnie, wringing her hands in front of her. 'She's been asking me about feeding the birds. Such ridiculous nonsense. As if I'd feed the damn birds that steal my raspberries. What is she doing in my house?' Her voice had risen and the expression on her face was suddenly a rictus of animosity.

Marnie took an involuntary step backwards. 'I'm so – I'm sorry I said . . . I mean, I didn't mean to upset you.'

'It's all right, Alison. Marnie didn't mean to upset you.'

'Well, she did upset me. Get her out of here.'

'Marnie's just going.'

'Yes. Yes, I am.' Hastily Marnie picked up her handbag, but she hadn't closed it properly when she was putting the photographs away and some of the contents spilled out as she picked it up. She stuffed everything back into the bag hurriedly. 'Goodbye, Alison,' she muttered. Her hand hovered over the book on clematis.

'Put that book down,' snapped Alison. 'It belongs to me. What do you think you're doing with it! Get her out of here, I said, Luke. Stupid old bag. And what does she mean by asking me all those fucking questions about school? I loathed the place and I detested all those idiotic girls with their prissy ways and their nasty boyfriends. Get her out of here!'

Alison made a sudden lunge for the tea trolley and grabbed a cup. There was the sound of breaking china as first one cup, then another, and then a saucer flew in all directions, the first one bouncing off Marnie's arm to land on a table behind her, sending one of the porcelain shepherdesses flying.

'Marnie! Please go. Right now!' Luke's voice was low but urgent.

Marnie needed no more prompting. She fled the room. In the

hall she paused. She needed her coat, but she had no idea where Luke had hung it. There were several doors leading off the hall. All of them were firmly closed. Marnie hesitated. She had no idea what she was meant to do now.

CHAPTER SEVEN

'Ssh, Alison. Alison, it's all right. Put it down, dear. That's fine. Never mind about the mess. She's gone. I promise she won't disturb you again. Oh, Alison . . .'

The tenderness in the man's tone brought tears to Marnie's eyes. Abandoning her coat, she opened the front door quietly and walked through it. Shivering in the sudden cold air, for the house had been very warm, she hurried to her car.

From force of habit, Marnie had locked it. For a dreadful moment she thought she had left her keys in her coat pocket but she found them eventually at the bottom of her handbag. She got into the car, put the key into the ignition and started the engine. It took her several attempts to turn the car in the space in front of the garage, and she stalled the engine twice. Eventually she calmed down sufficiently to steer the car down the drive and out on to the road.

It was the most appalling thing to happen. She would never have believed such a change could take place in a woman's personality – anyone's personality.

It was all her fault. Why had she come back to this country? Why wasn't she safe in the familiar surroundings of her Australian life? Marnie knew the answer to that one. She had come back to reclaim Chloë and in that she had succeeded, for she had found the beloved daughter she thought lost to her. She thought she had rediscovered a friend. But after today, that friend was surely lost.

Her other reason for coming back was still unresolved, for

Marnie knew that she was no nearer learning how to live on her own. What was worse, her confidence in coping with social situations had just received a severe dent.

Marnie was still trembling when she reached her B&B and parked the car. By the time she got out of it, locked it again and walked to the front door, she had begun shivering violently.

'Why, Mrs Edgerton, you never went out without a coat, did you? There, you Australians don't realize just how the temperature drops after four o'clock. Very unwise it was of you, but I don't suppose you'll do it again.'

'No, Mrs Jones. I don't suppose I will,' said Marnie. 'I even think I might go and have a bath to warm myself up.'

'The water's nice and hot. But are you going out again? You don't want to get a chill, going out so soon after a bath.'

'I had a large tea so I'm not in the least hungry. No, I don't think I'll be going out again, thank you, Mrs Jones.' Daphne Jones only supplied breakfast so Marnie alternated between the pub in the village, which she could walk to, and one of the Monmouth restaurants, sometimes eating out in the middle of the day and bringing back a sandwich, which her obliging landlady said she had no objection to, even providing Marnie with a large plate for the crumbs.

'You look as though you've had a bit of a shock, if you don't mind me saying so.'

'Yes, I think I have.'

There was an expectant pause.

Marnie went on unwillingly. 'I met an old friend. We were at school together. I was just a bit surprised how much she had changed.'

'Well, once you get past – erm – fiftyish – I suppose you have to expect a few changes,' said Daphne Jones, safe in the knowledge that she had at least fifteen years grace before such horrors happened to her. 'All right, poppet,' she called to her daughter, a spoilt and overweight brat of seven, who was demanding another chocolate biscuit. 'I'll open another packet in a minute, Lily. I tell you what, Mrs Edgerton, dear. You go and have that bath and after I've watched *EastEnders* I'll bring you up a nice cup of tea and one of them new chocolate biscuits. Would you like that?'

'That's very kind of you, Mrs Jones.'

'M-u-mm.'

'Coming, dear. I'm coming now.'

Marnie did not have her bath immediately. She sat in the small chair in her not very large bedroom and stared vacantly into space. Was that what Alzheimer's did to you? She had always understood that it was a memory loss; that you no longer knew where you were or what you were supposed to be doing; that frequently you failed to recognize members of your own family; that you couldn't be left alone in case you harmed yourself inadvertently.

This – Alison's behaviour – had been a total personality change. Alison had known who Marnie was, at first. At one moment she was a woman who remembered everything, every nuance of long past events that Marnie herself had quite forgotten – Alison even remembered them with humour and affection. The next minute she was a foul-mouthed harridan who threw things. It was terrifying.

That poor man. Her unfortunate family. Sad Alison.

Marnie began shivering again. She supposed it was shock. She went into her bathroom and ran a deep, scaldingly hot bath. When she had finished, she got into warm pyjamas over a turtle-necked shirt with the thick socks she used in her Wellingtons. She was still shivery, so she put on her new fleece jacket also.

Polly. Oh, God. Someone had to tell Polly what had happened.

Marnie found Polly's number and rang it. The phone was answered eventually, but by Simon Hunter.

'It's Marnie Edgerton. You're probably eating. I'm sorry to ring now,' Marnie said, apologetically. 'I really need to speak to Polly.'

'I'm sorry, Marnie. Polly isn't here right now. May I take a message and get her to ring you back?'

'It's just that something dreadful has happened. And it's all my fault,' she wailed.

'Marnie. Marnie, is this something to do with Alison?'

'Yes. Oh, yes, it is. Do you know what's happened?'

Simon did not know all the details, he told Marnie. Luke had phoned in some distress about an hour before and Polly had gone over immediately.

So Marnie told him exactly what had transpired. 'It was obviously all my fault,' she repeated. 'Alison was fine when I arrived. Either I stayed too long, or I said something to trigger her distress. I don't know. Maybe it was both. Anyway, it was just awful. I couldn't believe the change, especially when she began throwing the china . . .'

'Marnie. There are personality changes with Alzheimer's which, as you know, is a form of senile dementia. People turn against those they love quite unexpectedly. It hasn't actually happened before, with Alison, I mean, but Polly and Luke were warned that it was a distinct possibility. She has deteriorated quite rapidly in the last four months. It wasn't your fault, Marnie. Please believe that.'

They talked for a time, and eventually Marnie began to feel a little better about her involvement. She had the impression that Simon himself was happy to talk. She thought that maybe he was preparing to cope with a distressed wife when she returned that night. She wondered aloud how on earth Luke could manage that sort of behaviour on his own.

'Forgive me, but I suppose no one has mentioned professional help?' Marnie ended. 'I mean, something more than the drugs that I imagine she is on now.'

Simon sighed. The sound came over the line plainly. 'Both Polly and Luke are vehemently against moving Alison from familiar surroundings. Which is all very well . . .'

'But Polly works full-time and Luke and Alison live in a large house.'

'As I've pointed out.'

'It's a mess. Thank you for hearing me out, Simon. Please let me know if I can do anything. Whatever you say, I think I shall always feel a little responsible.'

There was a knock on the door and her landlady came in carrying a tray of tea things.

'You look less peaky, I must say.' Daphne Jones found a space for the tray on Marnie's dressing table. 'There's a nasty shock you must have had.' She stood by the dressing table, an expression of interested concern on her face.

'My friend has Alzheimer's,' Marnie said reluctantly. 'I wasn't expecting what I found.'

'Would that be that nice Mrs Firmer? Lives at The Dingle? She used to sell lovely jams at the WI stall.'

'You know her, then?' said Marnie, unconsciously verifying gossip.

'Why, of course. I'm an Otterhaven girl. Lived here all my life. My mother-in-law was at school with Alison Evans.'

'Was she? So was I. What was her name?'

Daphne Jones told her. 'Well, I never. Isn't it a small world? My mother-in-law'll be ever so interested you've come back. So Alison Firmer does have Alzheimer's. Poor woman. Nasty thing, that. Mind you, a lot of us suspected it was coming. At the WI stall in the market, in Monmouth, I mean. My mother-in-law has always baked sponge cakes for them. She has a very light hand with a sponge, does my mother-in-law. I've never had the inclination for that sort of thing myself. Well, the supermarkets do just as well, I'm thinking, and they're just as cheap. Though my mother-in-law does say they only keep for as long as they do because of E thingies. Alison Firmer made jams and marmalades. A few years ago there was a batch of strawberry jam that was uneatable, Mum said. She'd only gone and doubled up on the sugar. Alison, I mean. At least, that was what they thought had happened. Anyway, it couldn't be sold. Sandy Williams, she was the chairman of the WI at the time, she had to tell Mr Firmer that it probably wasn't a good idea for his wife to send anything more to the market. There's a lovely man Mr Firmer is. I expect he didn't like to upset his wife, so of course Mrs Firmer went on jam making. The poor man kept bringing it in, but most of it had to be dumped. Someone'd wash the jars and he'd take them home.'

'How sad,' Marnie said inadequately. She was wishing fervently that her landlady would go – and perversely she was glad of the small, human, contact.

Daphne Jones tutted as she straightened the dressing table.'Well, well, you never know when ill fortune'll come your way, do you?' She paused. 'You know, Lily and I are going to miss you when you go tomorrow. It's been a real pleasure having you here. Don't you go forgetting that we're only just round the corner, if ever you need a spare room.'

'Thank you, Mrs Jones. I couldn't have chosen better if I'd tried.'

'Got your things all ready for the move?'

'As you know, I've already taken one suitcase. There's just a smallish bag to go with me.'

'Now, Mrs Edgerton, dear, I hope you've put on your electric blanket. You just drink that tea while it's hot, then get into bed and have a good night's sleep.'

Daphne Jones waited until she was sure her guest and her daughter had gone to bed. She even went into the garden to check to see if Marnie Edgerton's light had been turned off. Then she telephoned her friend, Mrs Evans.

'Dor. You remember what we were talking about last week? Well, we were right. Alison Firmer has got Alzheimer's . . .'

'No, I've not met anyone who's had it, have you?'

'Your cousin's mother-in-law . . .'

'Did she. Oh, dear me . . .'

'Well, my Mrs Edgerton had a nasty shock this afternoon . . . No, I don't know any exact details, yet.'

Moving into 2 Church Lane was less hassle than Marnie had feared it would be. The gas-fired Aga, which was going to heat Marnie's new radiators warmed them up quickly; the washing machine and fridge-freezer were installed with no difficulty at all; the bed and bed linen ordered from Cribbs Causeway were delivered exactly when they were promised. The builders, having their cup of tea with a celebratory piece of cake (from the local shop that stocked a supply from a baker in Monmouth who still baked on the premises), could not believe there were no crises and they were full of dubious warnings about what could still go wrong.

Marnie was determined not to be intimidated and told them plainly that if anything did go amiss it wouldn't be for lack of forethought on her part and with the prospect of the bonus she'd promised if they finished when they said they would, and left the place tidy, the doom-laden prophecies fell silent.

The one thing that did exercise Marnie's mind, in the next few evenings once she'd completed all the tasks she'd set herself for the day, was just how was she to reclaim her only smart coat.

It was not possible to phone Luke Firmer, she decided. The man must have far too much on his mind to bother about a thing like a mislaid article of clothing. Yet she could hardly go round to The Dingle herself. She really felt she could never face Alison again – which might be feeble of her – but that face, that extreme loathing she had seen in it, was something that would stay with her for a long time. Marnie had tried phoning Polly, but all she could get was an answering service. Moreover, Polly's office would only tell her that Ms Firmer was currently away. She had left messages but in the meantime she just had to resign herself to doing without her coat.

Luckily Marnie still had her fleece so at least she could go out without freezing. It just had to be hoped that nothing too sartorially demanding came her way for a little while.

There came a morning when Marnie, in the throes of painting the sitting-room walls a delicate shade of mushroom, was disturbed by the doorbell.

Standing on her doorstep was Luke Firmer.

CHAPTER EIGHT

'Oh,' said Marnie, seeing Luke Firmer on her doorstep. 'What are you doing here?'

He held out her coat.

'Oh, gosh,' said Marnie, totally flustered.'I never expected . . . I never thought . . . I tried to contact Polly but . . . oh, dear.' She sighed. 'You must think I am a total fool. Please will you come in?'

'I thought you'd never ask.'

'Is it all right, though? I mean, have you left Alison on her own? I mean . . . Oh, God. Why is it I can't open my mouth without saying something quite fatuous?'

There was a glimmer of a smile on Luke's strained face as he said: 'Would you like me to go out and start again?'

'Yes. No. For goodness' sake, come into the kitchen and have a cup of coffee. It's obviously time I had a break.'

'I gather you're painting.'

Marnie wrinkled her nose as she put the kettle on. 'The smell is pretty invasive, isn't it? I put cut lemons on saucers in all the rooms, and at night I douse my pillow with lavender oil, but I can still smell paint throughout the cottage. And it's far too cold to have windows open except in the room I'm actually painting.'

'It wasn't that.' He leant forward and with his finger wiped at a smudge of paint on Marnie's cheek. 'Oh, dear, I think I've made it worse.'

She said shakily: 'I'm surprised my hair isn't covered with paint. I never remember to put on a scarf.' She was thinking that it was a long time since a man had touched her skin – other than in shaking her by the hand. The sensation seemed to burn her.

'Have you much more to do?'

Pull yourself together. She had to pull herself together. 'Just the spare room upstairs. I've been working very hard and the builders actually left me with less to do than I'd planned originally. You see, I only meant to have central heating installed and a new bathroom. You can't imagine what state that bathroom was in. At least, I very much hope you can't, though you never can tell with English bathrooms. Oops . . .' She paused. For heaven's sake, she was talking far too much.

Luke grinned. 'Polly's bathroom is a bit of a tip, but that's Simon. He never picks up his wet towels. Alison was always very particular about things like that.'

There was an awkward pause. The kettle boiled. It was a timely distraction. Marnie measured out coffee grounds into a cafetière and fetched mugs. She poured the coffee and indicated milk and the sugar bowl.

'No sugar, thank you. Marnie, I am sorry you had to leave your coat behind. You must have been so very cold.'

'You shouldn't be apologizing to me. I'm just so sorry about your situation. You should have told me that Alison didn't like visitors.'

'But that's just the point. She really enjoyed talking to you about the past. I could see that. You must have seen it for yourself. But I never imagined for one moment that she would become violent. It's something . . .'

'I've found out a bit about Alzheimer's since I saw you both,' Marnie said quietly. 'Is Polly with her mother now?'

'Alison is having a week or so in a residential care home. The consultant thought it would be a good idea and there was a room available in a place nearby that also cares for the elderly with personality problems. So that's where Alison has gone, for respite, and so here I am.'

60

'Stay for lunch,' Marnie said, on impulse.

Luke accepted the invitation with alacrity. It was then that Marnie realized that there wasn't much food in the fridge. She had intended driving into Monmouth in the afternoon for a supermarket shop. Most of the time she supported the general store in Otterhaven, but there were things the store didn't have and she knew that once a month she would need to stock up in Monmouth. She hoped it wouldn't make her too unpopular, but she guessed that was what most people inevitably did.

'I've only a few eggs, though,' she added apologetically. 'Would a herb omelette be enough?'

'That sounds good. It is such a change to have someone cook for me. Even bread and cheese would be great.'

'Bread, but no cheese. It'll have to be the omelette. Unless you want to go out?' She held her breath. She couldn't ever remember asking a man out for a meal before. Not even Felix. Come to think of it, she wouldn't have dared ask Felix out for a meal in the early days of their courting.

'I'd really prefer to eat here.'

'That's fine by me.' Of course it was. Luke probably wouldn't want to be seen having lunch with another woman while his wife was so unwell.

'It's peaceful here. I'd just like to sit quietly in your kitchen for a little while.'

'Then we'll stay here.'

They finished their coffee and decided that if Marnie made the omelettes straight away it still wouldn't be too soon for an early lunch.

'I tell you what,' said Marnie, again on impulse.'Why don't we have a glass of red wine with our lunch? I always make a point of not drinking on my own, so while I was staying at Mrs Jones' B&B I used to have a glass of wine when I went out for my evening meal, but unless I change the habits of a lifetime I'm not going to have much opportunity from now on. You'd probably be doing me a favour, seeing as how they think a little wine is good for you.'

He grinned.'Alison and I used to have a sherry in the evening but once we realized what was happening to her we decided to give up alcohol. Though I really don't know if that was a help or not. Anyway, I felt it was a little unkind to drink on my own. Wine, with you, sounds extremely sociable.'

While she was cooking, Luke admitted to Marnie that it was a number of years since he'd begun to wonder if his wife was in the throes of early dementia.

'It was all the classic stuff. You know, she'd forget things when she went shopping. She'd miss appointments.'

'Don't we all do that?'

'To an extent, I suppose. I know I often forget why I've gone to my study so purposefully, but it was far worse for Alison. There came a time when I had to shop with her and drop her off at the hairdresser's, for example, to make sure she kept her appointment.'

'Did Alison notice anything wrong herself?'

He grimaced. 'Oh, yes. And there were times when she wasn't very happy. Withdrawn, you know? She spent more and more time in the garden. But I thought that the exercise, the gardening, the fresh air, was good for her. Then, eventually I realized we did need professional advice and we went to the doctor. But at that stage there wasn't anything he would do except suggest palliative care, like the fresh air and the exercise she was already getting, along with lots of Vitamin E, that sort of thing.'

'Didn't he prescribe drugs?' Marnie asked.'I thought the NHS provided drugs for something like Alzheimer's.'

'Unfortunately, not in the early stages. Which seems to me to be quite crazy, not making life easier in the beginning, both for the sufferer and for the carer. You see, that's what I am: a carer. It's different now, of course, now that Alison is going through a really bad patch. She is prescribed drugs and they are making a difference, though there have been side effects.'

He did not say what these were and Marnie could not ask. She also wanted to ask how long Alison would stay in the care home, but it seemed unkind.

Luke seemed unwilling to go. He was easy company, some-times not saying anything for several minutes, then coming out with some query about the cottage, or Marnie's family, or her life in Australia, that proved he had been thinking about her all the time. It was a soothing experience, one that she could scarcely remember ever happening to her before. Felix had not been a man for handing out reassurance of any kind.

Luke had been with her for three hours when Marnie's phone rang. It was Polly, asking when it would be convenient for her to return Marnie's coat.

'How kind of you to offer,' Marnie answered lamely.

'Simon told me off about it this morning. He said I should have remembered to take it to you days ago.'

'Only, Luke brought it back this morning.'

'Did he? That's all right, then.'

There was a pause. Marnie had an uncomfortable feeling she knew what was coming next.

'I don't suppose Dad said anything about where he was going, did he? I've been trying to get hold of him.'

'Actually he's right here,' said Marnie cheerfully. 'Would you like to speak to him?'

'He's with you?'

The incredulity in Polly's voice made Marnie immediately feel exceedingly guilty. Wordlessly she handed the phone over to Luke who, she could see, was trying his best to look noncha-lant.

'There's nothing wrong, is there?' he asked guardedly.

The conversation continued, Marnie trying not to listen to the one side that was audible by quietly clearing up the debris of their lunch. From the placatory noises and the few comments he was able to make, it sounded as though Polly was expostulating vociferously.

'Polly's a bit cross,' Luke said expressionlessly, as he put the cell phone down on the kitchen table.

They looked at each other for a full minute, then a smile started in Luke's eyes. Unable to prevent it, Marnie giggled. After a moment Luke gave a guffaw.

'Oh, God,' he said. 'I didn't expect to be checked up on by my daughter for a good few years yet. How humiliating.'

'Tell me about it,' Marnie said fervently.

'Polly seems to have acquired a way of making me feel as though she's the adult and I'm the child. I'm not sure when it happened. I suppose it was when I'd been particularly crass in not picking up on something her mother had done.'

'Jack was so disapproving when I told him I wanted to buy the cottage, especially when I was stupid enough to describe the extremely boring house in the new development that I turned down. He was all for safety and an easy sale in the future. All the same, he made it sound as though I was being totally irresponsible with my money. And it's not as though he's got to worry about a mortgage himself.' As she ended that sentence, Marnie wondered if she'd been a little indiscreet. Oh well, she thought. It was too late to retract any of it.

'I should imagine you'd get a better sale price for this house than for a house on any estate. This has real character.'

'Hasn't it. On the other hand, a lot of Jack's disapproval may have come from his current dislike of his sister. Oh dear, I shouldn't be telling you about my dysfunctional family.' Another indiscretion.

'It doesn't sound that bad to me. After all, you were telling me that Chloë has been very supportive during your move. That doesn't sound dysfunctional in the slightest. Besides, all families have issues. That doesn't make them dysfunctional.'

'That's wise. I think Chloë was just relieved that I chose not to live too close to her. But after our traumas, I do think we're getting there,' said Marnie. 'Sometime I'll tell you more about the last few years, but I don't think I come out of the story very well, so maybe it would be better left unsaid. How long do you think it will be before Alison comes home?'

Luke sighed. 'I have absolutely no idea. Eve Morgan, who manages the care home, said that often the timing is dictated by the resident. If Alison was pining for home, familiar surroundings and faces, going home might be the best solution, but she would still need careful watching.'

'And at the moment you are far too tired to nurse her your-self.'

'That's right. When I think about carers who have fewer resources than I have, I feel humbled. There are so many, either looking after elderly parents or children with special needs – I still find it easier to think of them as disabled, which I know is politically incorrect.'

'It's our generation,' agreed Marnie.'The one with fixed minds.'

Again they grinned at each other, both quite certain that in this they did not fit the mould.

'Anyway, looking after either the young or the elderly is so draining. This respite is technically for Alison. I'm glad of it for me. As for how much longer it will be?' He shrugged.'At the moment there are days when Alison doesn't seem to know quite who I am.'

'That must be distressing.'

'It is. Actually she makes a terrific effort and before I leave she's usually said something that makes me know she does remember me. And sometimes the care assistant who lets me in announces to Alison that her husband has come to see her. That helps.'

'Is Alison up to having visitors?'

Luke hesitated for only a moment.'The staff at The Sycamores say that it would be a really good thing for her to have them. Unless – unless she's not feeling well.' He put it delicately. Marnie knew what he was implying.

'Then I'll find the time,' she said on impulse, 'and they can tell me whether it's a good idea, or not.'

'That would be a kind thing to do. Thank you, Marnie.'

He did not stay much longer, saying that it was time he went to The Sycamores for his visit. He liked to be there at teatime.'And not only for the cakes,' he said, with a glimmer of the humour Marnie was beginning to recognize as a part of the man's character.

'Thank you for my coat,' said Marnie, as she stood on the step to say goodbye.

'Thank you for my lunch. I look forward to our next meeting, Marnie.' He gave a sort of half-bow and walked down the garden path to the gate.

CHAPTER NINE

'Did I see someone leave just now?' The front door opened and Chloë came in without knocking. 'You know, you really should keep your front door locked. You never know who might just walk in.'

'And hello to you, too, dear. This is a nice surprise.'

'Hello, Mum.' Chloë gave Marnie a peck on her cheek. 'I thought you might like some help with the painting, if you've got a spare paintbrush, that is. Or have you stopped for the day? Did I see someone leave as I drove up?'

'That's right,' said Marnie cheerfully. 'That was Luke Firmer going.'

'Luke Firmer?' Chloë repeated sharply. 'Whatever was he doing here?' Marnie had described to her what had happened when she went to tea at The Dingle and Chloë had been visibly shocked.

'He was kind enough to return my coat. Didn't I tell you that I had to leave it behind when Alison became a bit violent.'

'Oh, yes. I think you did. So why did Luke return it himself?'

'I think he happened to be passing,' said Marnie, knowing full well that Luke had come out of his way to call at Church Lane.'Anyway, he thought I might be needing the coat, so he brought it back. Perhaps he felt responsible for the fact I didn't have it when I left so hurriedly.'

'Perhaps. Are you getting into the habit of leaving your wash-ing-up or did Luke stay for lunch?' Chloë nodded towards the two dirty plates in the sink. Beside them were the two glasses, both with a residue of red wine visible at the bottom.

Marnie noticed that her daughter had managed to put insinu-ation as well as accusation into her tone of voice as she asked the question.

'My, my,' she said drily.'Do you know, Polly Firmer rang just after we'd finished eating and I got a strong impression that she wasn't too pleased, either.'

'I don't know what you mean.'

'Dear, I am not inclined to explain, or excuse, the fact that I asked Luke to stay for an omelette by way of a thank you for bringing me back my coat. He's currently a lonely, depressed man whose wife has an incurable disease. I felt – feel – very sorry for him. Alzheimer's is something I wouldn't wish on my worst enemy, either to suffer from, or to have to pick up some-one else's pieces.'

'Of course not, Mum. Sorry. I didn't mean . . .'

'Of course you didn't. So, since you've come to help and I see that you're wearing torn jeans.' She ignored the implication of torn jeans. 'Why don't I find you a paintbrush and we'll get on with the living-room. You never know, we might even get it finished.' Inwardly she sighed. After two glasses of wine, Marnie would have preferred to have sat down for a little while, but there was no way she was going to relinquish the moral high ground she had scrambled her way on to.'And tell me, I thought you were coming over on Saturday. Have your plans changed?' Marnie handed a paintbrush to her daughter, picked up her own, which she had wrapped in newspaper, and led the way into the sitting-room. 'How do you feel about starting the gloss on the skirting boards?'

'OK,' Chloë agreed.'Um, about Saturday. The thing is, there's someone Nick wants to see in Swansea and he's asked me to go with him. It isn't going to take very long and then we'll have the whole day for ourselves. Would you mind very much?'

'Here, put a bit more newspaper down on the floor. Then you

can kneel on it.'

Marnie was thinking that this was another first in her new relations with Chloë. She couldn't remember when her daughter had mentioned a boyfriend before. She had only got to hear about the odd one or two in Sydney from comments Jack had made. (Particularly the odd ones.) Was this a boyfriend, or a friend who happened to be male? Tread carefully, Marnie, she warned herself.

'Is this Nick a student, like you?' she asked.

Chloë, whose tongue had been clenched between her teeth at the corner of her mouth in concentration – a gesture Marnie remembered from her childhood – carefully put her paintbrush into the corner of the skirting board before she relaxed and turned towards her mother.

'Oh, no. Nick's no student. Actually, he's a bit older than me. I met him through the Young Farmers' Club. He owns a market garden. I met him when I went there to ask for a Saturday job. You know, work experience? Though actually Nick pays me, which is great. He's nice. You'd like him.'

'I'm sure I would. Um . . . is this Nick more than just a friend, or am I reading too much into it?' Nick, she was thinking. Only recently someone had mentioned that name to her.

'Actually, I'm not sure.'

How interesting. Suddenly Chloë had become almost inarticulate. And she was blushing, her mother noticed.

'Well, I'm sure you'll have a splendid time on Saturday. Does Nick have another name?'

'Hunter. Nicholas Hunter.'

Nicholas Hunter; the brother of Simon Hunter, who was married to Polly Firmer, the daughter of Luke.

That was the trouble when you came to live in the country. There were wheels within wheels. You never knew who was related to whom. You had to be very careful what you said (especially if it was at all derogatory) because ten to one you were talking about someone's cousin, or niece, or whatever.

'You must mean Simon Hunter's brother,' Marnie said. 'Polly referred to him when I went to tea at the farm. I gather he had a row with his father before he died.'

'And as a result he and Simon don't speak. That's right.'

'Such a waste,' sighed Marnie.

'Perhaps. Not if the other one only speaks to criticize.'

'Is that what happens between the brothers? How sad.'

'Nick rowed with his father because the old man wanted him to go into the family farm. Nick insisted that the farm wasn't making enough money to support two families. At the time, neither of the brothers was married, but Nick was thinking about the future and he knew Simon was keen on Polly. I think he was in a relationship himself, but in the end nothing came of it. If you were wondering,' she added.

'I suppose that happens quite often,' said Marnie, choosing to ignore the subtle information that Nicholas Hunter was more than a few years older than her daughter. 'Quarrels between farming fathers and sons, I mean.'

'I guess it might. Their father said that it was up to Nick to make sure the farm did pay enough.'

'And that also sounds reasonable.'

'It depends on your point of view, Mum. Actually, it seems to me that they have more in common than they'll admit. They're both into organic methods, for example. It's just that Simon is developing his grasslands while Nick is into horticulture. He says there's more money in soft fruit and vegetables to sell locally than there would be if they merely expanded the farm.'

'So Nicholas does use family land?'

'No, that's the whole point. Nick managed to find land to rent. He has polytunnels and a greenhouse and at the moment he sells his produce at the farm gate. It would be so much more sensible for him to use family land. And what I think he should do is to open a proper garden centre.'

'Wow,' said Marnie.'There's a considerable difference between a small shop selling its own produce and a garden centre with, I suppose, all sorts of plants and stuff that might have to be out-sourced. No wonder Simon isn't too keen on the idea.'

'Well, I know about the out-sourcing, and so does Nick,'

'That's right,' said Marnie. 'Though my roots aren't Australian, you know. I was born and brought up in Chepstow.'

'Well, it's good to hear the traffic goes both ways, so to speak. I have a cousin who emigrated to Adelaide about ten years ago. She vows she won't ever return. Oh, dear. It would appear that size has already gone. Or . . .' She hesitated.'Have a little browse on the rails for a moment.'

Jo Edwards went to the back of her shop where several cubicles had been curtained off. 'How are you getting on, Vera?' she asked. 'Is there anything more I can bring you to try on?'

A disembodied voice replied, 'I'll take the cream trousers. Do you have the same ones in black?'

'I'll have a look.'

Jo returned to Marnie, a small grimace on her face. 'Sorry. I thought maybe my other customer mightn't like them. Vera buys a lot of my things. That's Vera Crawford. She runs the gallery just down the street. I'd introduce you, but she's a bit occupied right now. Is there anything else you would like to try?' Jo whipped a pair of black trousers off the rail before Marnie had a chance to pick them out. They were the same design and size as the cream. 'There's a nice pale grey here.'

'Thanks, but they won't go with my jacket. I'll have to leave it this time.'

'I could phone the supplier,' suggested Jo helpfully. 'They are very good at sending the odd item to me.'

'Thanks, but it seems they are a bit too popular for my taste.'

'Do call again, then.'

'I will,' promised Marnie, almost out of the door. 'This was really just an impulse visit. I can see you have some lovely things here.' As she left the shop she thought that she might not buy too much from Dolly's. Not if there was the chance of walking into it in the street every day.

'A bit too popular . . .' The customer who had been behind the curtain emerged wearing the black trousers that Jo had thrust into her hands. 'Who does she think she is?'

'She's the new owner of Bert's cottage.'

'I gathered. Don't think she's going to be much of an asset to

Otterhaven,' Vera Crawford said, smoothing the cloth over her hips. 'She hasn't been anywhere near me, for a start. You know, these do fit very well. I'll take both pairs.'

CHAPTER TEN

Sundays in Otterhaven were a time Marnie enjoyed because she took herself off into the countryside for a walk. These walks were very different from the occasional bushwalking she had done in Australia. Here she had bought maps and she was engaged in exploring footpaths – most of which were well walked. She had no difficulty in managing the stiles, she had discovered to her relief, because her hips were still in an excellent condition and the stiles were in good repair. Occasionally her map reading had gone astray, and so had she. But as she always took something to eat (and her anorak) a small detour had not, so far, brought her any serious consequences.

Since Chloë had come over during the week, Marnie had not expected to see her at all. But on her return from this walk, she found a strange car parked by the gate and her daughter and a man she had not met before sitting in the back garden. The man was in his late thirties, she guessed, fair-haired, with a thin and wiry body, from what she could see under his well-worn Barbour.

'Hi, Mum, where have you been?'

'Hello, dear. I'm not attached to a garden fork with a piece of string, you know.'

'Of course you're not,' said the man. 'Hello, Mrs Edgerton. I'm Nick Hunter, in case you're wondering.'

'Sorry. Hey, you've met now. Any chance of a cup of tea?'

'Just what I was going to suggest. Go in and put the kettle on, Chloë, while I take off my boots. There's cake in the tin, too.'

'I guess the boots mean you've been walking, Mrs Edgerton.'

'Why don't you call me Marnie?' She smiled at him.'Yes, I like to walk on a Sunday. I like the gardening, too, but it's good to have a change of scenery.'

'Thank you, Marnie. Where do you walk?'

'All over. I'm doing a bit of an explore, and when I find a walk I've really enjoyed, I write it down for next year.'

'That sounds as though you don't intend to return to Australia in the near future. Chloë'll be very pleased.'

That was perspicacious of him. His expression showed polite interest in her affairs; his voice was non-committal. Marnie made a vague 'Mmm,' sound, intending to convey whatever Nicholas Hunter took it to mean. She was not prepared to lower her guard entirely against this man, yet.

'Do you walk on your own or with a group of ramblers?'

'On my own. It's such a beautiful part of the world and I prefer to walk at my own pace and admire the views.'

'You'd do better to have a dog with you.'

'Even with sheep around? And what about disturbing the wild birds? No. I don't have a dog, nor do I intend having one at my age.'

'What's all this about Mum having a dog?'

They had walked into the kitchen by now and Chloë, setting out mugs and plates for the cake, which was now on the kitchen table along with a bottle of milk, had overheard the last part of the conversation.

'Nick thinks I ought to have a dog to take on my walks. Apart from being a cat person, I think a dog would be far too much responsibility at my age. Not to mention the kennel fees when I wanted to go away. Dear, can't you find a jug for the milk?'

Chloë grinned and gave a little shrug in Nick's direction, which Marnie saw. Nevertheless, Chloë took out a small milk jug from the cupboard and filled it.

'I can't really see Mum dragging a dog round with her.'

'Sometimes you can borrow a neighbour's dog to walk. The dog benefits, the neighbour is usually delighted, and you get the safety factor thrown in for free.'

'I do have a whistle,' Marnie said defensively, 'but it's kind of you to worry. So, how was your trip to Swansea?'

They spent the next twenty minutes or so telling her all about what appeared to be a modern and very efficiently run garden centre, exclaiming over the value of its stock and the sort of money it must be making. Chloë then explained that her course contained garden centre management, horticultural skills and plant management as well as organic horticulture.

Marnie listened carefully; not so much taking in the minute details as trying to read between the lines. Both were enthusiastic. It pleased her very much to discover that her daughter had found what seemed to be an abiding interest, and that she was aware of the pitfalls as well as the profits which could be made from this project. Marnie thought that Nicholas's awareness of what would be involved was tinged with a healthy caution. She considered that the animosity, which both Polly and Chloë had told her existed between the brothers, was all the more disappointing, given that a degree of co-operation had to be more lucrative for them both. But that was often the way of the world. It did occur to her to wonder whether Chloë might prove to be the glue that fixed an otherwise insuperable family dispute.

She also saw a look on Nick's face that pleased her. Compounded of pride – that Chloë fully understood his business undertakings – and awareness that she was a very attractive woman, there was also a tenderness in his eyes as he looked at her (which it seemed to Marnie that Chloë was oblivious of) and a softness to his lips that decided her he was no overt fortune hunter.

'I almost forgot to tell you,' she said, as they were finishing their tea.'I spoke to Jack this morning, and all the children. They all sent their love.'

77

Chloë grunted.'That's a first, then.'

Marnie ignored that.'They asked me for photos of the cottage. I said I'd send them a disk.'

Not long afterwards, the young people left.

The conversation between mother and son that morning had been entirely predictable. Jack expressed outrage at the very thought that his son was being bullied. Once he calmed down, though, he was equally outraged that Ellie had involved her grandmother.

'Dear, while I was living with you the children were in the habit of telling me all sorts of things about their school days. Oh, nothing like this, I assure you.'

'Isn't that just what I was getting at when I told you it was better for children to have someone at home for them in the afternoons? You were the one who chose to go away.'

Marnie sighed. Audibly.'Yes, Jack, but that remark applies as much to parents as it does to a grandparent. What I'm getting at is that Ellie seems to have felt more comfortable telling me about Josh's troubles than either you or Gemma. That is a problem you have to solve with your children, and preferably without shouting.'

There was a shocked silence. For a moment Marnie was convinced that Jack had put the receiver down on her. She waited. Just as she was about to abandon the conversation, Jack said softly:

'I don't shout at them, Mother.'

'Well, dear, let's say that sometimes you are a little short with the children. All of them. Gemma is, too,' she added, thinking that as often happens, a working mother had even less time for confidences than the children's father. 'I guess that Ellie knew that she would have my undivided attention.'

'Of course she'd have your attention if she e-mailed you. The main problem now, though, is what do I do about it?'

'Perhaps Gemma could have a quiet talk with Josh? It might be less confrontational than a man-to-man one. You know, a mother is less likely to demand to know why his son didn't sock the other boy.'

'Like Father did, with me. Do you remember?'

'No. No, I'd quite forgotten. Did you?'

'Did I what?'

'Hit the other boy.'

'Of course I did. I tell you, it hurt me far more than it did him.'

'But did it have the desired effect?'

'As a matter of fact, it did. We became friends, until Dan changed schools.'

'I never knew that.'

'Well, there you go. But I'll talk to Gemma and see what she says. After all, it may be nothing.'

'I'm sure there are rules and regulations about bullying nowadays. If you do have to approach the school, you mustn't let them fob you off with assurances that they've got everything under control.'

'Moth-er.'

'Right, dear. Hugs all round, and an especially nice one to Ellie.'

Marnie decided that she ought to be as good as her word and at least try to visit Alison. Eve Morgan at The Sycamores, who answered the telephone, was encouraging when Marnie told her of their longstanding friendship and it was arranged that Marnie should arrive about teatime.

'Mrs Firmer is often quite sprightly then. I'm sure she would like to have a visitor.'

The Sycamores was a mile or so outside Otterhaven. A Victorian house, it stood on a small hill above the River Trothy and in its heyday it must have been a delightful estate. A considerable portion of the original grounds had been sold off but the remaining gardens were charming. The estate had been acquired for use as a residential home several years previously, by its present owners. There was a small development of converted barns nearby for the elderly who were still alert and mobile, but who liked the reassurance of a warden's presence. A wing of the house itself was for the more frail.

As she expected, Marnie had to wait at the front door to be

let in, but once she had introduced herself she was ushered into a substantially sized and prettily furnished drawing-room, with plenty of easy chairs and occasional tables arranged in small groups, most of which were already occupied by the residents.

The atmosphere in the sunny room was pleasant. There was plenty of animated chatter, and at first glance it was impossible to tell who was the resident, who the visitor. On the whole, Marnie did not have much experience of residential care homes. She had so feared there would be a pervading smell of urine. There was not. The rooms smelt delightfully of beeswax polish and lavender.

Sitting on her own was Alison. There was something uncompromising about her body language that was unwelcoming. Alison, she noticed, was wearing a loose dress, floor length and purple. Marnie approached her with a tentative smile, wondering how much Alison remembered of their last encounter.

It appeared that Alison recalled nothing of it – or else she was sublimely indifferent to what had happened. She smiled back, quite unselfconsciously. 'Come and have a cup of tea, Marnie.'

Marnie sat down. After a moment she leant forward in her seat to pour for them both. There was a plate of biscuits on the table. 'It seems very comfortable here,' she commented.

'It is. The food's good,' said Alison, helping herself to two more biscuits. 'We have Sky TV. My husband wouldn't have Sky.'

'Ah. Do you have many visitors?'

'Only when I say I want them. Mary Beresford called but I told the silly bitch to get lost.'

Marnie tried not to register shock. 'I'm sure she was only trying to be friendly.'

Alison snorted scornfully. 'They gave me a new pair of knickers this morning. Do you want to see them?' She whipped up the skirt of her dress to display a voluminous pair of cotton knickers with a pattern of lilac flowers on them.

'Not now, Alison, dear.' A care helper deftly pulled down

Alison's dress. 'Why don't you show your friend where your room is? I think one of your favourite programmes is about to start. You can switch on your set yourself, can't you?'

'Stupid woman! Of course I can. Come on, Marnie. I'll show you my cell.'

Alison's room was on the top floor. It was not very big. Almost cell-like. Marnie guessed that it had once been a maid's room. She thought that there probably hadn't been much of a choice when Luke applied for his wife to go to The Sycamores. It was, however, tastefully furnished. The curtains and bedcover were new, as was the carpet, and Marnie had a distinct feeling that she had seen the small table and two of the pictures in the drawing-room at The Dingle.

But once Alison had shown her the room, she seemed to lose all interest in her visitor, for she turned on her TV and sat down in her chair.

'I think it's time I left you,' said Marnie inadequately. 'Thank you for tea. Do you think you'd like the flowers I brought you up here?'

Alison shrugged.'Doesn't matter to me. I don't like the smell of roses anyway.'

'Oh. Would you like me to come again?'

'If you want to. You always did do what you wanted, didn't you, Marnie?' She turned to gaze into Marnie's face. 'We all had to do what Marnie wanted. Still, I suppose it makes a change to talk to you rather than the chattering idiots who live here. Yes. Come again. Come next week.'

'You mustn't mind Mrs Firmer's language,' said Eve Morgan, who was hovering in the hall when Marnie got downstairs. She had introduced herself as the manager of The Sycamores. 'I'm afraid dementia brings out unexpected characteristics. I'm sure she doesn't mean to upset people.'

'You mean characteristics that were suppressed?' said Marnie faintly.

'In a way. It doesn't always happen, but someone who was very upright, who never swore . . . It can be very upsetting for the family. Then sometimes they do the opposite, become introverted. Alison did seem to be glad of your company, though. I'm sure she'd be glad of another visit, but better ring first. Just in case.'

CHAPTER ELEVEN

It was late morning and Marnie was in the general store in St Bride's Street. After selecting a few groceries along with a birthday card for Gemma for which she paid Mr Powell, she busied herself writing a note inside it before she bought a stamp from Mrs Powell, who ran the Post Office counter. By the time she had finished the card there was a small queue. As she had already found that Mrs Powell was garrulous, Marnie was resigned to a long wait.

'Hello, Marnie,' Luke greeted her, as he joined the end of the queue behind her.

'Hello, Luke.' Marnie hesitated. 'How is Alison?' Immediately she spoke she was aware that her query had emerged into an expectant silence.

'Oh, you know,' he answered dismissively.

Mrs Powell, from behind the counter, interrupted her business with a well-dressed customer of indeterminate age to say: 'Mr Firmer, we are all so very sorry to hear about Mrs Firmer. Such an unfortunate illness for anyone to be stricken with. And Mrs Firmer was always so much of a lady. It's a real pity.'

'Yes, it is, Mrs Powell. Thank you.'

There was a murmur of agreement from those present, from which Marnie gathered that Alison was popular with the villagers.

'Do give Alison my love when you see her next.' The woman who had been served by Mrs Powell picked up her change and moved away from the counter, pausing by Luke.

'Thank you, Vera. I'll do that.'

'Is Alison up to having visitors?'

'She has her good days. It's perhaps better to phone first at the moment.'

'Right. Well, just give her my love,' she repeated.

'Vera, have you met Marnie Edgerton?' Luke turned to include Marnie in the conversation. 'She has bought 2 Church Lane. Marnie, this is Vera Crawford who runs the gallery in Otterhaven. It's one of the delights of the village, Polly says.'

'How do you do? I've looked in your window several times. You have some interesting things.' So this was the woman who had taken her cream trousers. Nice figure. Marnie wondered if they would have looked quite so good on herself.

'Polly is one of my regular customers. You must come in, too, next time you have a moment,' Vera replied, with a constrained smile.

'I've been living in Australia for the past sixteen years and I've come home with very little so I'm furnishing my cottage more or less from scratch.'

'That's exciting.'

'Yes, but I'm still looking for essentials. Still, I'd like to see what you have some time.'

'Marnie was at school with Alison,' Luke interposed.

'Were you?' Vera Crawford's manner was no more friendly. 'So sad to come home to find an old friend in ill-health,' she commented.

'Yes, it is. Especially as there seem to be fewer of my old acquaintances in the vicinity than I thought there would be. My own fault, I suppose, for losing touch.'

'I went to school in Cheltenham, myself, so that happened to me almost every holiday. Ah well. I must go. So nice to meet you, Marnie. Goodbye, Luke.'

When Marnie also left the store, her transactions completed, she found Luke hovering outside. 'Didn't like to say anything in there,' he said quietly, 'lot of gossiping old biddies, but I wondered if I might buy you lunch, as a thank you for last week?'

'Oh. That would be very kind. Are you on your way to see Alison?'

'No. Thing is,' he said, 'I thought we'd find a pub today.'

'That would be excellent. Only I've got some frozen stuff here. I'll have to take it home first.'

'Why don't I drive you there now? My car's parked round the corner.'

Some three-quarters of an hour later they were sitting at a table at the Duck and Drake, a few miles outside Otterhaven, with low-alcohol lagers in front of them, both waiting for the day's special, a cottage pie.

'I'm looking forward to this. It's not a dish I'd cook for myself,' said Marnie, regretfully. 'I don't seem to have any left-overs nowadays.'

'Not a dish I've had for years,' said Luke. 'I'm not much of a cook, anyway. Leftovers are a bit arcane.'

'How did you manage? I mean, was cooking something you had to do for Alison?'

'You mean along with making sure she was dressed properly and that she ate at all? Sorry, that sounded bitter. There was a time when . . . Well, Alison was a fantastic cook when we were first married. Then she lost all interest. Long before I retired I had virtually taken over the running of the house. I told you about helping Alison with the shopping, didn't I? In the end I took it over completely. I confess ready meals have been a godsend.'

'That must have been difficult, if you weren't sure what to expect when you got home.'

'That was the point. Sometimes Alison decided to get a meal ready, sometimes she had lost all sense of time and I had to go looking for her. Admittedly I usually found her somewhere in the garden, even if it was raining. That was another complication. There was always the worry . . .' He paused, looking distraught. 'I've never told anyone that.'

'No. That's understandable,' replied Marnie, who was think-ing that it might be understandable, but it would have been better for both Luke and Alison if he had voiced these worries to someone else. 'How did you cope?'

'Not always very well. I did try to keep Alison interested in the house and our life together. Sometimes she seemed to resent my very presence.'

'That must have been extremely hard.'

'It was, when I remembered her as she was when we were first married. She was so house-proud, so full of energy.'

'And you had no outside help? Oh, sorry, it's presumptuous of me to ask, let alone expect you to answer.'

'That's all right. Of course I thought about it and a year or so ago we found a woman in the village who comes in twice a week. Alison says she can't bear the thought of a stranger snooping round the house. But Kylie has been a godsend. Like Polly, who has been marvellous. I can't tell you. A few months ago she even started spending the night with us in case her mother needed attention.'

'Tiring,' observed Marnie. She thought that if the state of things at The Dingle had got to that, it must have been exhausting for everyone. 'How often do you visit Alison?'

'So you did pick up on what I said in the shop? Alison's going through a really bad period. Hasn't recognized me at all for several days. She even got a bit violent yesterday, said she didn't know me and insisted that I was trying to molest her, so they suggested I should leave it for a few days before going again. If anyone does telephone the rest home, I do hope they're tactful.'

'It's a wretched business.' Marnie stretched across to touch Luke's hand, lying on the table.

He turned his hand over so that hers rested in his. 'I can't believe it's come to this, in such a comparatively short time. It seems no more than a few months since Alison could cope reasonably well, provided she was told whom she was going to meet or what she expected to be doing. Like when you came to tea.'

'Oh, God. I do feel responsible for what happened then.'

'That's total nonsense,' he said forcibly. 'Neither of us had the least notion what was going to happen. In fact, all that time I was congratulating myself on asking you to tea. It had been so long since I saw Alison so animated. It was great to see it. That was what made her breakdown so shattering.'

'Polly did tell me her mother hadn't been well when I first met her at the farm. She did mention Alzheimer's.'

'That afternoon when you came to tea was the first bout of a real personality change. Before that, when it appeared to be only vagueness, we could cope. The first time she was really violent was when you came to tea and she threw the china at you. It has been such a shock. Polly's taken it really hard.'

There was infinite sadness in Luke's face and in his voice. Marnie left her hand in his because she thought the human contact must be a comfort. The touch of another person, provided it was not just accidental – as it had become between Felix and herself in the weeks before he left her – had to contain the reassurance you were still part of the human race. It was the lack of this contact, especially from her grandchildren, particularly their spontaneous hugs, that Marnie missed most in her new life.

'Hello, Dad. Marnie. I didn't expect to see you here.'

The bell-like voice above them with its tone of accusation came from a young woman in a well-cut charcoal-grey pinstriped trouser suit who had stopped beside their table. It was Polly Firmer.

Under her hand, Marnie felt a sudden tension in Luke. It was because of that, as well as what she had been thinking in the moments before Polly's arrival, that made her leave her hand in Luke's for several more seconds before she gave his fingers a slight squeeze and laid her own hand in her lap.

'Hello, Polly,' she said. Not for the world would she show Polly, or the smartly dressed man with her (who certainly wasn't Simon) how rattled she actually felt.

'Polly. How's Simon?' Luke asked pointedly.

'Fine, Dad. Just as he was when he phoned you this morning. Ah, have you met—'

Luke rose. There were handshakes all round. Polly and her client (for so he was, Luke said afterwards) left the restaurant.

'Oops!' said Marnie, and grinned.

Luke expelled his breath and relaxed visibly. Their food arrived. Once the waitress had gone, Luke said, 'Marnie, you are so sane. You do me so much good. Thank you for not throwing a wobbly.'

As Polly would have done, if she had not been accompanied by a client, Marnie surmised.

'But there was nothing to become agitated about, was there,' she said, and it was not a question.

'I guess a daughter doesn't much care for the sight of her father holding the hand of another woman.'

'Not if she's another woman in the sense I think you mean. For heaven's sake, Luke, this is only the third time we've met.'

'The fourth, as a matter of fact.'

Marnie shook her head. 'If you're going to start counting, I think I shan't be able to ask you to have another meal with me in the cottage.'

'Which would be a pity.'

'Indeed it would. You see, it's good to have someone to cook for. I miss being needed. I never thought I would say that, especially as there were times when I was even becoming a little resentful of the demands my family was making on me.'

'But you miss them.'

'I do miss them very much, especially Ellie and Josh and Felicity.'

'I should like to meet your Chloë sometime. It's good you have her in the background. I'm sure her brother is glad of that, too. I expect he was concerned when you decided to move so far away.'

'He certainly was,' Marnie declared. She explained briefly the current rivalry between Jack and Chloë. Then she remembered Nick Hunter and gave a small groan.

'What is it?' Luke asked, alarmed.

'I've just remembered about Nick.' She told him that Polly's brother-in-law and her daughter appeared to be something of an item. 'Such a weird description. What it seems to mean in this instance is that they are becoming fond of each other.'

'How extremely interesting,' said Luke, his eyes gleaming. 'I always thought the boys were so stupid, quarrelling over their father's will. You see, Simon may have got the land, but it was Nick who got the old man's money. There was quite a bit that was not tied up in farming.'

So Nicholas Hunter was not in dire need of Chloë Edgerton's fortune (such as it might or might not be).

'The brothers would do so much better if they joined forces.'

'That is what Chloë told me.'

'I do hope she's successful in reconciling them.'

'In the meantime, perhaps it would be more diplomatic not to mention to Polly about Chloë? I mean, I expect she'll hear about Nick's new girlfriend soon enough.'

'Oh, she will, Marnie. You'd never believe what a hotbed of gossip Otterhaven is.'

'Do you know, I think I would.'

They finished their lunch and Luke drove Marnie home. It had already been decided that Luke would come to lunch with her in five days' time.

'Unless it turns out to be a day I have to visit Alison.'

'Naturally,' agreed Marnie. It was sometime afterwards that she noticed that Luke had referred obliquely to his visits to his wife as a duty.

CHAPTER TWELVE

Both Luke Firmer and Marnie Edgerton returned to their respective homes thoughtfully. Luke felt rested. It had been the meal, he decided, his current lack of appetite tempted by good food eaten in congenial company. Marnie was a good sort, there was no doubt about that. He did regret that she had not come to live in Otterhaven before Alison's health deteriorated so drastically. Marnie would have been a good friend to them both, he was sure of that. Maybe Marnie might have been able to counsel him to do the sensible thing. Exactly what he meant by the sensible thing he could not admit, even to himself, but he had a distinct feeling that it would have saved himself, not to mention his daughter, a great deal of anguish.

Marnie went into her garden pensively. It was so sad that a desire for the world not to impinge on a family's trauma sometimes ended in their ordeal being worse than it might have been. She did like Luke and she did so hope they would be friends. It would be good to make a friend of Polly also, she thought, though she was not quite so sure about that young woman, judging from the look on her face when she had caught her father having lunch at the Duck and Drake with a woman not her mother. Caught? What total nonsense!

What neither Luke nor Marnie had been aware of as they said goodbye was that Vera Crawford was walking past on the opposite side of the road. She did not pause, or wave, or give any impression that she was in the least interested in the couple who were standing close together at the garden gate. But a keen observer would have seen how her lips were compressed, how her eyes narrowed and her pace quickened.

Eve Morgan, who let Marnie in through the locked door of The Sycamores the following afternoon, said confidentially, 'Alison is having one of her good days. The only thing is, she hasn't been outside for some time. The garden is lovely at the moment and I'm sure some fresh air would do her the world of good.'

'Doesn't Alison get out regularly?'

'Our residents are encouraged to walk in the gardens. That is, only those who . . .' she hesitated.

'Quite so,' said Marnie, who realized at once that there must be residents whom it would not be at all safe to leave on their own in the garden. 'I'll ask her when we've had our tea.'

After they'd had a cup of tea (and Alison had eaten four biscuits), Alison hesitated when Marnie mentioned a walk. Then she said: 'They told us a water feature was being installed. I suppose they mean a pond. I can't abide poncey language, can you? But I suppose we might as well go and have a look at it.'

The water feature was no pond. In the middle of a small lawn was a stone fountain in the shape of a water nymph carrying an urn. From the urn flowed a trickle of water that fell on to pebbles contained in a circular basin. The water rose and fell rhythmically, making a soothing, splashing sound and a gurgle that Marnie found pleasing.

Alison was entirely scornful.'Pond, indeed! It's nothing but a bowl of bloody pebbles with a concrete gnome.'

'I quite like it,' Marnie answered. 'It's the sort of feature I could easily see in my own garden. But the roses are gorgeous. Shall we go and have a look at them instead?'

Alison turned away from the fountain. Then she changed her mind, instead sitting down on a semi-circular stone bench that had been placed just above the water feature. She swung her legs to and fro like a child. 'I'd rather stay here,' she said. 'I don't like roses any more. Their smell makes me feel sick.'

'Then of course we'll stay here.'

'That's why I don't come into this garden,' confided Alison.

'The flowers stink and there are no weeds anywhere.'

Marnie laughed. 'There's many a gardener who would be envious of a weed-free garden. Don't you remember how you felt when . . .' She stopped.

'When I was a gardener?' supplied Alison. 'Of course I remember, Marnie. I remember a lot of things.'

'You remember me.'

'I remember you perfectly well. I also remember that I forgot who you were the other day and that I threw a cup and saucer at you.'

Marnie had not expected that. 'You didn't exactly hurt me, you know,' she pointed out.

'No. But your expression was a study.'

'It was a surprise. Did you enjoy throwing crockery at me?'

'Yes. At the time it was just what I wanted to do.'

From the satisfaction in her old friend's voice, Marnie was under no illusion that Alison felt any remorse. 'And do you always do what you want to do nowadays?' she asked cautiously.

A look that Marnie could only think of as calculated cunning crossed Alison's face. 'It depends on how bad it is.'

'Bad!'

'Have you never wanted to do violent things? Pull up a plant by its roots and just chuck it away? Take a bread knife and gouge a scratch on a smooth surface, like a mahogany table?'

Marnie suppressed a small shudder of distaste. 'No. Of course not,' she protested.

'Well, I have,' said Alison complacently. 'I felt like throwing the cups and saucers that afternoon. So I did. It was . . . liberating. The only thing is . . .' She threw up her chin defiantly. 'The only thing is, it was like the time when I cut down all the roses in the front garden. It made Luke unhappy.'

'What did Luke do when you cut down the roses?' asked Marnie, not sure if this was a question it was wise to ask, or even if she wanted to know the answer.

'Oh, he didn't exactly scold but there was a look in his eyes . . . Later he got in a contract gardener to plant new ones. And he said he thought I shouldn't work in the front garden again. So I didn't. Do you know Luke?'

'Not as well as I know you, Alison. I've only met your husband a few times, you see. I've known you for years.'

'But you never came to see me in all that time.'

'No, I didn't, because I was living in Australia with my family. Alison, I know you have a few difficulties with your memory. How much do you remember about the last few years?'

'You mean, after that day when I knew there was something wrong with me?'

'Did that happen suddenly?'

'Losing my mind must have happened gradually. Knowing what I was going to face happened one afternoon.'

'Do you feel like telling me?' Again, Marnie wasn't sure if she should be talking to Alison about something so very private but she thought it might help to understand Luke if Alison talked to her.

'I needed to do a supermarket shop in Monmouth. I fancied some fish. Luke likes his fish with the skin off, you know. So I took the car. I drove out of Otterhaven and went to Waitrose. I bought the fish, but when I came out of the car park I discovered that I didn't know where I was supposed to be going.'

'How appalling! Whatever did you do?'

'I'd got to traffic lights. But I didn't know whether to go left, right, or straight on. I waited to see if I could remember, but there were drivers behind who began hooting at me, so I had to do something. I panicked,' Alison replied simply. 'I just turned left and drove, and drove, hoping that I would see a landmark that would tell me where I was.'

'Did you remember about Otterhaven?'

'Oh yes. I knew where I lived. I could picture the house quite clearly. I just couldn't remember how to get there.'

'So what happened?'

'I was on a dual carriageway and eventually I turned off, but that was no better so I just went on and on. Then I found myself passing another supermarket. I'd got to the outskirts of Hereford, you see, by various routes that I didn't remember. It

93

was a supermarket that sold petrol. By then the petrol tank indicator was into the red and I knew that if I ran out of petrol it would be a disaster, having to explain what had happened. So I turned the car, went back to the supermarket and filled up. Then, when I was paying, I asked which was the best way to Monmouth and if they knew which side of the town Otterhaven was. I tried to sound like any stranger, asking directions. There was a nice man in the garage who insisted on writing down his directions. So I did what he told me, and once I got within a mile of the house I knew exactly where I was.'

'Did you tell anyone what had happened?'

'Do you mean, did I tell Luke? I wasn't going to, but unfortunately I'd been gone the whole afternoon. He asked me where I'd been and I burst into tears. So then I had to tell him. And then he made me see a doctor. After that, I never drove again.'

'Oh, Alison. How dreadful.'

'Yes. But there you go. And you know, now that I'm here I feel quite safe.'

'You feel safe? Weren't you safe at home? Didn't you feel safe there?' She'd not expected to hear that. 'Didn't you feel safe with Luke, with your family?' There were implications here that she hardly liked to voice. 'Oh, Alison, you aren't suggesting that your family . . . that Luke was violent towards you . . .'

Not Luke, Marnie was thinking, her mind reeling. Not the man who was patently so distraught about his wife's deteriorating health. Instinctively her eyes went to Alison's wrist, her left wrist, the one on which she had seen bruises on both occasions when she had gone to tea at The Dingle. Alison's skin was perfectly clear. There was not a sign of any mark at all.

Alison was looking at her, an entirely knowing expression on her face, as if she were well aware what was going through Marnie's head. But she did not say anything more about her feelings of safety at The Sycamores, or of what might – or might not – have occurred at home. Instead she gave a broad smile, which itself made Marnie uneasy. 'You liked Luke, didn't you?' she said.

'Well, of course I like Luke,' Marnie replied, as if it were the most normal thing in the world to be discussing one's feelings about a friend's husband with that friend.

'Well, of course you did,' said Alison mockingly.

Marnie noticed that once again Alison was referring to her husband in the past tense. She made no comment about that, saying softly instead,'Luke never hit you, did he, Alison?'

'I was always worried about how Luke would react to what I did. Half the time I was on edge, waiting for his expression of concern. I can't tell you how utterly irritating that was!'

'I'm sure he meant well,' said Marnie weakly. But she persisted: 'Did Luke ever hit you?'

'Of course not. It's just . . . I suppose he did mean well. He was just a pain about it. Here it doesn't matter what I do, or say. I can't tell you how refreshing that is. All the same . . .' She stopped.

'All the same . . .' Marnie prompted gently.

'My family doesn't come to see me now,' said Alison sadly. 'They've left me here all on my own. It's hard, being abandoned among strangers.'

Marnie swallowed a lump of pity. 'I thought Luke came regularly.'

'There is a man who visits. I think he must be a doctor. Yes. That's what he is. A doctor. He's not the man I married. I liked the man I married. He never hit me. Now, I'm not so sure about that man who comes to visit. I don't like him. I have a daughter, too, you know. But I'm glad she doesn't come often.' She shivered suddenly. 'I'm cold. I want to go inside.' As they both stood up, Alison said crossly: 'Call that a pond! I suppose they thought we might drown ourselves if they installed a proper one. Idiots!'

Eve Morgan met them at the side door and escorted Marnie to her car. 'It was good of you to take Alison outside. I hope she liked our new water feature.'

Marnie shook her head. 'I think Alison was expecting something a little bigger.'

'Yes, well . . . Health and Safety, you know. There are all sorts of constraints imposed on us.'

'That's what Alison said.' Marnie paused. 'May I ask you

something? You see, it was something Alison said. About feeling safe here.'

'I'm glad she does feel safe with us.'

'It's just that there seems to be an implication there, an accusation about her family?'

'Mrs Edgerton, you couldn't really expect me to comment, could you?'

'No. No, certainly not. But . . .'

'There has never been any suggestion that Mrs Firmer's husband was anything but kind and caring,' the woman emphasized.

And with that, Marnie had to be satisfied. Except that something niggled, and continued to do so.

CHAPTER THIRTEEN

'She went to see Alison the other day,' Mrs Powell confided to Vera Crawford, who was sending a large, first-class letter.

'Who did?' asked Vera, searching in her purse for change.

'Marnie Edgerton, that's who.'

'After what happened? Bit of a nerve, if you ask me.'

'Exactly. Our Lisa was visiting her aunt and uncle who've just gone into one of them cottages at The Sycamores. Ever so nice they are inside, Lisa said. Of course, the kitchen is very small but they don't do much of that nowadays. Cooking, I mean. You don't, do you, when one of you's recovering from a heart attack and the other's overweight.'

'I suppose not,' Vera replied. 'It'll have to be a note, I'm afraid, Val.'

The postmistress heaved a sigh. 'Anyway, she said she saw Marnie Edgerton talking to Alison Firmer in the garden. Lovely gardens they have, at The Sycamores. But them fees must easily pay for a gardener, don't you think? They was there for a long time by the new water feature. Alison and Marnie Edgerton. Too long. A nasty wind got up all of a sudden and Alison was looking proper frozen when they went inside. Our Lisa said she thought Alison was crying.'

'I suppose it could have been the wind.'

Mrs Powell gave Vera Crawford an old-fashioned look. Then she handed over a fistful of coins. 'Sorry about that, Vera. I'm quite out of five-pound notes today.'

'Still, I don't like to think of Alison being made to cry.'

'I should say not.'

When the shop door clicked behind Vera Crawford, Mr Powell said to his wife reproachfully, 'I thought we'd said we weren't going to slag off Mrs Edgerton no more, Val. On account of her being a customer, like.'

Val Powell shrugged. 'I only speak as I find.'

'Anyway, you know there was never no suggestion that Luke Firmer caused them bruises we saw and that was weeks before Marnie Edgerton ever came on the scene.'

'They was nasty, though.'

'Just remember, we don't want to lose no customers, dear.'

It was several days after Marnie and Luke had gone out to lunch. Very little had happened since, apart from Marnie's visit to Alison, which she did not feel like repeating too soon. There had been a brief e-mail from Jack telling his mother that Ellie had, indeed, been correct about the bullying and that he and Gemma were going to do something about it. Just what they were proposing to do was unspecified. Marnie had made a face at her laptop and resigned herself to feeling redundant.

Then she told herself not to be so pathetic. After all, this was what she had intended: that her son should take full responsibility for his family and not rely on her quite so much for support. If the result was more extreme than she liked, she had to face that this was the way of the world.

She did e-mail a well-done note to Ellie, and hoped that she would hear more from her Australian family soon.

Nor had Marnie seen anything of Chloë. Again, that was perfectly understandable. That young woman had been a great deal more supportive than Marnie had anticipated when she made the decision to come back to the UK principally to find her daughter. Now that Marnie knew there was a man in the background (or was Nick very much a formidable force in Chloë's life?), she could hardly expect that daughter to come running at every opportunity. Not that she ever would expect Chloë to do that now she was settled in her cottage, Marnie thought, as she looked round her sitting-room, which already contained several good pieces of furniture and two pleasing watercolours, though neither had come from Vera's gallery.

What she needed next, Marnie decided, was a distraction or she'd be found talking to herself.

Just how to distract herself was another matter. Marnie was not much of a joiner. She already knew that the WI was an important part of village life; certainly it was in Otterhaven. Jam and Jerusalem played little part in the WI in the twenty-first century, Daphne Jones had declared, its members being enthusiastic about subjects as far-ranging as 'Pornography and the Family' to 'How to Keep Your Hives Healthy'. Marnie thought that she might think about joining sometime in the future but she could raise little enthusiasm for the idea. She had picked up a leaflet about the University of the Third Age whose members walked together, swam together, philoso-phized together and did almost every other activity you could name. But Marnie preferred her own company when she walked, as she had told Nick. She certainly couldn't imagine anything worse than getting undressed in this climate then swimming in cold water, even if it might be good for her, and she did not want to stretch her mind beyond the daily cross-word.

There was another tiny concern about joining anything. Village life could be claustrophobic. Lurid tales of village life and how established villagers closed ranks against an incomer were not so different from the attitudes that prevailed at school in her day, when a new girl arrived. Marnie wanted to integrate, but she did not want to throw herself into things and run the risk of seeming pushy and being frozen out. Or had that already happened?

Marnie was almost certain that Vera Crawford had cut her dead in St Bride's Street the day before.

Marnie had been for a walk. She was returning past the pond when she saw Vera Crawford walking towards her. She had not spoken to anyone for two days so she was pleased to see a familiar figure and hoped that Vera might engage her in a small conversation. As they drew near, although Marnie was smiling tentatively, there was not a flicker of recognition in the other woman's face; not a hint of a smile to indicate that she acknowledged the presence of another in her village. Worse, just before they drew abreast, Vera Crawford crossed the road. To an onlooker it could have been coincidental. To Marnie, it was quite deliberate.

After twenty-four hours, though, Marnie decided that she had to be charitable about Vera Crawford's behaviour. Vera could have totally forgotten they had been introduced. She might have been deep in thought and genuinely not realized who Marnie was. There had been no snub.

It was the day before Luke's visit. In the morning Marnie had gone into Monmouth for a supermarket shop. She had intended gardening in the afternoon but a fine drizzle had put paid to any idea of that and as she had stale bread in the bread bin and she was feeling restless, she decided to go and feed the ducks. There was a mallard nesting in the reeds at the far end and Marnie thought she deserved feeding. The duck was nowhere to be seen, but two drakes came swimming across the pond and Marnie spent several minutes sitting on a bench seat and watching them squabble over the pieces of bread that she threw in their direction.

Deciding to complete the circuit on her way home, she set off for the churchyard and the footpath that would bring her out into Church Lane. As she approached St Bride's, she realized that, for the first time, the church door was open.

Marnie always went to church on Christmas Day and usually on Easter Sunday but for the rest, it was weddings and funerals only. She did, however, remember fondly the country churches of her childhood and she had discovered on her walks that there were many churches in the vicinity that were not locked. St Bride's was an exception. Marnie thought this was because it was less isolated than some with therefore more potential for theft.

The whole idea of theft from a church scandalized her. It was an aspect of modern UK life that was profoundly shocking. Now she was merely curious to discover what her parish church was like inside (and without having to wait until Christmas). But as she pushed open the door to enter, it was wrenched violently from her hand.

'Gerroff you silly old fool!' Looming over her was an agitated young man, his voice rough with anger and apprehension as he found his way blocked.

Marnie froze.

He swore and shoved her aside and she staggered, turning her ankle on the floor of the porch, its ancient surface badly worn, and she yelped as she landed heavily on the unyielding stones.

'Stop, you little devil! Come back! How dare you! Oh, my God! Are you hurt? Did that wretched boy hit you? Let me help you up.'

'Just a minute. Wait, please!' pleaded Marnie, her heart thudding from the shock. 'I think I'm all right.' She rubbed her hip, which had hit the ground first, then she flexed her left arm. 'Ouch, I shall be covered in bruises, but I don't think anything's broken. It's all right,' she said firmly, as once more the woman who had come to her rescue bent to help her. 'I'm better getting up on my own.' With a little difficulty, she hauled herself to her feet.

The woman was looking at her anxiously as she said:

'I need to report this to the police, but should I call a doctor first?'

'Heavens, no,' declared Marnie.'I tend to fall quite well. I was a gymnast in my youth and relaxing as I fall seems to have been a lesson well learnt. Whatever was going on?'

'Wretched youth. The church is usually kept locked because of opportunist theft. Not that we dare keep anything of any real value out of the safe nowadays. So sad. Come in and sit down for a minute. Would you like a glass of water? I could get you that. You do look a little pale.'

'I suppose it's a bit of shock. I certainly didn't expect quite so forceful a welcome.'

The woman, who was possibly older than Marnie but still in her sixties, was dressed in a tweed skirt of unfashionable mid-calf length, stout shoes and a navy waxed jacket. She sat Marnie in the nearest pew and bustled off to the vestry for a glass of water.

Marnie rubbed her elbow as she looked round. St Bride's was small, but well proportioned. It had a Norman chancel arch, and what appeared to be a Norman font by the door, which was oak and heavily iron-banded. The walls were white-washed except for the north wall on which was an ochre-coloured mural of the Ten Commandments in a reasonable state of repair. There were a few memorials on the walls, but little other decoration.

'Here, sip at this. I'm Linda Griffiths, by the way. Are you a visitor? So unfortunate. I am so sorry. What must you think of Otterhaven?'

'My name is Marnie Edgerton. I've bought—'

'Bert Wilson's cottage.'

'That's right. I was returning home through the churchyard and I saw the door was open so I thought I'd come in.'

'Wretched youth!' Linda Griffiths repeated forcefully.'I suppose you didn't catch much of a glimpse of him?'

'All I saw was this young man in jeans with a dark, hooded top which was pulled right over his face . . .'

'And they tell us to hug a hoodie. I know what I'd do to that one.'

'I think I would, too, Mrs Griffiths.'

'Linda.'

'Linda, but I suppose not all hoodies are hooligans.'

'I was in the vestry filling a can to water the flowers,' said Linda Griffiths.'I was only gone a moment. As you see, there isn't anything small to steal. I even make a point of opening the donations box once a week after the Sunday service, just in case. I suppose he saw the door open and came in. He wouldn't have got anything. Still . . . I don't know what the world is coming to. You've come back from Australia, haven't you?'

'Is that my accent, or is that common knowledge?'

'Common knowledge, as a matter of fact. I gather you have come back to meet up with Luke Firmer.'

'Wherever did you hear that?' exclaimed Marnie, who was almost more shocked by that piece of information than she had been by being knocked down at the church door.

'Ah,' said Linda. 'I think I should lock up and take you home for a cup of tea. Much better for you than plain water.'

'Oh, I . . .'

'I live just opposite. At St Bride's Cottage. Looking after the church, and being a key-holder, and in the summer clearing up a bit in the churchyard is my way of doing voluntary work. Come on, let's go and put the kettle on. And, by the look of you, I should think you could do with a tube of arnica.' Without waiting for assent, Linda Griffiths produced a huge iron key with which she locked up. Then she led the way back down the church path and across the road to a small stone cottage opposite in its well-kept garden.

'I hope you don't mind the kitchen,' Linda said, setting mugs on the table. 'I get the afternoon sun in here. Now, tell me all about yourself.'

So Marnie did, as she rubbed arnica into the more accessible of her bruises. She took pains to explain that it was Chloë she had come to see and that she had lost touch with Alison and that she was so shocked to discover . . . There she hesitated.

'That Alison's gone doolally? It's all right. That's common knowledge, too.'

'I think Luke was hoping it could all be kept secret.'

'My dear, you can't keep anything a secret in Otterhaven. Mind you, a lot is believed to have happened long before it actually does, if you get my meaning.'

'Strictly conjecture.'

'Gossip, pure and simple, if gossip can ever be called pure. Anyway, it is conjectured that Alison became violent when she saw you and Luke together. Luke being your old flame. Or is that the other way round?'

CHAPTER FOURTEEN

Luke her old flame? Marnie listened to Linda Griffiths in total disbelief. The whole thing was outrageous! She bristled, her annoyance perfectly plain.

Linda put her head to one side and said, 'Oh dear. Is this another case of village gossip getting everything wrong?'

So Marnie decided she had no choice but to tell Linda the whole story, beginning from when she decided she did not want to move to Canberra with her son and his family and finishing on the day when she finally met up with Alison Firmer after all those years – and stressing that she had never even met Luke before that day.

'It was such a shock,' Marnie ended. 'You see, at first Alison seemed to remember so much more than I did about our school days. It was such fun, reminiscing. I really thought she'd be able to put me in touch with friends I hadn't seen for years. And then . . .'

'She flipped? Alison threw things at you. Kylie's told everyone she found china on the drawing-room floor.'

'The Firmers' cleaning lady? Luke is going to be devastated.'

'There is worse,' said Linda gently. 'You see, you and Luke were seen canoodling in the Duck and Drake. There was a scene with Polly— Ah. You've never been to the Duck and Drake.'

'That's the trouble with gossip,' said Marnie wryly. 'It always contains a germ of truth. More than a germ of truth.' She explained. 'What is more, Luke is coming to lunch tomorrow.'

Linda Griffiths laughed. 'I'll say this for you, you really do believe in giving a V-sign to the village.'

'Not at all,' protested Marnie. 'The trouble is, Luke is totally innocent of any shocking intentions towards me and I just never gave appearances a thought. It's because of having lived in a large city, I suppose. Sandgropers don't give a damn what their neighbours get up to. It's like living in a time warp here. That's what people born and bred in Perth call themselves,' she explained, seeing Linda's puzzled expression. 'Sandgropers.'

'Yes, well, you'll either have to abandon any notions of helping Luke through a domestic crisis or bear the consequences.' It certainly was an entertaining slant on village life, though Linda had her doubts whether any man could be said to be entirely innocent. 'Anyway, whatever you do will turn out to be no more than a ten-day wonder, I don't doubt. And now, I must report the incident at the church. Won't be a minute.'

Tending her bruises while she was left on her own, Marnie regretted having mentioned anything to Linda Griffiths, who seemed very friendly now, but she could so easily turn against her. Like Vera Crawford appeared to have done. Before tomorrow morning a whole raft of new gossip would probably be running round the village.

'Someone'll come by tomorrow and take a statement,' said Linda, returning to the kitchen. 'Have you treated all your bruises now? It's best to do it as soon as possible. Will you be in tomorrow? I expect the police'll want to interview you. Oh, I forgot. You're expecting Luke for lunch.'

'It would be a bit disconcerting to have a constable taking a statement during lunch,' agreed Marnie. She decided she needed to change the subject. There was a series of unframed pictures laid out on a side table. 'Are you a painter?' she asked, gesturing towards them. 'I couldn't help noticing them while you were on the phone.'

'Goodness me, no. Come and have a look at them. As you came into St Bride's this afternoon, you might be interested,' said Linda, walking over to where the paintings were displayed.

There were four of them, painted in acrylic. 'If you weren't too preoccupied by your ordeal, you probably saw that the church is very bare nowadays. Not so long ago we were left a small legacy for either cushions for the pews or kneelers. As kneelers are a bit out of fashion nowadays, we've decided to make cushions. I swear those pews in St Bride's have to be the most uncomfortable I have ever sat in, so this will be a great improvement. But it's not an easy task to find stitchers, I can tell you, as so few young women seem to have been taught to sew. The parochial church council commissioned Tom Gillard, our local artist, to design them. He's come up with four basic designs, three scenes from the life of St Bride and these otters playing on a river bank.'

'Who was St Bride?'

'St Brigid of Ireland, an early sixth-century saint, sometimes called Bride. And don't ask me why our foundation was called after her because I'm no church historian. But there are several churches named variously after her in the locality, including the church of St Bridget in Skenfrith. She's the patron saint of all sorts of people including dairy maids, printing presses and children whose parents aren't married, which I think makes her a pretty useful sort of saint.'

'I can't say I've ever heard of her,' admitted Marnie.

'I can lend you a pamphlet we had printed several years ago for visitors to the church, if you like.' Marnie nodded her head politely.

'We've drawn Tom Gillard's designs on to canvas,' Linda continued, 'and I painted in the colours. Fairly crudely, I confess, but the shading will come with the stitching. I've just started one of them.' She picked up a wooden frame on which was stretched a piece of canvas, some of which was worked. 'You don't sew, do you, Marnie?'

'You're not asking me to embroider a cushion, are you?'

'Well, that's the general idea. The canvas is fourteen holes to the inch and we shall use a variety of stitches, from a simple half-cross stitch to an encroaching gobelin for interest, and we have some gorgeous shades of wool. What do you say?'

Marnie laughed uncertainly. At school she had enjoyed doing all kinds of stitching but what with one thing and another, using a sewing machine to make something for her grandchildren's school plays was about all she had managed for many years.

'Don't tell me the bridge brigade has you in its toils already.'

'Bridge. Heavens, no,' exclaimed Marnie.

'Round here, it's an accepted pastime for a widow. You know, regular sessions with like-minded people. Keeps the loneliness at bay, if you see what I mean. And it's a powerful stimulant for the brain. I don't play. I keep the vestments in good repair and now I'm going to make cushions so that I can sit and listen to the bishop's sermons in relative comfort.'

'All right,' agreed Marnie.'I'll do it. But I'm going to need more than a little guidance from you.'

'That's not a problem. What about starting on Tuesday morning?'

Marnie thanked Linda for both her rescue and the tea, and they parted, Marnie shaking her head in bewilderment that she had permitted herself to be talked into a village activity so easily.

As a distraction, it was unquestionably different.

'Did you manage to visit Alison? I heard you and Luke mentioning it in the shop the other day.' Sandy Williams accosted Vera Crawford in St Bride's Street. Sandy was the manager of Monmouth's Citizens Advice Bureau. 'How is she getting on?'

Vera shook her head and replied: 'Not too well, by all accounts. I took Luke's advice and rang The Sycamores, but the woman I spoke to was discouraging. Didn't actually say I couldn't visit but, you know, said she was a bit tired that day.'

'Poor Alison. Dreadful business, Alzheimer's.'

'And it's not as if I knew her all that well. She wasn't one for buying presents from me. Not like her daughter.'

'It's an awful thing to happen to any family. My uncle had Alzheimer's. And he lived until he was ninety,' said Sandy.

'Fortunately I think Luke is getting a fair amount of TLC, if you get my meaning.'

'From Polly? I suppose that's only natural.'

'It isn't Polly I'm talking about.' When Sandy maintained a carefully interested expression that masked more than a little curiosity, Vera continued: 'I don't know if you've met Marnie Edgerton?'

'The woman who's bought old Bert Wilson's house in Church Lane? Wasn't she knocked unconscious by a young thug who stole more than £50 from the church? Absolutely appalling.'

'I don't think she was hurt all that badly.'

'Thank goodness for that. Not the sort of welcome we want for an incomer.'

Vera sniffed. 'It depends on the incomer, if you ask me.'

'Vera, what do you mean?'

'Well, it seems Marnie Edgerton's been nursing a torch for Luke Firmer ever since he married Alison. She came back from Australia especially to get in touch.'

'How very romantic.'

'I'd call it predatory, myself.'

'Goodness. Surely not!'

'I guess we'll find out what her motives are, soon enough.'

Marnie thought that it would be unfair of her to provide too simple a lunch for Luke after his declaration that a lot of his meals came from the supermarket. She decided on lamb chops with a tomato and olive sauce, new potatoes and green beans.

He arrived very much on time, filling her low-ceilinged sitting-room with his bulk and his gravelly voice and making her quiet existence of the past few days seem something of a dream.

She asked after Alison.

'Oh, you know.' He shrugged.

There was something in his face that persuaded Marnie not to mention Luke's wife again until after they had eaten. She did not know the man well enough to judge whether he genuinely preferred not to discuss his wife's condition or if he were trying not to distress her. He had brought a bottle of wine – said he'd walked – and she thought the alcohol would relax him sufficiently for him to be able to talk to her more familiarly after lunch. It wasn't always easy to confide in the younger generation, as she was only too well aware. Luke probably felt the same way about Polly and might welcome unloading some of his angst on to a comparative stranger.

They had just finished the pudding she had made – a rhubarb fool – when the doorbell rang. As she feared, it was a young policeman. 'Would it be convenient for me to take a statement from you, madam?'

Marnie hesitated. 'I do have a visitor.'

'Hello, Constable Watkins. What are you doing here?'

PC Watkins paused. 'Good afternoon, Mr Firmer. Madam?'

'Should you mind, Luke? The policeman has just come for a statement. It's about the attempted theft at the church.'

'Don't tell me you were involved in that!'

'I was knocked down as the thief ran away. Though I probably mean failed thief since he didn't manage to steal a thing. Oh, let's get it over with. I guess it won't take too long. Coffee, Constable, or would you prefer tea?'

PC Watkins declined both. Laboriously Marnie's statement was copied down, read back to her and eventually she signed it. 'I've written down my name, madam, and your crime reference number. Victim Support will be in touch in case you want to talk to them.'

'Victim Support?'

'Counselling,' muttered Luke, looking as though he were trying hard not to laugh.

'Precisely, sir,' the policeman said reproachfully.

'I don't think so,' declared Marnie.

'Anyway, they are there to help.' He put away his papers and got to his feet. 'Thank you, madam.'

'Victim Support,' snorted Marnie, when she had shut the door behind the policeman.

There was a splutter of laughter beside her. She turned to find Luke with his face quite contorted with merriment. 'Oh, Marnie, I do enjoy my encounters with you. They are so refreshing. I never know what you're going to come up with next. If only the young man knew, he was probably extremely lucky he got away unscathed.'

'There's nothing to laugh about. That fall hurt very much!'

'I bet it did. I had noticed you are limping a bit.'

'This is just one of my huge bruises,' said Marnie. She rolled back her sleeve to display a dark discoloration on her arm. 'I'm afraid Linda's arnica didn't entirely work.'

'Poor Marnie, what an introduction to Otterhaven.' He reached out his hand and touched the bruise gently. 'Well, I suppose there are some people who are glad Victim Support exists.'

'I guess a bruise or two is probably the least of my worries,' grunted Marnie, disconcerted by his touch and very unwilling to show it. She wasn't used to tactile sympathy. 'I'll put the kettle on.'

'What do you mean, the least of your worries?' asked Luke, sauntering back into the kitchen after her. 'That sounds serious.'

She told him about the gossip that Linda had picked up and about Vera Crawford. She omitted to mention Kylie. Domestic help was never easy to find. She would not want to be the cause of Luke's losing his. 'I'm not too sure I like being considered a Jezebel, though,' she added.

'Lord, no! That's very unkind and most unfair.'

'It would be even worse if it got back to Alison.'

'Fortunately that's most unlikely.'

'But you can't be sure. Oh, Luke, I don't know what to do. This is so stupid. You know, I love this cottage, but I'm beginning to wish I'd never set eyes on Otterhaven.'

'You don't mean that.'

'Don't I?'

There was a strange expression on his face. He made a move towards her. Marnie thought for a moment that he was going to take her into his arms, which would be a complication definitely too far, even though she would have enjoyed a comforting hug. She evaded him by slipping past and she reached into a cupboard for coffee cups. When she had set them on a tray and looked at him again, she decided she had read too much into his face. Of course she had!

'Coffee,' Marnie said. 'Coffee's ready. With no sugar.'

CHAPTER FIFTEEN

'You asked about Alison earlier,' Luke said, as he accepted his cup of coffee. There was no sign that anything untoward had been in his mind a minute before so Marnie was sure she must have imagined it. 'The fact is, sometimes Alison doesn't even recognize me. Eve Morgan tells me that the doctor is trying to stabilize her on drugs, but that's one of the reasons I'm not there every day.'

'What does Polly say about this?' Marnie asked cautiously.

'Not much. When it happened the first time to her, she was totally shocked. I think she tries to avoid having to visit at all now, which is a pity because I get the feeling the staff think Alison would benefit from the occasional visitor.'

'I can understand that. But it must be so sad for her, watching her mother's condition worsen day by day.'

'What's even sadder is that Polly says she feels guilty.'

'Why does she feel guilty?' Marnie asked, her voice neutral. Surely Luke was not suggesting that their daughter had anything to do with Alison's bruises.

'She says the family should be able to cope. She thinks we are letting her mother down by keeping her in The Sycamores.'

'That's not true,' said Marnie emphatically. 'With some victims of Alzheimer's there comes a time when their families need professional help. You can't be expected to look after a sick wife for twenty-four hours at a time.'

'Some families have to.'

'It's a dreadful indictment on modern life.'

112

'It's also Polly herself I'm thinking about. She and Simon have been trying for a family for two or three years now, obviously without success,' he said, with a grimace. 'Life can be so cruel, can't it?'

'How old is Polly?'

'She's just turned forty-one and Simon is forty-three. So it's getting a bit urgent for them. Lisa and Rupert have plenty of time because she is only twenty-five. That's probably another niggle for Polly, though she never says anything about it to me.'

'Forty-one isn't so very ancient for modern women, though. Is there any reason why it hasn't happened. Don't answer that if you think I'm being intrusive.'

'Well, it's not something to repeat. Which I know you wouldn't. Apparently six months ago they found Polly had a blocked tube which they were able to clear, so now there is no reason why she can't conceive. And for the moment they certainly don't want to go down the IVF path. Polly's been told that her best natural way is to avoid stress. The state Alison has been in recently obviously hasn't helped. That they were trying for a baby was one of the reasons why I held out for so long when Polly first suggested she should come and spend the night at The Dingle to relieve me. She thought we were managing. The illusion went the first night she saw her mother get into a state and become foul-mouthed.'

'Oh, Luke.'

'We conspired to keep it in the family, you know. And it wasn't too difficult to hide it from strangers. Everyone knew Alison loved her garden. I let anyone who called asking after her assume she was busy outside.'

'When she was no such thing?'

'When at the best she was pulling up flowers and carefully transplanting weeds, or just sitting and staring into space.'

'But not doing herself any harm.'

'I've said before that when Alison threw the china it was the first time she'd been violent. You really mustn't blame yourself,' he added, seeing Marnie's face.

'No,' she agreed. 'And after a while lots of people stopped

asking after Alison, I suppose. That's the way of the world. I did promise I'd visit her again. Would it be a good idea?'

'I honestly don't know. You'd have to ask first.'

'I would do that, anyway.'

'The problem is . . .' He hesitated. 'You see, along with the occasional violence there's some inappropriate behaviour.'

Marnie did not ask for details. Nor did she mention how Alison had shown her her knickers in full view of other residents.

Inappropriate behaviour probably meant that Alison was exposing herself, using explicitly sexual gestures, and generally behaving in a fashion that was totally alien to her former self, all of which were symptomatic of senile dementia.

'I'm so glad that twice I had at least twenty minutes' rational conversation with her at home,' she said simply. When she found sufficient courage to look Luke in the face again, she saw that he was crying, his tears sliding down his furrowed cheeks unchecked.

'Oh, my dear,' she said. Without a moment's thought she got up from where she was sitting on the other side of the table and went over to him and put her arms round his shoulders.

He rested his head against her for a long minute. She felt a deep shudder go through him. Then he pulled back. Marnie moved away, fearful that she had been the one to cross an invisible boundary. As he began fumbling in his pocket, tactfully she went over to the coffee pot.

'Would you like another cup?'

'No. Yes. I suppose you wouldn't have a brandy instead?' he asked wistfully.

'No brandy, sorry. I do have a bottle of whisky.'

'Just as good,' he said.'Do you mind?'

Privately thinking that a sweet coffee might do Luke better than a whisky, Marnie nevertheless fetched the bottle and two glasses. They spoke no more about Alison. They spoke about nothing very much. Luke finished his whisky fairly quickly. Then he got up to go. At the door he thanked her.

But on the doorstep he suddenly turned back, took her face

between his hands and, without warning and very briefly, he kissed her on the lips.

Her eyes wide with disbelief, Marnie stared after him as he went through the gate without looking back at all. Swiftly she looked from right to left and back again. As far as she could see, there was no one walking along Church Lane. Had anybody observed that little scene? It was anyone's guess, for at least three houses had net curtains at the windows.

With foreboding, Marnie reckoned up her chances of escaping censure. At that moment they didn't seem very high.

What Marnie was beginning to call the local Mafia met by chance in the general store the following day. Unsurprisingly it started with an innocuous query about the state of Alison's health, this time from Jo Edwards from Dollys.

'It's not poor Alison you need to worry about. If you ask me she's a lot better off where she is than she would be at home.'

'Not that it's Luke I blame.'

'Whatever do you mean, Vera?' asked the bewildered Jo.

'You mean you haven't heard, dear?' said Mrs Powell.

'What haven't I heard?'

'About Luke Firmer's piece.'

They told her, in considerable (and untrue) detail, dwelling on the aspect that most appalled them, that Marnie Edgerton had come home knowing that Alison Firmer was in the final stages of Alzheimer's and determined to win over Luke for herself. Apparently she had been devastated when he had asked Alison to marry him instead of her and she'd married a much older man on the rebound.

'But surely she couldn't guarantee Luke would fall for her now?' protested Joan Graham, one of Otterhaven's more elderly divorcees.

'That one wouldn't care about riding roughshod over Luke's feelings.'

'I don't think we should be talking about Luke's feelings at this dreadful time in his life, and I'm not sure you can call a sixty-year-old woman a "piece",' Mary Beresford objected

115

mildly, 'if, indeed, there is anything to substantiate what is really only gossip.'

'Holding hands in the Duck and Drake?' objected Mrs Powell. 'That's fact, not gossip.'

'Kissing in the street?'

'No!' But no one took Mary Beresford's defence of Marnie Edgerton too seriously. After all, she was Castle.

'That's not gossip, either,' said Vera Crawford. 'I heard it from Mrs Pritchard next door to Marnie Edgerton and she happened to be looking out of the window when it occurred.'

Marnie's first stitching session with Linda Griffiths was tiring, but enjoyable. Linda was handing out no concessions. First she asked Marnie to choose the design she preferred.

'I like the otters. Wouldn't it be more sensible if I worked on St Bride's cross instead?' It was a curiously squared-off cross that, it was believed, St Bride had made from rushes as she sat by the bed of her dying father. Tom Gillard had placed the simple design, to be worked in shades of ripe corn, on to a background which was the colour of a bullrush.

'What's the point of being sensible? There's no merit in being bored. If you like the otters, do them. The cross is probably best done by an absolute beginner, and I know you are not that. Choose your colours then you'll need to frame your canvas.' Linda made Marnie work a few trial stitches on a piece of spare canvas and make some notes about the stitches she might use in various places.

'I think we may be joined occasionally by Hetty Loveridge who's only teaching part-time now. By the way, I do hope you'll offer to take this home. A few extra hours will make such a difference. You'll like Hetty. She's ever so nice and Tom Gillard's partner, or whatever you call people currently who sleep together. Personally I can't see why they don't get married because they always are together. It's just that sometimes Tom stays at Hetty's house in The Lane, at other times you'll find them both on Gaer Hill.'

'I suppose if you are a working artist you need periods of

peace and quiet,' said Marnie, thinking there was a lot to be said for enjoying the best of both worlds. She thought, also, that when people said you'd like someone, it didn't always work that way. And she desperately needed someone else on her side in Otterhaven. She had gone to the general store before she came to Linda's to post a birthday card to a friend in Perth and though Mrs Powell had served her without comment, Marnie had been sure there was a definite withdrawal of goodwill.

'Yes, well. Living together without the benefit of clergy just seems a bit odd to old fogeys like me.'

'I doubt very much if you've ever been one of those, or ever will be,' Marnie said cheerfully, as she picked out shades of green wool.

Linda had heard through the Mafia (in this case Kylie, who also did for her one morning a week) that Luke had lunched with Marnie. The girl had also told her that it didn't look as though Mrs Firmer would be coming home all that soon. Tactfully, and without mentioning the lunch, Linda began talking about Alison.

'So sad. I don't think I'll try to visit. I'd prefer to remember her as she used to be. Alison always had such style, you know. Idiosyncratic, but a definite style. Do you know that poem by Jenny Joseph, 'When I Am Old I Shall Wear Purple'? Alison has worn purple for years. Long skirts and trailing scarves. And in the summer she had a straw hat with huge silk flowers in it. And lace gloves. She said she wore those because they hid her hands, which were roughened from gardening. She was gorgeous. But she wore Luke's old corduroy trousers in the garden. Sometimes you couldn't tell which was which from behind.'

'Were you very friendly?'

'Alison wasn't the type of woman you were very friendly with. I don't think she ever had a real confidante. You know, the person you tell your deepest secrets to.'

'I'm not sure I've ever had one of those myself,' said Marnie.

'Nor I, come to think of it. But I guess Hetty and Mary Beresford have that sort of relationship.'

'I've not met Mary Beresford, though I did meet Ian.

117

Goodness, it was the first day I went to tea with Luke and Alison. It was the next visit that was the start of it all.'

'Whatever do you mean by that?'

'How do I cope with a corner? Do I just miss a hole?'

'Let me see. Think of it as painting in threads. Look at the outline and see if it should be the colour you're working in or if it would be better as background. It's your decision ultimately. So, what did you mean by saying your visit to the Firmers' was the start of it all?'

'The start of Alison's change of personality, of course.'

'What utter nonsense,' declared Linda. 'Alison hasn't been well for years. The fact that you happened along on a particular day has nothing to do with where she is now.'

'Luke said that, too. All the same, I do feel responsible,' said Marnie stubbornly.

'Isn't that a bit arrogant? You just concentrate on keeping Luke sane and let the medical profession deal with his wife.'

'Ah. Someone told you he kissed me goodbye after our lunch.'

Linda sighed. 'I'm an idiot. I wasn't going to mention anything about the two of you having lunch together.'

'It was no big deal. He was just saying thank you.'

'Of course he was.'

'I told you he was coming. Though it might have been a better idea if he'd kissed me indoors.'

'I think some of the gossips have already decided what went on behind closed doors.'

Marnie put down her frame and stood up. 'Perhaps I'd better go.'

'I can't think why.'

'You'll get into terrible trouble harbouring a Jezebel.'

Linda laughed out loud. 'As if that's going to worry me. Besides, if the gossips know you are helping me with the church cushions, some of them may think twice about condemning you out of hand. Now have a good stretch and come and sit down again. I reckon we can do another hour before you need a proper break.'

CHAPTER SIXTEEN

Marnie decided that she really should make the effort to visit Alison once more. Five days after she had spoken to Luke, she phoned The Sycamores.'I'm sure Mrs Firmer will be happy to see you,' was the reply. From which Marnie deduced that the drugs were having the desired, calming effect on Alison.

Remembering that Alison had expressed an aversion to flowers, she took with her a box of chocolates. Then, when they met in the same drawing-room to which she had first been shown, Marnie wondered if she had done the right thing. The drugs might be having a calming effect on her friend, but something was making her bloated. From the almost emaciated woman of their first encounter not all that time ago, Alison had put on a considerable amount of weight. She also pounced greedily on the chocolate box, tearing off the wrapper and throwing it on the floor.

'Goody, goody,' she said, cramming a violet cream into her mouth. 'Creams. I hate hard centres.'

A care assistant, who had come in with a tray of tea, gently took the box from Alison.'Shall we keep the rest of these until later, Alison? There's a digestive biscuit for your tea.'

'Suggestive digestive,' sniggered Alison.'I'd much rather have another choccy,' she said wistfully, helping herself to three of the biscuits on the small plate.

'How are you, Alison?' asked Marnie, wondering what on earth they would be able to talk about, with Alison in this mood.

Alison shrugged.'I'm all right.' She leant forward.'You heard that woman call me Alison? They only call me Mrs Firmer when I'm good. It's fun being naughty. Who are you?'

Taken aback, nevertheless Marnie had been expecting something like this.'I'm a friend of yours. Just visiting.'

'I guessed you were a friend, idiot. What's your name?'

'Marnie.'

Alison shook her head. 'No. I don't have a friend called Marnie.'

'We knew each other a long time ago. Don't worry about not remembering. I find I forget things nowadays.'

'Patronizing cow. Are you married, Marnie?' Alison took the last biscuit.

'Not any more.'

'I don't think I'm married. I used to have a husband but he was a bit of a nuisance. Always expecting me to cook for him. I liked him but I hated cooking. There's a man who comes here sometimes. He molests me.'

'Does he? Whatever does he do to you?'

'You know. He tries to kiss me. I have to tell him to fuck off.'

'Perhaps he's just trying to be friendly.'

'Then he shouldn't. Well, we've finished the biscuits and I want to watch the telly.' She expounded on her favourite programmes of the moment, more animated than Marnie had seen her before. 'So you'd better go,' Alison ended pointedly.

'Right. It was good seeing you, Alison.'

'No, it wasn't,' said Alison sharply. 'I'm as much of a pain as that man who comes to see me, but at least I know what I'm doing. You can come again, if you like. If you bring me another box of choccies.' She turned and marched stolidly out of the room, leaving Marnie sitting back limply in the easy chair.

'You mustn't mind Mrs Firmer.' The care assistant who had brought the tea tray had come to see her out. 'Really, she's so much better than she was.'

'But now she doesn't know me at all.'

'No. I'm afraid that happens, sometimes.' She led the way to the door and unlocked it. 'Do come again. Though . . .'

'Maybe without the chocolates?'

'You could bring a magazine. One with a lot of pictures.'

Old age was hell, thought Marnie as she went to her car. Quiet, reflective, intelligent Alison reduced to a chocolate-guzzling blob, fixated on television and magazines for the semi-literate.

At the weekend Marnie had two visitors, though she had only expected to see Chloë. She had gone into Monmouth on the Saturday morning for shopping and she had spent all Saturday afternoon and part of Sunday morning working outside, putting in a few bedding plants, planting out lettuces and mowing the lawn and edging it so that the garden was looking colourful and well tended.

She noticed it immediately: an air of suppressed excitement as Chloë and Nick emerged from the kitchen door and on to the terrace, where Marnie had already placed cups and saucers on the old wrought-iron garden table which, along with four chairs, she had picked up from a yard specializing in architectural memorabilia. The furniture was in fairly good condition and Marnie thought the table and chairs blended into the surround-ings much better than they would have done had they been brand new. She had also bought green and white striped cush-ions for the seats and the seat backs.

'Wrought-iron can be so cold, especially if you aren't wearing anything thicker than a shirt,' she said, when Chloë admired the effect. 'What's up with you two?' she asked, suspecting that they were dying to tell her. 'Are you going to tell me now, or shall I make the tea first?'

'We're going to have a baby! Chlo's pregnant,' Nick burst out, quite unable to wait to tell Marnie their news. 'Isn't it the most fantastic thing? A baby.'

He sounded exhilarated and proud and proprietorial, all at the same time, as he picked Chloë up and whirled her around.

'Hey, oaf,' said Chloë, leaning against him weakly. 'Not a good idea in my present state, remember?'

'Oh, hell. I didn't think. Are you all right? I've not made you sick, have I? I'm a total fool!'

'I'm fine. It's only first thing in the morning.' But Chloë sat down carefully.

Morning sickness. Whatever Marnie had expected, somehow it was not this piece of news.

'Oh, wow. Goodness. Gosh. Well . . .' Marnie said. She looked at her daughter, not quite sure if Chloë's feelings matched Nick's but there was a kind of smugness on Chloë's face that told her that the event was not unwelcome. 'Well, congratulations,' she said heartily. 'I'm going to have another grandchild,' she said. 'Isn't that lovely? Let me give you both a hug.'

It was while she was giving Nick his hug that she remembered Polly and her difficulties, and that Polly was married to Nick's estranged brother. Oh, Lord. It was a beastly, selfish thought, but Chloë's baby would be yet another nail in her own coffin as far as Polly's reaction to this news was concerned.

The baby was due in the New Year. 'The timing is great,' said Nick.

'Though we hadn't planned for a baby,' said Chloë hurriedly.

'Because though Chlo won't have finished her course, she'll be able to take the baby to college with her and we weren't planning on setting up the garden centre until next autumn anyway.'

'So you are going ahead with that?'

'Most definitely,' said Nick. 'I wouldn't have had the courage on my own, but with Chloë and her ideas it can't fail.'

'It would be better if you had your own land,' Marnie pointed out. 'Then whatever buildings you have to erect will be permanent structures.'

'I know. I haven't entirely ruled out the possibility that Simon might change his mind, especially when I put a proper business plan before him. He is family and the garden centre will profit us all once it gets going.'

'Wasn't there a business plan before? When you told Simon you weren't interested in farming as such, I mean.'

Chloë smiled fondly at Nick. 'He hasn't much of a head for figures, have you, love? I can understand why Simon was cautious. It'll be different now. I'm working on it.'

Marnie bit her tongue. She did so hope Chloë and Nick were

right and that Simon wouldn't permit himself to be overruled by his wife. Then, Polly had legal training. Surely she would be able to see the advantages in amalgamating the two businesses.

'I know you'll probably condemn me for being very old-fashioned, but is it permitted to inquire if you two are going to be married before you have your baby and set up this business venture?'

'It really isn't necessary, Mum.'

'Of course we're going to be married, Marnie. Apart from anything else, Simon wouldn't even think of a combined family venture if Chlo and I weren't married.'

'Ah,' said Marnie. 'Do I detect a divergence of opinion? I tell you what, I'll go and put the kettle on while you two have a little discussion about the merits, or otherwise, of weddings.'

She wouldn't look out of the window, Marnie decided. She'd give them plenty of time. It was great news and she was almost certain that Chloë would agree. It was true that her daughter had not had the best example of married life from her parents. But her mother and father had not split up until she was eighteen – or was that just as bad? Marnie thought, then, that maybe it was as difficult to watch your parents part when you were in your twenties as when you were very young. There was always that black hole in your life; that feeling of disintegration that took away all your stability. But at least if you were married when you produced a child, if you tried to stay together, that child had some foundation, some sense of permanence. Marnie felt very strongly that a child needed two parents. That was why she had turned a blind eye to Felix's philandering over the years (not all that often and always discreetly, until the advent of Bella), in an attempt to maintain the integrity of the family.

It was Felix who had destroyed their family; Felix who had taken her daughter away so that Chloë had been lost to her for all those years. Then, she had to share the blame for Chloë's abandonment, didn't she? She had made very little attempt to ensure that Chloë continued to feel a part of her family. It was strange how a man's death could rehabilitate him in the eyes of his family. Yet despite her feelings about her former husband,

Marnie did so hope that Chloë remembered the good things about her father and not the selfishness of a man who always had to have things his own way.

She went to the bathroom and splashed her face with cold water. Her eyes were only a little pink. She thought it was most unlikely that either Nick or Chloë would notice, being far too preoccupied with their own momentous affairs.

Then Marnie went back to the kitchen and made the tea.

On the terrace, Chloë and Nick were sitting very close. They were holding hands.

'Let me take the tray,' said Nick, letting go of Chloë's hand and springing up to take the heavy tray from Marnie, then putting it on the table. 'Chlo has said yes. There is going to be a wedding. We must speak to the vicar. An autumn wedding'll be perfect in St Bride's.'

'I said I'd marry you. I said nothing about a church wedding,' objected Chloë.

'No church wedding?' Nick sounded horrified.

'We never go to church, do we, Mum?'

'Not in the past. Perhaps I'd better confess to a small interest.' Chloë already knew about the incident with the young thief at St Bride's. Now Marnie told them that she'd agreed to stitch cushions for the church pews. 'I may find myself at the odd service. You know, in the sense of taking part in a village activity.'

'That doesn't mean I have to get married in church,' said Chloë stubbornly.

'It's a lovely setting,' Nick said coaxingly, but when Chloë shook her head he added, 'It's a lot more important to me that we get married than where it happens.'

Her answering smile was dazzling.

'I know,' said Nick. 'Ian and Mary up at Ottergate Castle have recently been given a licence for civil marriages. What about having it there?'

'I've not seen the castle yet,' said Marnie, 'but that sounds a very grand location.'

'I think you'll find it's not quite on the lines of Windsor Castle,' said Nick, laughing. 'Ottergate is only a very small border castle, but its setting is wonderful. We must check it out, Chlo. Announce the engagement . . .'

'No announcement.'

'All right,' he sighed. 'No formal announcement. But a ring. You will let me do that, buy you a ring?'

She grinned. 'I think I'll let you buy me a ring.'

'Great. Buy the ring. Go and see Simon. Look at the castle. Decide on a date. Do you think your brother would come over for the wed–ceremony, Chlo?'

'Not for one moment,' she replied firmly.

Marnie thought she would have a say in that.'I think they'd be delighted to have an excuse to come over.' Then she realized the difficulties.'But the terms are different in Australia. Schools have a fortnight's holiday in the middle of July and another fortnight at the beginning of October. We'd also have to check on the uni terms.' There was a week in early July and one in October but they didn't always coincide. It might be that Jack could come over on his own. Ellie would be furious to miss out on her aunt's wedding – especially if it were to be in a castle. But Marnie didn't dare mention the word 'bridesmaid', not yet at any rate. That was the problem, prickly family relationships and living the other side of the world.

CHAPTER SEVENTEEN

It was Hetty Loveridge who took Marnie to see Mary Beresford at Ottergate Castle. Hetty and Joan Graham had joined Linda and Marnie for the stitching sessions. Joan was plump and elderly, with not very much to say for herself – though she was a talented embroiderer. Marnie had the distinct impression that Joan had been got at by the Mafia but that she was too polite to be anything more than a little aloof.

It was extraordinary that she, who had been in the village of Otterhaven for such a short period, should have made enemies of certain inhabitants who were determined to cast her in an unsavoury light, taking sides against her. She wondered if they intended actually hounding her out.

Hetty Loveridge, on the other hand, was charming. She was entertaining company with a wry sense of humour. One of Tom's designs depicted the wish of St Brigid for 'a great lake of beer for the King of Kings'. This was a small pond near the bottom of his design. Hetty said she was going to enlarge this and stitch it as though a breeze was wafting across its surface.

'How will you do that?' asked Marnie.

'Linda will tell me,' said Hetty confidently. Linda rolled her eyes.

Marnie had not been too sure about telling anyone that her daughter was going to marry Nick Hunter. She need not have worried. Joan Graham had already heard the rumour from Mrs Powell. All Marnie had to do was confirm it.

'That is so good for you, to have your daughter married and living close by,' said Linda warmly.'Now you really won't want to leave us and go back to Australia.'

'Were you thinking about it?' asked Joan.

'I was not,' said Marnie firmly. 'I always intended giving it a year. Now I won't even consider leaving until Chloë and Nick are settled.'

'Good for you,' said Hetty.

'They are talking about a wedding at the castle,' said Marnie. 'I haven't seen it yet.'

'Lovely setting for the photos,' exclaimed Linda.

Ian and Mary Beresford had taken over what was little short of a ruin some years previously.'They live in a modernized wing and they have already restored the Great Hall which they use for medieval banquets,' Hetty explained.

'Medieval banquets!' Marnie interrupted, imagining with horror all kinds of vulgar interpretations, mainly concerning wenches with cleavages. 'I don't think that sounds terribly suitable for a quiet wedding.'

Hetty laughed.'I can assure you it's all very tasteful. Mary and Ian do a couple of these feasts each year to raise money for charity. They use vegetables and herbs grown in their walled garden and authentic recipes. But now that they're offering a venue for weddings they have opened up another room and that is kept looking immaculate. I tell you what. Why don't I ring Mary and suggest I bring you over on Saturday? I have promised her a candle-making session. You can prowl round while I make the candles.' Hetty occasionally helped Mary produce goods for the shop the Beresfords ran in conjunction with their organic garden.

'Won't the Beresfords think it a bit odd? I wouldn't want to be seen prowling,' said Marnie anxiously.

'Of course not. They haven't done too many weddings yet so I think they'd be glad of your interest.'

Joan Graham sniffed. Linda, who was sitting beside her, stiffened. Turning her back on Hetty and Marnie, who were now both engaged in matching wools, she said quietly, 'If you've anything to say, perhaps you'd better say it to me.'

'I should think when Polly Firmer's had her say to Mary Beresford there won't be any Hunter wedding at the castle.'

'Oh, I do so hope you're wrong, Joan. You see, if Mary and Ian do find it necessary to refuse Marnie, I might feel the need to ask you to leave this group. Which would be such a pity. Not only are you a talented needlewoman, you do actually have the opportunity to get to know Marnie properly. Unlike some of the villagers, if you get my meaning. It's so unwise to take sides before you know the truth, don't you find?'

Ottergate Castle dated back to Norman times. Small and unpretentious and off the main trading routes between the Welsh and the English, it had escaped the defenestration of Oliver Cromwell's soldiers and had fallen into disrepair only because each successive owner had been unable to afford its upkeep, maintaining just a small portion as a family home. Ian and Mary Beresford had acquired the castle and some land, paid a great deal of money to begin the restoration (from a considerable sum Ian had made in the City), and they were now intent on re-couping their finances.

Though Mary and Hetty had not known each other for very long, they had discovered a kindred spirit. If Mary had not already been impervious to malicious gossip, therefore, she would have been inclined to accept Marnie for herself. Hetty had seen fit to introduce them: Mary would judge for herself whether she would make of Marnie another friend.

'It's a lovely afternoon. Do feel free to wander around,' Mary said, after she had explained the candle-making process to Marnie and she and Hetty were putting on their aprons.

Marnie laughed. 'Hetty said I was to prowl. Are you sure you don't mind? I should very much like to tell Chloë all about the castle. Nick is so keen to have the wedding here.'

'If you were a perfect stranger I daresay Ian would want me to give you the guided tour, but I think you'd get a better feel for the place if you are on your own. We've had brochures printed and they are in the Great Hall. Do take a couple. Make sure you go and see the garden,' she called after Marnie. 'Clive is working there today, so he'll tell you all about it.'

Marnie had forgotten how enchanting ruins could be. A practical part of her said that ruins could be most impractical in bad weather. If it rained, they'd need a pile of umbrellas to get from the cars to the Great Hall where the reception would be held. The actual ceremony would take place in what it was believed had been the original, small chapel, though nothing remained of any religious artefacts. The stone walls, flagged floors and Norman-arched windows gave it a tranquil atmosphere, while flowers and cushioned wooden chairs promised modern comfort. She thought that Jack would hate the place; Ellie wouldn't want to leave.

After Marnie had spent some time there reading the brochure, she wandered into the courtyard which was cobbled and laid out simply with a few tubs and hanging baskets to give colour. Across the empty moat there was mown grass and a few shrubs, none of which detracted from the view of surrounding pasture with its several huge and ancient trees under which grazed some red Herefordshire cattle.

There was a discreet signpost to The Grange that she followed, passing along a paved path through a newly planted arbour of climbing roses and wisteria with rose beds on either side. At the other end of the arbour there was a gravelled car park and a large wooden shed that served as the shop. These fronted a high stone wall in good condition in which was an ancient wooden door. The Grange was a two-acred walled garden and it was divided into sections by box hedging. In these were healthy-looking vegetables, raised herb beds and flowers for cutting. There were also espaliered fruit trees against the walls. There was a man working near the gate who straightened as she approached.

'Hello,' Marnie said.'Mary Beresford said I was to look around as I am hoping to persuade my daughter to be married from here.'

'That's good news. Mary and Ian are keen to develop that side of the business. I would also have flowers for decoration, unless your daughter is into the exotic kind.'

'I don't think so. They're talking about July.'

'Excellent. There would be so much to choose from.' They talked colour schemes enthusiastically for a while. 'Excuse me,' the man said. 'I really should have introduced myself. I'm Clive Makepeace and I run The Grange with a few volunteers. And you . . .'

'I'm Marnie Edgerton.'

The smile on Clive Makepeace's face froze. Marnie's heart sank. Oh, Heavens. Not another member of the Mafia!

'We are talking about your daughter's wedding, Mrs Edgerton. I hadn't realized who you are. I was under the impression . . . Ah, no matter.' His voice was suddenly expressionless, his face equally so. Only his eyes betrayed an avid curiosity that was quite chilling.

She was appalled by his change of manner. 'Yes, Mr Makepeace. As I said, my daughter's wedding. She is to be married to Nicholas Hunter. I cannot imagine what other impression you might have got, or from whom. But I'm so glad to have met you and I shall be sure to tell Mary Beresford how helpful you've been. Good afternoon, Mr Makepeace.'

Marnie spent some time sitting on a bench in the sun in the cobbled courtyard. She felt stunned. How could it be that a man whom she had never met thought it acceptable to judge her and find her wanting? She shut her eyes and leant her head against the warm stones of the castle and tried to make sense of it all. Why should so many people in Otterhaven have decided to range themselves against her?

There was a creak as someone sat on the bench beside her. A man said: 'Are you all right? You look a little pale.'

She opened her eyes with a start to see that it was Ian Beresford. He was looking just as disreputable as he had done the first time she had seen him, in his Land Rover outside The Dingle. She was extremely embarrassed and tried to hide it. 'I-

I'm fine. Really I . . . I mean, I . . .'

'You don't look it, Marnie. May I help?'

'Do you know, you are one of the very few who has uttered my name without implying that I'm not only "that woman from Australia", I'm a she-devil,' she answered wildly.

'Good heavens! Is that so?'

'That I'm a she-devil? Half the village seems to think so.'

'Well, Mary and Hetty don't. Neither does Linda Griffiths and she has excellent judgement. Luke seems to like you, too.'

At that Marnie began to laugh. It became a little hysterical and she had to force herself to sobriety. 'Yes. Well, the fact that Luke likes me is part of the trouble.'

'You know, Marnie Edgerton, I think you should come into the kitchen and while I'm making you a fortifying cup of tea you should tell me all about it.'

Afterwards Marnie decided that though she liked the Beresfords very much, she would never be more than an ordinary friend of Mary's. There had been no instinctive rapport, though she liked the younger woman for her warmth and practicality. Ian, on the other hand, had been so very kind and level-headed, so sane. He had talked her through the events of the previous weeks (she'd even confessed that, as it happened, that kiss had occurred) and he had persuaded her that she had nothing to feel ashamed about.

'Villagers do try to exclude newcomers. I think it's fear. I think they bristle when they imagine they are being judged.'

'They think they are being judged!'

'Why not? You have to find your place in their lives as well as they in yours. You have seen things, been to places they can't imagine. No wonder they are protective.'

'And are they being protective of Alison or themselves?'

'Assuaging their guilt in terms of Alison, more like. You see, it was you who was there when she had her collapse. Some of them are envious . . .'

'Envious of a horrible episode like that!'

'Maybe not envious, perhaps I mean resentful that you, a stranger, happened to be there instead of someone who had known her for years.'

'A weird kind of jealousy, if you're right.'

'I didn't mean it was commendable, only understandable.'

'So what am I to do about it?'

'I don't think there is anything you can do. Be discreet.' He shrugged.

'Linda more or less accused me of indiscretion.'

'Though anyone with sense would know that if you really had anything to hide you would have hidden it. It will all blow over, you know. In good time.'

'And how long is good time?'

Again he shrugged. 'You could always run away,' he told her.

Marnie's eyes narrowed. 'I damned if I'll do that.'

'Good for you.' He had put his arm round her shoulders and given her a hug. And Mary had walked in on them followed by Hetty. They had all laughed and Hetty had driven Marnie home.

'That woman has the most amazing propensity for trouble,' Mary said to her husband, as she watched Marnie and Hetty cross the courtyard.

'You're referring to that hug, of course.'

'Of course.'

'She'd just had a set-to with Clive. She was a little distressed.'

'With Clive? He's a fool, we all know that. A good gardener, but a shockingly bad judge of character.'

'Precisely. Marnie is convinced there is a village Mafia whose aim is to chase her out of the village.'

'I daresay she's right.'

'I do hope you're not a part of it.'

'Ian, I only met her for the first time today,' protested his wife.

'She only met Luke for the second time that afternoon.'

'That's what Hetty says. Hetty also remarked that there have been times when she's found Vera Crawford thoroughly irritating though they've never actually fallen out and she's known Vera for years.'

'So are we going to host Marnie's daughter's wedding?'

'The little Chloë to Simon Hunter's brother?' Mary Beresford smiled.'Oh, I think we are. I think we're going to have a most interesting summer.'

CHAPTER EIGHTEEN

A few days later, Marnie was stitching with Linda's group when another woman, whom Marnie had not met before, arrived unannounced. Fortyish, she was clad in jeans and a cotton sweater over a flowered blouse. Her figure was trim and her dark hair, peppered with grey, was cut short. She wore a pink lipstick and on her fingers were several large rings.

'Hi, folks,' she said breezily. 'I've come to see how you're getting on. I must say, you do look industrious and there wasn't a sound – not even a gossipy murmur – when I let myself in. You don't mind, do you, Linda?'

'Morning, Ginny,' said Linda. 'Not at all. It saved me from having to extricate myself from my frame. Do have a good look, now you're here. By the way, I don't think you've met our new arrival, have you? Come and be introduced to Marnie Edgerton who has been kind enough to lend us her skills. Marnie, this is our vicar, Virginia Ingoldsby, otherwise known as Ginny.'

'How do you do, Marnie? I hope you don't mind the informality.' Ginny Ingoldsby beamed and held out her hand as she spoke. 'And I hope you are enjoying Otterhaven. I'm so glad your rude introduction to the church hasn't put you off us totally.'

Marnie shook Ginny's hand. She wondered if the woman was really as ingenuous as she sounded. Surely she must have heard the gossip about herself and Luke.

She said instead, 'I'm very lucky to be permitted to be a part of this, since I'm not a regular church goer.'

Ginny shrugged. 'Who knows? Once we've got comfortable seats the congregation may increase by leaps and bounds.'

'Ginny has already held several concerts in the church, which our former parish priest refused to countenance. It's such a lovely little church which deserves to be better known,' said Linda.

'When it's decorated it's a real picture,' Joan added. 'What a pity your daughter isn't getting married there.'

'Do you have family in the area?' asked Ginny, tactfully passing over the subject of the wedding venue. 'You must forgive me. I should do a lot more parish visiting than I do, but you may already be aware that I have three parishes and have to divide my time accordingly.'

Marnie explained about Chloë.'I'm afraid she has persuaded Nick to consider a civil ceremony at Ottergate Castle, Vicar.'

'Oh, "Vicar" is so formal, don't you think? Everybody calls me Ginny. The castle is a splendid venue. I'm sure it'll be a beautiful day for you all. Anyway, now I've met you, I'll make a point of calling in one day.'

Ginny declined the offer of coffee, saying that she'd be running to the loo all morning if she drank it, but she spent several more minutes examining each woman's work, full of praise and assertions that she couldn't so much as thread a needle.

Linda went with her to the door and Joan said she'd make the coffee. As the front door closed behind Ginny, Joan was heard to say distinctly:'Ginny does so love to get her teeth into projects, doesn't she? Cushions for the pews and now a sinner to bring back into the fold. It makes you feel quite sorry for Marnie.'

There was an appalled hush.

Hetty said feelingly, 'God, Joan can be so bitchy. She reminds me very much of Laura Blackstone.'

'That's hardly surprising, Hetty. They are cousins, after all,' said Kath Bowman, a woman of Marnie's age, who had joined Linda's group shortly after Marnie herself.

'I never knew that. It explains a lot, of course. My mother thought very highly of Laura's bridge-playing abilities but I found her a bit terrifying. You mustn't mind Joan's tongue, Marnie.'

'I believe I'm becoming a little more used to Otterhaven ways. I must say, though, people are very much more opinionated than the Aussies I lived with.'

'Goodness. And I always thought Aussies were very forthright,' said Kath.

'Perhaps it's because I always lived in cities out there.'

'Anyway, I'm sure Joan was only referring to church-going,' said Hetty soothingly.

Linda came in with a tray of mugs. The moment passed, but all the same, Marnie was left with the conviction that Joan had not been referring to church attendance, or lack of it, at all.

The group of stitchers, including Marnie, left Linda's house soon after midday. Marnie took with her the canvas she was embroidering and instructions for what she might be able to finish before their next session. The morning sun was warm, the sky almost cloudless. There was blossom on the trees and forget-me-nots in Linda's garden. Marnie's shoulders felt tense and the air smelt so sweet she decided to return home via the pond and see how the ducks were getting on. Only a few people were near the pond but there, striding towards her, was Polly Firmer.

Marnie's stride faltered only for a moment. The women drew abreast. Marnie smiled and said brightly, as if nothing untoward had occurred between them, 'Good morning. Isn't it a lovely day?' as she passed.

'Mrs Edgerton!'

Marnie paused. She noted the formality and she wondered fleetingly if what was going to be said would be uncompromisingly uncivil. She turned back, her face impassive. 'Ms Firmer?'

'Am I right in my understanding that your daughter is to marry Simon's brother, Nicholas?'

'Why, yes. Isn't it splendid news?' This time there was no forced pleasure in Marnie's voice. 'Nick is such a nice man.' She smiled more warmly. 'Do you remember I actually asked you if your husband had a brother when you were kind enough to invite me to tea? Of course, that was long before I knew Chloë had even met your brother-in-law. Such a coincidence.'

'I can't think of any connection I would like less than one with you,' Polly Firmer hissed. 'And stay away from my mother!'

Marnie was considerably taken aback. Hostility exuded from the younger woman. 'The Sycamores seems to think my visits provide Alison with some distraction,' she said. 'I never go without phoning first to see if it's convenient. I shall, of course, do what the family thinks best.' She emphasized the word, 'family'. 'I recall that you also mentioned that your husband and his brother are estranged,' she continued quietly. 'At the time I replied that I thought this was a pity. I do know, from my own experience, how these things happen but it saddens me you feel this way about Chloë. After all, you've never even met her.'

'Nor do I want to. She is your daughter.'

'Polly . . . Ms Firmer, I do wish you would believe that I mean no harm to you, or your family, especially your mother. That afternoon, when I first met Alison again after all those years, was just like it used to be. I was amazed how much more she remembered from our schooldays than I did. She seemed genuinely pleased to see me and to have the opportunity to talk about old times.'

'Are you seriously suggesting that you came back from Australia for another reason? That you didn't come back here on account of my father?'

'I met your father for only the second time on the afternoon your mother became . . . um . . . ill. I'm sure I mentioned that to you in your office when I consulted you.'

Polly Firmer said: 'If you did, I don't remember it.'

'I wasn't able to attend your parents' wedding,' Marnie said. 'I think I had flu. Then we moved, or they moved, and then Felix and I went to Australia. Though I corresponded with Alison for a few years, eventually we lost touch. Luke might have read my letters, they were not written with him in mind.'

'I don't believe you.' This time, though, it was said with considerably less conviction.

'Then I'm afraid that is your problem, not mine.' Marnie

turned to walk on.

'Mrs Edgerton!'

Again Marnie turned back. This time she remained silent.

'Mrs Edgerton. If what you say is true, that is, if you only met my father for the second time that day, how is it you have become his mistress so quickly?'

'Excuse me?'

'It is an old title. It is one that is particularly apt. I said—'

'I heard what you said. If you were to repeat that in front of anyone from the village . . .' Marnie began furiously, then she hesitated. She had been about to threaten Polly with the law. *Threaten Polly, Luke's daughter?* She shook her head. 'It is not true.'

'My father spends all his time with you.'

Marnie laughed shortly. 'Not quite all his time, my dear. I haven't seen him for at least two days. But if he were spending time in my company, do you not think there might be a reason? That he is very lonely, living in that large house with all the memories of your mother around him, knowing where she is and why she is there? I offer him company, human warmth. And, please don't say it,' she warned, her voice suddenly hard so that Polly's eyes widened. 'I should dislike it very much if Luke's daughter and I were to fall out. Especially if we were to fall out over something that hasn't happened. Your father and I are not lovers. Nor are we likely to become so. That my daughter is to become the wife of your brother-in-law is one of life's ironies. I should like to think that Chloë might help to cement the brothers' relationship sometime in the future. I should hate to think you disapproved of it so much you jeopardized that rapprochement. Good day to you.' She nodded curtly and without pausing to see what effect this speech had on Polly, she strode off in the opposite direction.

Inwardly, though, Marnie was seething as she walked away. How dare Polly speak to her in that manner! How dare she accuse her of something that was just not true! Yet, when she had fed the ducks and her temper had cooled somewhat, Marnie began to consider the situation from Polly's point of view.

This woman – Marnie Edgerton – had come back from Australia on what seemed like a whim. Marnie remembered that she had been quite frank with Polly about her concerns over her daughter when she consulted her in Polly's professional capacity. But, and as she had also explained to Polly, this was a daughter whom she had not seen for seven years. Hardly a committed mother/child relationship. They had met up; there had been a reconciliation. Then, instead of the mother returning to the bosom of her family in Australia, to a son and grandchildren, no less, there she was, buying a house in the very village where her old friends, Luke and Alison Firmer, had lived for years. This was a woman, moreover, who had been abandoned by one husband.

It was not so very unreasonable for Polly to assume that Marnie and Luke went back a long way. Not when Polly could see just how ill her mother was, and how miserable and alone this made her father. Polly, who, along with these feelings of guilt she harboured on her mother's account – whatever they were – longed for the distraction of the child she could not have.

Thank goodness it appeared that so far Polly had not heard about Chloë's pregnancy.

Then there was the small matter of how Marnie herself felt about Luke. Whatever the rights and wrongs of it – and however incongruous it was at her age to have felt an instant attraction for the man – Marnie had to admit to herself that she was attracted to Luke. Very attracted. It had been a devastating blow to her self-esteem when Felix left her. It was true that theirs had long since ceased to be a close, fulfilling relationship. Nevertheless, Marnie had never, in all their years together, considered the possibility that one day they would part; that one day Felix would decide he much preferred to be with another woman. Subsequently her life had been devoid of male companionship of her own age. Life with Jack and Gemma, caring for their children, had excluded her from all but a few old friends, and these were mainly women living on their own. There had been colleagues of Jack's with whom they socialized, some nearer Marnie's age, but these were transitory acquaintances, they were not her personal friends.

Absurdly, Marnie had felt like a teenager when she stood on the doorstep of Luke's house that first time she had been invited there. She, a woman of almost sixty-two, had been made aware of the stirring of emotions that she had all but forgotten existed.

She had no illusions about Luke's feelings towards her. It was obvious to her that she appeared as a lifeline; a sort of guardian angel who had come to his rescue at his very great time of need, with companionship, food he had not prepared for himself and occasional laughter.

But that still made Marnie guilty. She was guilty in Polly's eyes.

The seat by the pond was unoccupied. Marnie sat down on it. She thought to herself: *I should never have come back. I don't belong here.*

Then she thought that Ian Beresford was right; it was entirely natural that the villagers were wary of her, for Alison had lived among them almost all her life. They would regard any interloper with misgivings but once rumours began circulating that she was a predatory female, out to wreck Alison's marriage and Polly's home, they would feel it obligatory to show her how much they disapproved of her.

Marnie thought of the warmth of Perth. She thought of the extreme heat, too, and still it did not seem so hard a thing to bear as the coldness that was evident all around her. She remembered sights, the sounds, the pungent perfumes of the bush; the stars, too, though these were not the stars of her youth (which indeed had been so much brighter than those anyone in this country saw today) but the starry nights of the Australian sky which she had seen in her young womanhood, the stars of the Southern Cross.

She could, and would, go home, she decided. And this time she did not spell it in her mind with the capital H, which she had used to see the word all those years when she had yearned for the Home of her childhood.

Then Marnie remembered Chloë. Of course, she could not go home yet. There was a wedding to arrange. Her family would come to them. They would all celebrate Chloë's marvellous day together. Nor could Marnie return to Australia immediately after the wedding. There was the baby to welcome.

Polly would have to come to terms with what was happening in her own family. Luke would have to learn to bear with an invalid, confined wife. Then, when the dust had settled, Marnie could return to Australia.

CHAPTER NINETEEN

Nick hid his disappointment that the wedding would not be held at St Bride's, saying that he was thrilled that Chloë had agreed to be married at Ottergate Castle. They had both gone to see Ian and Mary Beresford and all the details for the July wedding were quickly in place. It was salutary for Marnie to discover that both Nick and Chloë knew exactly what they wanted for their day and that what with Ian and Mary's expertise there was very little for her to do.

Over the next week or so there was a flurry of e-mails and phone calls between Canberra and Otterhaven, most of them inconvenient because of the time difference. Initially Jack was not at all keen on the idea of spending vast sums of dollars to buy air tickets to London but Ellie was ecstatic about the wedding, more so when Chloë, without any prompting from her mother, suggested that Ellie should be a bridesmaid.

'A bridesmaid in a castle, Granny, that's what I'm to be! Cool! I've never ever been a bridesmaid before. What'll I wear? Will it be a beautiful, long dress?'

This, from a girl who would wear shorts and T-shirts all year round, if permitted.

Chloë said: 'Why don't you and Gemma choose something pretty for you to wear and surprise me?'

'Are you sure?' asked Gemma dubiously, on the open line. She was having difficulty in reconciling her dislike of the Chloë she thought she knew with the woman who was about to be married and who seemed so keen for her entire family to be present.

'Why not? I'm having posies of garden flowers so it wouldn't really matter what Ellie prefers: gold, cream, or a pastel shade. Make it a long skirt and a pretty camisole top. Beads, if she likes. Then Ellie could wear the skirt with a T-shirt and the camisole with jeans afterwards.'

'Beads . . . and sequins?' requested Ellie hopefully.

Gemma, in Canberra, had now seen the merits of an overseas trip, even if it were only for a short time. She began to work on Jack.

'We should all go. The children would like to see a proper castle, wouldn't you?'

'Will there be a cannon and archers?' asked Josh.

'There'll be ladies with long skirts and tall, pointy hats, I 'spect,' said Felicity.

'I daresay there'll be ladies with long skirts,' laughed her mother. 'I'm taken with the idea myself, but I don't think any of us will look as though we are living in the Middle Ages.'

'What's the Middle Ages?' asked Josh.

'It was when the castles were built, but I think you'll find much of Ottergate Castle is in ruins nowadays,' said his father, warming to the idea himself.'But perhaps you could go to the Tower of London on your way home.'

In the end it was decided that the whole family would fly over, arriving a few days before the wedding. Gemma would have to return to Canberra for the new semester immediately after the wedding and she would take the younger children home with her, but Jack had discovered that a conference on gene therapy was being held in London. His department agreed that it would be beneficial if he attended it, even arranging for him to read a paper there. Jack would leave Ellie with her grandmother for a few days while he attended the conference and then take Ellie home with him.

Marnie was making her way to Linda Griffiths' house for a stitching session. She decided that she had just enough time before they started to call into the general store for some eggs.

Just as she got to the shop she thought she caught a glimpse of Luke Firmer's back, but she could not be sure. It occurred to her that she had been absolutely right in her assumption that he regarded her as a minor support, for she had not seen him to speak to for well over a week. So much for any romantic notions she might have harboured.

Mrs Powell was behind the post office counter as usual when Marnie entered. Mr Powell was serving Vera Crawford. Marnie's heart sank. After her encounter with Polly by the pond and her subsequent thinking session, she had determined to be more robust. Marnie had decided that she could cope with most people in the village, but Vera Crawford seemed to be an exception.

'Good morning,' Marnie said, as she entered the shop.

There was silence from Vera Crawford; an almost inaudible grunt from Mr Powell. Mrs Powell disappeared beneath the counter as though she'd not heard the greeting.

Marnie helped herself to eggs, a piece of cheddar and a cauliflower that looked as though it had been picked that morning. She paid her money and left hurriedly. As she closed the door behind her she heard Vera say:

'I wonder how long that'll last?'

'Best all round if she goes back to where she came from, if you ask me.'

'Oh, I don't know, Vera,' Mr Powell said. 'Mrs Edgerton seems civil enough. I speak as I find. After all, she does use the shop. Not like some of the incomers I could mention. And Daphne Jones says there's nothing to all the talk . . .'

Marnie fled.

They were almost all there: Linda, Marnie, and Kath. Hetty was working. It was only Joan who was late, but she was not a good timekeeper. When she did arrive, she was pink-cheeked and breathless.

'You'll never guess,' she declared.

Needles poised, the others regarded her questioningly.

'Alison Firmer has gone missing.'

'What do you mean by missing?' asked Linda. 'She's in The

Sycamores. You can't go missing from there. They keep their front door locked.'

'You can, if you're determined enough. Anyway, Alison hasn't been seen since yesterday evening when they gave out the sleeping pills. The police are there now, and the last thing I heard is they've sent for the rescue helicopter and they're going to search the river bank.'

Alison Firmer had disappeared. That much was known. When she had left her room and how she had managed to leave The Sycamores undetected no one could say. That she had left deliberately was certain because she had bundled a few clothes under her duvet, which had been enough to give the impression to the member of the staff who had done a brief check around midnight that the bed was occupied.

Apart from anything else, it was an enormous embarrassment, for the wellbeing of their more frail residents was an important feature of The Sycamores' sales pitch, which ensured that there was usually a waiting list for an available room. Yet Alison had got dressed and put on a cardigan and her slippers were also missing. She had gone downstairs undetected and managed to leave the house by the side door, which was used exclusively by the staff.

The month's weather had been atrocious with a heavy rainfall, so that the rivers were running high and fast. The night had not been particularly cold, but it had rained quite hard for at least an hour earlier in the evening, though at the time when it was suspected that Alison must have left, the moon was up and the sky was virtually cloudless.

The grounds of The Sycamores were situated above the River Trothy. The river bank was the first place to search, after it had been established that Alison was neither at her own home nor at her daughter's, Polly's farm being in any case altogether too far for a woman who was not in the best of health to reach on foot.

There was no sign of her on the river bank, no sign of her on the roadside. She had vanished.

Luke and Polly were distraught, it was said. Of course they

145

were, Marnie thought, debating whether she should phone Luke. Much better not, she decided cravenly. There was the possibility that a phone call would be intercepted by Polly. Marnie had not gone to see Alison again, after that altercation with Polly. Now she felt remorseful. She had not visited because of Polly? Not entirely true. She had not gone because her visits had become uncomfortable. They had been a reminder that such was the human state that she could very well end her days in just such a way as Alison Firmer. But it could well be that Alison had missed this tenuous contact. Perhaps she had regarded this as yet another betrayal in her time of need.

In the end Marnie wrote a short note to Luke, telling him how very sorry she was to learn about this latest misfortune and offering to do whatever she could, if he needed any help.

There was no reply.

Alison's disappearance was the talk of the village.

'I had an aunt in Yorkshire who used to wander regularly,' said Daphne Jones to a queue in the general store.'In the end they used to pin a little note to her back when she got dressed in the morning. It said, "Return me to . . ." Wherever it was.'

'I don't suppose you could do that sort of thing, nowadays,' observed Ginny Ingoldsby, who was waiting to post a parcel. 'Not very PC.'

'More's the pity.'

'That's why they have to have locks. I had to wait ages for someone to let me in that time when I went to visit,' said Jo Edwards.

'My aunt loved walking into the village. She didn't do any harm.'

'Alison Firmer wouldn't go out in her slippers. She always dressed like a lady,' said Mrs Powell, waiting for her machine to spew out a printed stamp for the vicar's parcel.

'She didn't behave like no lady, though, did she, at the end?' observed another shopper.

'Took her clothes off at the drop of a hat . . .'

'Now, now, Mr Powell. Mrs Firmer was a good woman,'

chided Ginny. 'Is a good woman,' she corrected herself hastily. 'We all know that people suffer a personality change with senile dementia.'

'And you never know when it mightn't happen to one of us,' pointed out Daphne Jones, lugubriously.

'Precisely,' added Jo Edwards, with a small shudder. Her own father had turned into a foul-mouthed, dirty old man before he died, to the extreme distress of his wife and family.

'I wonder when Marnie Edgerton saw Alison last?' said Vera Crawford meaningfully.

There was a small pause as the implication of what Vera had just said sank into her audience.

'Vera! I do hope you're not suggesting . . .'

There was a mutter, more than a hint of sides being taken, new battle lines being drawn.

'Certainly not, Ginny. I was merely thinking aloud,' Vera Crawford said hastily, aware suddenly that the pack, of which she had been the undisputed leader, was in danger of turning against her. 'We must just pray Alison is found soon.'

'As I am and will continue to do,' said Ginny crisply. 'I don't suppose anyone would care to join me in St Bride's right now?' There was no immediate agreement, the response, *But it isn't a Sunday*, clear as if it had been spoken aloud. Turning on her heel, she marched wordlessly out of the general store.

There were a few uncomfortable shiftings as she left. 'Well, no prize for guessing which side our esteemed vicar is on,' said Vera, anxious to regain her ascendancy over the Mafia.

'I don't think I like being given a side,' said Jo. 'After all, this is just a horrible accident, isn't it?'

Horrible accident or not, it continued to exercise the village for another three weeks during which time there was no sign of the missing Alison.

Marnie came face to face with Luke about ten days after his wife's disappearance. He had plainly lost weight. His face was pinched, grey and haggard. He had still not answered her note. Not that she had expected to hear from him, though her heart ached for the experience he was going through.

Luke stopped. He could see that Marnie was undecided about speaking to him. That hurt, because he desperately needed to talk to someone.

'Thank you for writing to me,' he said simply.

They stood together, a foot or so apart. Marnie decided that if they only exchanged a few sentences no one could criticize a chance meeting.

'How are you? Are you getting enough to eat?'

He smiled wanly. 'Polly and Simon are feeding me.'

'Are you staying with them? That would be a comfort.'

'I daren't. Suppose Alison came home?'

'So how do you manage?' asked Marnie. She was beginning to think, along with most people by then, that as the days went by it must be increasingly unlikely that Alison would be found. Or at least, found alive.

'I spend most of my time in the house, or the garden. I just go to Polly for an evening meal. When I do go, I leave the house open. Just in case, you understand.'

'Oh, Luke. I am so sorry. Look, do ring me, one evening. Just to talk. For company.'

'Yes, I might do that.'

Both knew that he would not.

CHAPTER TWENTY

During that dreadful time of Alison's disappearance, the plans for the wedding had to continue. There were the invitations: Nick said that of course his brother and sister-in-law had to be invited. It was entirely up to them to decide whether they would come. He thought that as it was only going to be a small wedding, Polly's father might be omitted from the guest list.

'Invite him,' said Chloë, firmly. 'Luke's important to Simon and once we are married you might find Luke is on our side.'

Marnie wondered if they might include Linda Griffiths. 'She's been so good to me.'

Of course they would, Nick said, and all her stitching group, if she liked. Marnie smiled to herself as she gave names and addresses. There would be some villagers who would be positively green with envy at missing a wedding at Ottergate Castle.

There was Chloë's dress to be bought.

'I don't want anything fussy, Mum,' Chloë insisted.

'Who said anything about fussy?' asked Marnie. 'You're not the fussy type. I know that. But you aren't intending to be married in white jeans, I hope? Although the amount of time you've left yourself, that might be the only option. I mean, barely a month.'

Chloë spluttered over her coffee. 'I hadn't thought about trousers! I suppose I could always buy maternity ones.'

149

Marnie frowned.'Ellie's wearing a long skirt,' she said austerely. She was very glad her daughter was going to be married, but there was no getting away from the fact that Chloë was already putting on a little weight.

'I know. And I know what I'd like, but I don't know where to find it.'

'Have you thought of asking Mary Beresford?'

Mary knew exactly what to do. She introduced Marnie and Chloë to a designer friend who lived nearby and who said she would be absolutely delighted to make up something bridal.

'Ankle-length, looseish, little sleeves and a low neck to show off your lovely curves,' the designer said, sketching quickly.'Clotted cream, I think, for your skin tones. I've some gorgeous material that I've been saving for a special bride. And I won't sew up the final seam until the day before to allow for any expansion.'

Marnie saw that Chloë was enchanted by the thought of having something made exclusively for her.

There was Marnie's outfit, too. She'd intended to go to Bath, for she also knew what she wanted to wear, and it wasn't anything that would hang in her wardrobe for ever after, unused and unloved.

'A printed silk dress and a plain short-sleeved jacket?' suggested the designer.'I've some swatches here you might look at. Afterwards you can wear the jacket with trousers anywhere and the dress will be very useful, too.'

'And to think I was afraid we'd be spending hours pounding the streets,' said Marnie to her daughter.'That was one of the nicest afternoons I've ever spent shopping for clothes.'

Chloë said that she'd think about having her dress dyed after the wedding and next year, once the baby had come, she could wear it to the Pony Club Ball, so it wouldn't be that extravagant.

'I don't think extravagance comes into this wedding,' said Marnie.

Marnie had been filling her freezer with dishes she could bring out when her family was with her. They had decided that Jack and Gemma, Josh and Felicity would stay with Daphne Jones for the five nights they were to be in Otterhaven, in the main eating with Marnie at the cottage. But as Ellie would be staying on, she would use Marnie's guest room. Salads would be the thing to serve, Marnie had decided, but some basic tomato sauce would be useful as a standby. On impulse, she made a pasta dish with some of her sauce which she thought she'd take round to Luke.

Just to see how he was, she reasoned. One morning, when Polly was bound to be working . . .

Luke seemed very glad to see her when she arrived on his doorstep. Marnie thought for a moment that he was going to embrace her so she sidestepped adroitly and he made no further move towards her. She explained why she had come, holding out a supermarket bag.

'It's only a simple pasta dish. You can either re-heat it today or freeze it for an emergency. There's enough for two meals.'

'Or you could stay and eat it with me?' he suggested. 'Apart from Polly and Simon, I haven't spoken to a soul for days. I don't think people know quite what to say to me,' he ended simply.

Marnie's heart smote her. 'No. I guess they do find it difficult.'

'Just for a bit of lunch?'

'If you eat with Polly and Simon in the evening, you won't want this now. It might spoil your appetite. Do you have enough bread and cheese for us both?'

'I bought some pâté yesterday.'

'Excellent. Let's put the pasta in the freezer first.'

They had almost finished their lunch when the knock came. They both froze. Marnie felt as though she'd been caught with her hand in the till. She wondered whether Luke was feeling the same, then she realized that his fears were running on something a little more serious than being discovered eating lunch with a friend.

Luke got up and went to open the door. Marnie thought that it might be better if she left by the back door – they were eating in the kitchen – but she remembered that her car was sitting in full view in front of the garage. She stayed where she was.

'It's PC Watkins,' Luke said, ushering the policeman and a

151

male colleague into the room. What colour there was nowadays in his face, which had begun to drain when they first heard the knock on the door, had now gone completely, leaving him ashen.

Marnie got up clumsily, already knowing what they were going to hear.

'Good morning, madam. It is Mrs Edgerton, isn't it?'

'Good morning, Constable Watkins. You are obviously here on business. Would you like me to leave? Luke?'

Luke shook his head. 'Please stay.'

'Mr Firmer, I am so sorry. We have found Mrs Firmer.' He shook his head. 'There's no easy way to tell you this, sir. I'm afraid she's dead. Mrs Firmer's body was found in the river by a fisherman, early this morning.'

'I thought you'd searched the river thoroughly.' Luke sat down heavily.'How was her body missed?' His voice was ragged.

'You're not suggesting that she has only just drowned, are you?' said Marnie, aghast.'I mean, she couldn't possibly have been anywhere else all this time, could she?'

The second policeman said,'Mrs Firmer wasn't found round here, sir, madam. She was found in the River Severn.'

'That's not possible!' exclaimed Marnie. 'Is it?'

Unfortunately, it was not only possible; there had been a few well-documented cases of people who had fallen into the River Trothy, been carried downstream to Monmouth where the river met the Wye, then taken further downstream to Chepstow, to where the Wye entered the River Severn. That river being tidal – and given the right circumstances – strength of tide, height of water – it was recorded that bodies had then been carried upstream, taken from one river to another without there being any unnatural circumstances involved.

'Sir,' the policeman continued, 'we were going to let you know today that one of Mrs Firmer's slippers was found by a water bailiff yesterday on the banks of the Trothy near the bridge just below The Sycamores.'

'What was it doing there and why wasn't it found before?' Stupid questions, Marnie thought. She was dreading the next information they would receive; that Alison had committed suicide by throwing herself into the river.

The constables did not answer Marnie directly.'Mrs Firmer left The Sycamores – for whatever reason – and lost her footing by the water. Her slippers were never meant for a greasy river bank. We'll never know why she was by the river – or why she must have gone into the river, madam. There is always the possibility that she might have been trying to walk home . . .'

'Suicide?' suggested Luke quietly.

'That's also possible, sir. But Mrs Firmer had never given any suggestion that she was that way inclined,' PC Watkins said gently.'Mrs Morgan at The Sycamores is quite adamant about that, and she's known for her care of her residents. A feisty lady, Mrs Morgan called Mrs Firmer. I gather Mrs Firmer was a bit . . . of an exhibitionist in her way, but no one thought she'd want to commit suicide.'

'She could have just wanted to go for a walk,' said Marnie.

'Exactly, Mrs Edgerton. That's possible, too. At any rate, that's something the coroner will have to decide.'

The policemen discussed practicalities with Luke. Then they left.

'I must go, Luke,' said Marnie, when they were alone.

'Don't go.'

'I must. You have got to tell Polly what's happened, for a start.' Polly was not going to like it that it was Marnie who had been there when her father received the news about her mother's death. Marnie sighed.'Once before I said to phone me if you wanted to talk. I shall still be there, if you need me.'

The village Mafia had a field day.

'Of course Alison could have wanted to go for a walk,' commented Jo Edwards, who had come from Dolly's to buy a bag of apples. 'I'd want to go for a walk if I was living in a place like that.'

'At that time of night and after all that rain!' scoffed Vera Crawford. 'Alison might have gone peculiar, she wasn't a total fool.'

'They do say Eve Morgan is distraught.'

'Well, she would be.'

There was a pause while they pondered the implications of Alison Firmer's death on Eve Morgan's business.

'And what about Alison's presence of mind to shove clothes in her bed,' said Joan Graham.'That sounds like something out of a boarding school story.'

'So, do you think it was suicide?'

'No,' said Vera definitely.'I think she was trying to get home to see what her husband was up to with that woman.'

'I think all of you talk a lot of arrant nonsense!' declared Ian Beresford, who had entered the general store unnoticed and who was standing at the back of the post office queue. 'If, by that woman, you mean Marnie Edgerton, you are quite wrong. She's a nice woman who has only ever tried to be a friend to Luke since his wife became too ill for him to nurse her at home. You should be ashamed of yourselves, talking about them both like that. What's more, Eve Morgan is a caring woman.'

Dead silence greeted his outburst.

'I'm in no hurry, Mr Beresford,' said Joan, now at the front of the queue. 'Would you like . . .'

Jo Edwards had already sidled out of the shop. Mrs Pritchard, who was next in line, and Vera Crawford behind her, both muttered something inaudible.

A grim-faced Ian strode to the counter and asked for a book of first-class stamps. Mrs Powell handed them over without speaking. In the silence that continued, Ian took his stamps and strode purposefully towards the door.

He was to tell his wife later: 'Vera's face. I really thought I was going to be lynched.'

'Ginny would have been proud of you, at any rate.'

Back in the general store a communal breath was being dispelled as the door closed firmly behind Ian Beresford.

'Friends are a good thing to have in this life,' commented Vera unctuously.

Joan Graham did not deign to reply. She concluded her business and left without meeting anyone's eyes. Mr Powell took

Mrs Pritchard's money for a loaf of bread and a bottle of milk, their conversation confined to, 'Would you have anything smaller than a twenty pound note?' 'Sorry.' That reply was followed by a resigned sigh as a fistful of pound coins was handed over.

As Marnie had predicted, Polly was incandescent when she learned that Marnie Edgerton had actually been in her father's kitchen when the police had arrived to tell him that her mother's body had been found. She and Simon had hurried round to The Dingle immediately Luke telephoned with the terrible news.

When they had comforted each other and had begun to talk about what happened next, Polly produced a bag of groceries that she began to put away. She found a strange container in Luke's waste bin and queried him about it. So, perforce, he had to tell her about Marnie. Polly had the sense to do no more than purse her lips when it emerged that Luke had not had to suffer alone when the police called, but once they were on their way home she began screaming at Simon.

'How dare that woman interfere with my father! How dare she go round to comfort him in his distress!'

'Dear, I don't think it was quite like that . . .'

'You don't know anything of the sort.'

'But no one knew that the police were about to have to break the news to Luke,' protested Simon mildly.

'It's just as well they came when they did. Who knows what the two of them might have got up to if the police had arrived any later.'

'Polly!' His voice was so outraged that Polly was silenced.'You're talking about your father, for God's sake. You know very well he hasn't a bad thought in his head.'

'Well, I guess I know that about Dad,' she answered truculently, 'but I certainly don't know any such thing about Marnie Edgerton.'

'How can you be so uncharitable? You liked her very much when you first met her.'

'That was before I knew she was a – a scheming colonial.'

155

Simon actually laughed.

At the sound of her husband's derision, Polly burst into hysterical tears.

CHAPTER TWENTY-ONE

Simon left Polly to weep while he negotiated the track into the farm. His wife cried very seldom. When she did, it was noisy weeping with heaving shoulders and shuddering sobs, with copious tears that left her face blotched. This time the hint of hysterics alarmed him though he said nothing more until he had parked the car. Then Simon released their seat belts and took Polly into his arms.

'Ssh,' he said gently. 'Poor you. Poor Luke.' They sat together for some minutes. Gradually Polly's sobs lessened. She gave a final hiccough and expelled a long, sighing breath. Then she was quiet. 'At least now you know what happened,' he said reflectively.

'But we'll never know what happened!' exclaimed Polly, threatening floods of tears again. 'We'll never know whether it was an accident or . . .'

'What do you mean? Of course it was an accident.'

'She might have decided to do away with herself, because – because . . .'

'Yes, it might have happened that way. Then again, Alison might have decided, using a twisted logic, to prove to everyone that she was capable of getting herself home and so therefore that she was capable of living at home. You are right about one thing, love, no one will ever know the truth. So . . .'

'So. . . ?'

'So it would be much kinder to decide to believe in the most innocuous of explanations: that Alison decided she'd like to go for a walk. There was a moon that night, we know that. So, like a naughty schoolgirl, she hid clothes in her bed and crept out for this walk. She got down the drive and crossed the road to the bridge. I expect the river looked beautiful in the moonlight. So then she went down by the side of the bridge to the river bank.'

'And slipped.'

'I daresay Alison thought she'd be able to walk a lot further than she did, but because her mind had gone a little AWOL, she forgot that slippers are no substitute for outdoor shoes. And so she slipped on the river bank.'

'Does it hurt, to drown?' Polly pondered in a small voice.

'I don't know, dear. Maybe Alison thought at the very end that it was as good a way to go as any and so she didn't fight the water. I certainly think you should hold on to that.'

Fervently Simon hoped the coroner would think that that was what happened, too.

In the event, the coroner's verdict was a simple 'Accidental Death by Drowning'. There was no medical evidence to suppose otherwise.

It was known that Eve Morgan was extremely distressed that such a thing had happened. Luke Firmer, who refused to blame the care home for the death of his wife, was relieved that all the coroner had to say in addition to his verdict was that the night staff should ensure that all the outside doors were locked and the keys removed for the safety of the more vulnerable residents, that one door should be designated a fire exit, kept unlocked at all times. With the correct opening bar to the door, it was thought, there would be sufficient noise if it were opened unofficially for night staff to be alerted.

The funeral, which was to be held at St Bride's, was arranged for two days after the inquest.

It was the morning of Alison Firmer's funeral. The weather, which had been warm and sunny, had changed overnight when it had rained. Now the sky was overcast.

Marnie Edgerton had thoughtfully provisioned her fridge

with everything she might need for several days. There was no need, therefore, to go anywhere near any of the villagers. Instead she intended spending the time in the garden, weather permitting. Her lawn needed mowing, the edges were ragged, and she had discovered ground elder in a patch by the far wall. Chloë had warned her the only way to get rid of that was the hard way, by hand.

Marnie was just about to go into the garden when her doorbell rang. Linda Griffiths, wearing funeral black, stood in the doorway.

'Why aren't you dressed?'

'Excuse me?'

'Why are you wearing what I assume are your gardening clothes?'

'I'm going to wage war on my ground elder.'

'I came to collect you for the funeral.'

'The funeral? Alison Firmer's funeral? I'm not going to that!'

'Oh, yes, you are.'

'Linda, you aren't seriously suggesting that I should go to the funeral, are you?'

'I most certainly am.'

'But I can't. Of course I can't!'

'You'll never live it down if you aren't in church with the rest of us.'

'I'll never live it down if I am there.'

'You mean, damned if you do, damned if you don't.' There was the glimmer of a smile on Linda's face.

'That's precisely it. So, on balance, I decided that I'd rather be damned for not being there. At least it'll be less painful.'

'The whole point of a funeral is not your comfort. It's to comfort the bereaved family. Or do you do things differently in Australia?'

Marnie shrugged. 'I guess not.'

'Then you have ten minutes to go and get changed. And please don't tell me you haven't anything suitable to wear because I don't believe you. Besides, I deliberately came early because I thought you might be requiring a little encouragement. Anyway, ten minutes is quite enough time for someone of our age to change.'

Linda sounded so infuriatingly justified that Marnie had to smile though she made no move to go upstairs.'I still think it'll be regarded as making a very rude gesture to the whole village if I attend this funeral.'

'Look, you didn't come home to take Luke away from his wife.' Linda stated rather than asked the question.

'I most certainly did not!'

'You are not having an affair with Luke.'

Marnie shook her head. The stupid thing was that she did feel a tiny bit guilty for harbouring feelings towards the man that were not, strictly speaking, those of a totally disinterested bystander. Still . . .' No, I'm not having an affair with Luke,' she said positively. 'In spite of what Polly thinks.'

'If you stay away, everyone will think they know that there really is something in the wild rumours that are going the rounds.'

'If I go to the funeral, they'll accuse me of terrible bad taste.'

'No, they won't. They'll just put it down to your being a colonial. Do you have a black skirt?'

'I have a black trouser suit,' said Marnie reluctantly.

'You've now got seven minutes. Hurry up!'

When Marnie came downstairs Linda looked at her appraisingly.'Smart suit,' she commented.'Not too many people wear trousers to a funeral in Otterhaven but trousers merely point to the fact that you've come from exotic parts. I like the black and white spotted blouse. It lifts the black suit from deepest mourning. Now, I think we'd better go or there won't be any seats left.'

They were among the last to arrive and were forced to sit near the front, filling up an already occupied pew. The early comers had filled the back pews first, as is the wont of funeral-goers who do not care to be considered pushy, unless they can claim family connections. The coffin was already in the church. To Marnie's surprise it was a plain deal coffin with rope handles and a bunch of flowers obviously cut that morning from Alison's own garden.

160

'Very recycleable,' murmured Linda, 'I suppose. Myself, I intend to have a much more upmarket version with brass handles.'

Marnie was saved a reply by the entrance of the vicar and the family. Polly entered, clinging to her father's arm, and they were followed by Rupert and Lisa Firmer, Simon Hunter and a man she thought might be Alison's brother. There were various other family members who were strangers to Marnie. She had glanced surreptitiously around as she and Linda had entered the church but, apart from the villagers, there did not seem to be anyone else she recognized. She could not be sure but it did not appear that there was anyone present from the time before Alison was married.

It seemed the whole village had turned out. There was no choir, but the singing was lusty, with old favourites like, 'The Lord's My Shepherd', and 'Jerusalem'. Marnie considered that 'Jerusalem' was a bit militant for a woman like Alison, then she remembered Alison's WI interests and thought that that explained the choice of hymn.

There was a short eulogy from a member of the family whom Marnie did not know, and another from Sandy Williams. Then there was a short pause during which, unaccountably, Marnie met Ginny Ingoldsby's eyes.

The vicar gave Marnie a significant look and a nod, then she stepped forward and said, 'We have with us today one of Alison's oldest friends who would like to add a few words. Marnie Edgerton.'

As she stood up and stepped out of the pew to walk the few paces to the front of the congregation, Marnie was aware only of a sharp intake of breath beside her. She knew that this was the last thing Linda Griffiths had expected to happen. Indeed, when Marnie had changed out of her gardening clothes reluctantly and into her black trouser suit, this was the very last thing she had on her own mind. If Linda was startled, Marnie knew that a lot of the villagers were outraged. She half-expected Polly, or another member of her family, to leap out and physically restrain her.

Then she reasoned that Polly was sitting with her father's arm round her and that her brother was there, on her other side. Rupert might be intrigued by this unforeseen inclusion into the service, but he would have no reason to be alarmed and his reassuring presence would calm his sister.

'I am not sure, but I think that I am the oldest of Alison's friends in the church today,' Marnie began.

Her voice was well modulated and, picked up by the church's sound system, it carried to the very back. Like many new-Australians, over the years she had picked up the Australian inflexion. To Australians born and bred, she sounded British. To the British when she came home, she sounded Australian, but soon and unconsciously she had reverted to the tones of her childhood. Now, instinctively and as if to underline her foreignness, she allowed the Australian accent full rein.

'Alison and I first met at school when we were eleven,' Marnie continued. 'I leave you to work out how many years ago that was. We remained close friends until we left school. I remember particularly Alison's love of nature and natural things.' She gestured towards the coffin. 'In those days we studied physics, chemistry and biology. Alison excelled in our biology classes, so it is no surprise to me to discover how much she has loved her garden ever since. We also studied Latin. I remember that when her daughter, Polly, was born, Alison wrote to tell me of the birth. Pollyanna, she was to be called, because that was the name her father chose. But her second name was to be Erica. I am struck by the bed of heathers that line the driveway of Alison's home. I am sure that every time she tended those heathers she thought about her family, and with pride and joy.

'I am so glad that my return to this country was not too late to renew our friendship and reminisce about times past. It amazes me just how much Alison remembered of those years and it delights me that she could still think of them with fondness. I was so looking forward to continuing those discussions and, perhaps, with her help, finding other old friends we would both enjoy meeting again. It was not to be.

'I condole with the family in their grief. I remember and will

162

continue to remember Alison fondly.'

And then she sat down.

During the committal prayers that followed, Linda was aware that Marnie was trembling. It had taken a considerable degree of courage to do what she had done. Linda did so hope that Luke Firmer appreciated it.

The coffin was taken outside and into the churchyard where a plot awaited. Marnie and Linda followed the rest of the mourners outside and stood a little way apart while the burial was taking place. They were not alone, for only the family stood at the graveside. As they waited for the proceedings to end, Marnie mentioned to Linda that she had not thought to come across a burial in a country churchyard because of the lack of space.

'Apparently Luke and Alison bought a double plot soon after they moved into The Dingle,' said Linda.'What do you want to do about the wake afterwards?' The congregation had been issued with an invitation to meet the family and take refreshments in the village hall after the burial.

'I want to go home,' said Marnie fervently, 'but after that little exhibition of mine I'm not sure it's quite the thing to do.'

'You're right. I think we should brave it out.'

'You are good to me,' said Marnie impulsively.'I wouldn't blame you if you just walked away from me and my troubles.'

'Oh, I don't know,' said Linda, smiling.'At least life is never dull, with you around. And who'd finish your cushion, I ask myself, if you left Otterhaven because no one ever talked to you? Anyway, we needn't stay long.'

CHAPTER TWENTY-TWO

At the entrance to the village hall, Marnie and Linda encountered Ian and Mary Beresford. Neither of them mentioned Marnie's unscheduled eulogy but both of them enthused about the simple coffin.

'I have a hankering to be buried in a wicker basket,' said Mary.

'You can bury me in a black sack, for all I care,' said Ian.

'Only if it's one of those starch sacks,' Mary objected. 'There's no point if it takes a hundred years to biodegrade.'

After a while Marnie realized that Linda had drifted away. Apparently an unspoken pact had been made that she was now the responsibility of the Beresfords. She smiled inwardly as she accepted a glass of white wine from Ian and a smoked salmon sandwich from Mary, wondering who would take her over next.

It was Simon Hunter who approached her. 'That was an interesting comment about Polly's name,' he said. 'Do you know, I'd quite forgotten she was baptised Pollyanna? Polly says she hates both her official names and I'd forgotten that Erica is the Latin name for heather, if I ever knew it.'

'Do any of us like our second names?' asked Marnie. She continued quietly, 'Is Polly absolutely furious with me for interrupting the service?'

'As a matter of fact, she isn't. I think it was only when you were speaking about your childhoods that Polly realized just how far you and her mother go back.'

'We don't do that sort of thing in Australia, you know. Unscheduled eulogies are definitely not the norm. But Ginny

164

looked at me and seemed to be inviting me to say something. So I did.'

There was a tap on her shoulder. Marnie turned to find Ginny Ingoldsby behind her. The vicar was wearing a pinstriped grey suit with a pale grey clerical shirt, her dog collar and a large, intricately wrought-gold crucifix.

'That was well done, Marnie,' Ginny said.'I do so dislike it when people form an opinion that is quite erroneous. It leads to such unpleasantness. I'm sure you've well and truly scotched those horrible rumours now.'

'It was certainly not my intention to be quite so forthcoming when I arrived in the church, I do assure you.'

'Was it Linda who persuaded you to come to the funeral?'

'It was, indeed. I was going to get rid of my ground elder.'

'A noble project, if somewhat unsustainable. I'm glad you came. Ah, Clive. Marnie, you do know Clive Makepeace, don't you?'

'Mrs Edgerton. Yes, we have met, Ginny. I see you have an empty glass, Mrs Edgerton. May I top you up?'

'Thanks, but please, do call me Marnie.'

'I had such a delightful session with your daughter a couple of days ago, Marnie. You'll be glad to hear we are in complete agreement about her flowers for the wedding.'

'Simple, I think she says. Like the flowers on Alison's coffin.'

'Exactly. In the midst of life, and so on.' Clive bent down to her solicitously. 'Such well-chosen words, if I may say so.'

They turned together and there was Sandy Williams.

'I gather that speech in church wasn't planned,' Sandy said. Her tone of voice was friendly enough, her body language less so.

Marnie replied that Ginny Ingoldsby seemed to be urging her to say something.'Not that I am usually so susceptible to the clergy.'

'An unusual priest, I agree. Still, Simon and Polly appear pleased enough. You're stitching cushions for the church with Linda, I hear.'

They talked canvas work and other embroidery for a bit,

Sandy's manner appearing to thaw by the minute. Then Marnie was reclaimed by Linda.

'I'm ready to leave. How about you?'

'We need to say goodbye to Luke, I guess,' said Marnie. This was the point in the day she was really dreading.

'He is over there, by the door.'

They waited their turn. Luke looked away from the guest who was leaving and into Marnie's face. Before she could stop him, he stepped forward and kissed her on the cheek.

'Thank you,' he said. 'Rupert says he is so sorry no one thought to ask you if you would like to say something at the service. You were right, there are none of her old friends here today. You know how it is, either moved too far away or not well themselves. So we are very grateful.'

'And Polly?'

'I think she'll come round, given time.'

'Well,' said Linda, as they walked away from the church. 'That was a good day's work.' She laughed at Marnie's expression. 'You've converted Simon, Clive and Sandy. It's a start. Do you want to come in for a cup of tea?'

'No, thanks. I'll go home. I think I need to sit in the garden in peace and quiet. But thank you very much for today. I owe you.'

Marnie did sit in the garden for a while. She even had a short nap. Then she decided she had better things to do, even if it did not include zapping the ground elder. Chloë dropped by later with sample menus to discuss with her mother. She had other news, too, that she couldn't wait to share.

'Nick is going to see Simon on Saturday,' she said. 'He's going to tackle his brother about using the field I told you about. It'll be the first time they've spoken for three years. I can't believe that Simon has actually agreed to see him! And do you think this means that Simon and Polly will come to the wedding now?'

'It's a lovely idea, though I wouldn't set too much store by it,' said Marnie cautiously. 'Where are they meeting?'

'I suggested neutral ground,' said Chloë, 'so they're meeting at the Duck and Drake.'

'Are you going with Nick?'

'I'm not sure,' the girl replied.'What do you think? Part of me is sure they will be freer to say what they think if they are on their own. Part of me is a bit worried . . .'

'They'll say too much? Personally I think you'd be a calming influence. Why don't you talk it over with Nick?'

'You don't think Simon will feel intimidated with me here, do you?' Chloë asked Nick, as he pulled up in the car park of the Duck and Drake on the Saturday morning.

Nick laughed ruefully. 'There's not much that intimidates my brother. I thought we'd gone over all this. Don't tell me you've got cold feet?'

'Not really. It's just that I don't want to make things worse between you. Estranged brothers and all that.'

'That, my dear girl, is something that is most unlikely to happen, given our history,' he said drily.'Come on. Simon's here already. His car is parked over there.'

As Chloë was to tell her mother the following day, the meeting was quite different from what both she and Nick had expected. It was clear that Simon was taken aback by Chloë's presence. His greeting to them had sounded impatient, as though this was the last place he wanted to be, his brother the last person he wanted to have anything to do with, but innate good manners forbade Simon to be downright rude to her. He was even more taken aback by the fact of her pregnancy, which that morning she had done nothing to conceal.

'It was an unfair advantage, Mum,' she confided to Marnie.'He could hardly take his eyes off my belly. Quite sweet, really.'

Marnie took the plunge into indiscretion.'I think that Polly and Simon are having a few problems over starting their family. I expect Simon was a little envious.'

'Surely you're wrong!' exclaimed Chloë. 'Whatever gives you the impression that Polly wants anything as messy as a baby in her life?'

167

'Oh, you know,' answered Marnie, uncomfortably.

'Hang on. Are you telling me you know something I don't?'

'I'm just saying I think you should be a little more circumspect when you make value judgements about someone.'

'Ah. You mean Luke has said something. Well, well.'

'I'm saying nothing of the sort,' said Marnie hastily.

'Of course not, Mother. So, anyway, far from being unhelpful and condemning Nick's suggestions outright, after we'd ordered coffee, Simon began to listen to Nick. Actually, he listened attentively. Of course we did take a comprehensive business plan with us so we had proper figures to show him.'

'Was that your doing, or Nick's?'

'Actually, it was mine. I knew Simon would be scathing unless we'd costed everything out and projected profits for the future. Anyway, we insisted he took a copy of the plan away with him to study.'

'Polly wasn't there with you?'

'No, thank goodness. Nick and I both got the feeling that she was very much against any partnership or anything to do with a scheme that would mean diversification.'

'I thought diversification was the buzz word in farming nowadays.'

'Basically Polly isn't a farmer.'

'She is a lawyer, though.'

'Precisely. It was having a proper business plan to show her that seemed to appeal to Simon. Mind you, I'm not sure if that's because he's sure she can find holes in it, or if he's sympathetically disposed and with facts and figures he can talk her round. Anyway, he promises to get back to Nick soon.'

'And are they coming to the wedding?'

'Yes. Simon said that naturally they will be there. Nick's really pleased. I do hope Polly doesn't change his mind for him.'

Nick Hunter's father had left him one of the farm worker's cottages on the family farm that Simon now worked alone. This, of course, did not have the land that Nick so longed for, but at least the land he rented for his market garden was only just across the valley. The cottage itself had been left untenanted for several years before their father's death, though both Simon and Nick – for different reasons – had persuaded the old man not to sell it off despite a number of tentative enquiries as to a likely price. At his death the cottage had been ramshackle. Because of their row, Simon had refused to help his brother out, so Nick was obliged to use the cash his father had left him to re-roof the cottage, put in a damp-proof course, replace some windows and install a new bathroom in what had been a tiny box room. When he moved in, the cottage had still needed a lot of work doing to it. This would have cost money that Nick did not have to spare from his market garden, so any further schemes for improvement were put in abeyance.

Once Chloë discovered that she was pregnant, she and Nick decided the time was right for her to move in with him. The cottage remained chaotic, the only other room that had received proper attention being the kitchen. At least that was warm and cosy, for the one item that Nick had considered important was an Aga that also heated his water. Chloë assured her mother (who was even more appalled than she had been over 2 Church Lane when she was taken to see her daughter's new abode) that the redecoration of their bedroom was going to be finished before she actually moved in and that the other bedroom would be ready for the baby by the time they wanted their bedroom back for themselves.

It was a week before the wedding. Chloë arrived on Marnie's doorstep one evening in a state of extreme excitement.

'Mum, you'll never believe it! Simon has given Nick his and Polly's wedding present.'

'A sewing machine? A tractor?' Marnie asked, much amused, because Chloë had sighed for the first while Nick had said that he yearned for the second. She had offered to pay for a week's honeymoon, though this they would have to wait for until that period between the end of the growing season and before the build-up to Christmas. Nick had decided that his one assistant could manage alone for a week with the help of an itinerant labourer they used occasionally. The two were going to Beddgellert in North Wales as, by then, it would not be a good idea for Chloë to fly to a warmer destination.

'Much better than that. Simon has agreed that Nick should have the land he wants. Isn't it just the most splendid thing!'

A combination of Chloë's business plan, the sense that the idea itself was worth pursuing, Simon's approval of the woman his brother had chosen to marry and, just maybe, thought Marnie, the knowledge that he had been unfair to the brother who might be the only one of their generation to pass on the family name, all had brought this about.

'Oh, I am glad,' Marnie said, hugging her daughter. 'You deserve it, both of you.'

Chloë laughed happily. 'Not only that,' she told her mother. 'I'm getting a mixer as well. Mum, do you think it's about time you taught me to cook?'

It was two days later that Jack and his family arrived from Australia. It was all new and strange to the jet-lagged Gemma who had never been out of Australia before.

'Everything is so old looking,' she exclaimed. 'I'm not sure whether I think it's quaint or tatty.'

'I guess it's a mixture of both,' her mother-in-law said.

'And on the map the distances look so small, but you'd never believe how long it took us to get here from Heathrow!'

'Oh, yes, I would,' said Marnie feelingly. 'Would you like anything to eat or drink now?'

'I think we all want our beds,' said Jack. 'We had a break at a motorway service station. The children had chicken and chips.'

'Ellie and I will come with you to show you where Mrs Jones lives, then I'll bring her back here. Do you have your own case, darling?' she asked her granddaughter.

'I'll take it upstairs,' said Jack, picking up Ellie's case from the hall.

'Watch the low ceiling!' warned Marnie – too late.

Daphne Jones was solicitous, knowing already that her guests were going to arrive late. Marnie did not linger as she could see

Ellie yawning surreptitiously.

'I can't wait to show you my bridesmaid's dress,' said Ellie later, as Marnie helped her unpack her night things.

'In the morning, my love.'

'You don't sound Australian any more, Granny. It's very weird.' Ellie yawned hugely, then she fell asleep.

What would Jack and Gemma make of that? thought Marnie.

CHAPTER TWENTY-THREE

Both Josh and Felicity were a bit overawed, meeting Chloë and Nick for the first time the following day. Chloë had met Marnie in the afternoon and they had gone to pick up the wedding dress and Marnie's outfit, both utterly delighted with the final result.

'Ellie has shown me her outfit,' Marnie told Chloë. 'I do hope you like it.'

'Pink, naturally,' Chloë sighed. She smiled. 'I expect it's pretty.'

'It is. A dark pink, so not too sugary. The cream roses you've chosen for her headdress and to put in her little basket will look charming. I also told her about her hairdressing appointment. She was ecstatic.'

They arrived in Church Lane to a commotion. A bored Josh had discovered the old apple tree at the end of Marnie's garden and he was almost at the top.

Gemma, standing underneath, wringing her hands, was petrified that he would fall.'Marnie. What'll we do? Thank heavens Jack is taking a walk round the village with Felicity. He'd go ballistic. Josh, don't put your foot on that branch!' she squealed in horror, as the branch in question creaked.

'Don't worry, Mum. It's perfectly safe,' the boy, who was plainly enjoying the adults' panic, called.'Oops!'

'Josh!'

'It's all right. I think,' said Marnie quietly.'He is quite safe, so long as he doesn't do anything stupid. Josh,' she said more loudly. 'Don't be in a hurry. Try to remember which branch you used to climb the tree. Then you'll get down safely.'

'Don't worry, Granny. It's easy-peasy. Look at me!' In seconds he was on the ground.

'Don't you ever do that again!' his mother insisted.

'Well, not unless you have an adult nearby,' said Marnie, who considered that all small boys should know how to climb trees. 'Sometimes old trees can be a bit fragile, though I think this one is sturdy enough.'

'It was cool,' exclaimed Josh.'I like this garden. We don't have trees as good as this for climbing at home. Can we plant one when we get home, Mum?'

'I think it would take too long to grow,' said his mother, sounding a little less scared now that her son was on solid ground.

'How old is this apple tree, then?'

'At least sixty years, I should say,' replied his grandmother.

'Well wicked!'

Nick arrived at 2 Church Lane to join them for dinner and this first meeting with Chloë's husband-to-be was a welcome distraction for Gemma from the escapade of her son. Jack and Felicity returned and the family was complete.

Jack opened wine and Ellie helped set the table. Marnie was thinking, as she served a vast shepherd's pie, that she had quite got out of the habit of coping with ravening hordes at mealtimes.

'Granny's shepherd's pie,' said Ellie, replete at last and sighing with pleasure. 'No one makes it like her.'

'Chocolate soufflé, anyone? Fruit?'

There was a final discussion about the proceedings for the following day and since the Australian contingent was beginning to droop, they departed for an early night.

'You look very smart, Linda,' Jo Edwards said, as the two met outside the general store on the morning of the wedding. 'Going anywhere special?'

'I'm off to the wedding at the castle,' said Linda, with a nice degree of smugness.

'Which wedding?'

'Chloë Edgerton and Nick Hunter's, of course.'

'Oh, that one.' There was a mixture of disapproval and envy in Jo's voice, which Linda noted with some satisfaction. 'I hope it's not going to rain.'

'It certainly doesn't look like rain to me.'

'Do you know anyone else who's going?' asked Jo carefully. There had been some speculation about the guest list when it was discovered where this wedding was to take place, but no one Jo knew had admitted to receiving an invitation; either because they did not care to admit they had, or because they did not care to be thought to brag.

'Marnie's invited all our stitching group. Such fun!' said Linda.

'Come to buy some confetti, I suppose,' said Vera Crawford, who had come up behind Jo and was listening to this exchange with avid ears and could not prevent herself from adding her contribution.

'Of course not, Vera. You must know that the Beresfords won't have anything thrown in the castle's courtyard that isn't biodegradable. Besides, I've picked rose petals and stripped some of my lavender. It smells gorgeous. I'm just going in to buy a card.'

'It's a fact the bride won't be needing rice for fertility,' commented Vera, with a sniff.

'Vera!' Ginny Ingoldsby, who was coming out of the shop and who had heard Vera's remark, muttered reprovingly. Vera actually looked a little abashed. 'I'm sure you know that rice isn't good for the birds, anyway,' the vicar went on. 'The grains swell up when the birds swallow them.'

'I didn't know that,' said Jo.

'Enjoy the wedding, Linda,' said Ginny. 'And do give the bride and groom my very best wishes when you speak to them.'

It was a beautiful day: bright, shiny and balmy. The timings were impeccable. The guests were elegantly attired. The bride and groom were both inclined to be dewy-eyed.

Marnie had been afraid that the forty they had invited would look lost in the dramatic surroundings of the castle – particularly when she had discovered that ninety was the maximum number of guests the Beresfords were permitted to accommodate in the Great Hall. But Mary knew just how to arrange the seating for the ceremony, and for the meal that followed, so that it appeared as if an intimate gathering of a family that belonged in the castle was involved.

Clive Makepeace had worked wonders with his cream roses and garden grasses to create a charming bouquet for Chloë and the wicker basket that Ellie carried, while in the rooms of the castle that they were using there were huge containers of lupins and delphiniums, more grasses and ornamental greenery that positively glowed against the sombre stonework and old oak.

Everyone agreed that the bride was gorgeous. Chloë's high-waisted wedding gown in an ankle-length, heavily figured cream silk fitted her perfectly, emphasizing her beautifully lush curves and drawing the eye away from her belly.

Nick was debonair in a new dark suit. Gemma was a little disappointed when she learnt that the men were not wearing morning dress but Nick had firmly refused, saying that he needed a new suit and would much prefer to spend his money on something that would be used again. He had not asked his brother to stand as best man. Marnie felt that that would have been a little too much to expect, given their former animosity. Instead, Nick had asked an old school friend, a barrister who worked in Cardiff. Chloë had met both Rod and his wife, Rachel, and she said that they were both enormous fun and that she hoped they would see more of each other in future.

'Nick needs a social life, Mum.'

'Of course he does,' agreed Marnie.'Once you're married I expect you'll find it happens naturally.' It certainly would, she thought, if the old Chloë had anything to do with it.

Chloë had agreed readily to the lack of formality. She had not protested when Marnie insisted on paying for a trousseau, but Chloë said that anything other than her dress had to have a useful afterlife. This was a sentiment that Marnie thought showed such maturity that she was only too happy to include working clothes in the package, in maternity sizes.

Chloë said that she couldn't have chosen an outfit for Ellie that would have pleased her more, which made Ellie very happy (and relieved Gemma, who had wondered if the spangled skirt and pink top was too much for a country wedding).

Marnie admired the little knitted wrap that Ellie wore round her shoulders during the ceremony. 'Such a good idea to have your bare shoulders covered. I'm sure you must be feeling the cold.'

'Not really, Granny,' Ellie had said, while she was getting dressed. 'After all, it is winter at home.'

'So it is. I'd quite forgotten.'

'My nana in Sydney knitted this,' Ellie offered. 'And she sewed the beads on it once I'd chosen the wool in the shop.'

Marnie experienced a pang. She had always been the grandmother who produced the small extras that the children required. 'Your nana is very clever,' she said diplomatically. 'You'll be able to wear it lots when you get home.'

There had been some discussion about including the other children in the ceremony. Josh had been adamant that he was not going to dress up for anybody at his age. Felicity declared that all she wanted was to give the bride and groom a silver horse-shoe once the ceremony was over. Both of them seemed perfectly happy to allow Ellie the limelight. Ellie had also been asked to play a piece on her flute after the speeches.

Among the guests were assorted Hunters whom Marnie had not met – she had only spoken to Simon twice – but now that it was generally known that Nick and Simon were going to work their father's land together, there was approbation and warmth and good feelings on both sides.

During the course of the afternoon, Marnie found herself face to face with Polly. She had seen Polly make what looked like animated conversation across the room while they were eating but now, caught off-guard, her expression was brooding and there was an unhappiness in her eyes which was all too plain to read.

'Polly. I'm so glad you and Simon are here on this happy day,' said Marnie, determined to maintain optimism.

'Are you? Then you obviously haven't been told that I am here under duress.'

'Why should that be?' countered Marnie softly.

'You must know that I'm not happy about Simon and his brother going into the business together. I think it's a bad move that is going to lose Simon money.'

'That's strange. Chloë seems to believe that Nick's plans have won you both over.'

Polly shrugged. 'Simon is more impressionable than I am.'

'Or maybe he is glad for the opportunity to mend fences?'

'What's more, I think Chloë is far too young to be marrying Nick,' Polly persisted doggedly. 'If Simon hadn't insisted, I wouldn't have come today.'

'Well, I am very glad that Simon did talk you into it. Both Nick and Chloë are delighted to have you here. Nick truly thinks this means he is part of his family once more.'

'Why didn't you tell me that Chloë is having a baby?'

Marnie had known all along that this was the cause of Polly's unhappiness. 'It wasn't a secret for me to confide. Besides, I haven't seen you for several weeks. Does it really matter so very much to you that your sister-in-law is to have a child?'

'Of course it does!' Polly snarled.'Chloë and Nick have already started their family. Now everyone can see just how I have failed Simon.'

'My dear, you haven't failed. It's not a question of success or failure. It just is. Or rather, unjust as it is, it happens. That's something that I am sure your mother would have told you, had fate decided not to be so unkind to her also. I imagine your father has said as much? At least, I am sure he would have done, had you given him the opportunity.'

Polly was simply standing there, in front of Marnie. She blinked, and closed her mouth which had literally dropped open while Marnie delivered what she was well aware was a dangerous speech.

Just what Polly would have said – her eyes were glinting with something that was much more akin to anger than tearfulness –

Marnie was never to know, for a Hunter cousin, a bear of a man in his late fifties, came up behind Polly, twirling her round and enfolding her in a huge hug.

Marnie breathed a sigh of relief and turned away to discover Luke behind her.

'You didn't send whatever his name is to Polly to distract her, did you?' she asked accusingly.

Luke grinned sheepishly. 'I had the distinct feeling that you and Polly were about to have a difference of opinion.'

'Goodness! I do hope it wasn't too obvious.'

'Not at all. It's just that – well, I know Polly and that expression she has. I'm also beginning to know that straight back you adopt when you know you are right.'

'Or think I know I'm right? Luke, I'm so glad you felt you could come today. How are you?'

Marnie had seen very little of Luke since the funeral. She knew that he needed space, time, to come to terms with what had happened to Alison. There was no relationship between the two of them. No bond except the need of a man who was suffering and who had found that a stranger offered a more comforting shoulder than his kith and kin. What might, or might not, happen between them in the future was another matter.

'I'm fine. Well, you understand, don't you, Marnie? I'm hellishly lonely, bereft. Yet, in a macabre way I'm thankful that it's all over. At least Alison is at rest, even if those of us who are still here aren't. But now that Alison is at peace, I am free to remember her as she was when I fell in love with her. It is such a relief.'

Marnie swallowed an uncomfortable lump in her throat at his words, simply spoken. Of course that was how Luke felt now. It was only natural, especially after everything he had done for his wife.

'I'm glad you've found the real Alison again. You deserve it. Everyone knows how much you did for her.'

'Grudgingly,' he sighed. 'If I'm honest with myself, there were times when it wasn't entirely wholehearted. It was so hard . . .'

'Dementia is a dreadful curse on the elderly,' Marnie said softly, into the pause that followed Luke's words. 'And I – we are all so glad you are here to support Simon. And Polly.'

'I'm sorry about Polly.'

'I expect we'll both get over it,' Marnie said enigmatically.

'Granny. Chloë and Nick are leaving. Come and see!' Ellie grabbed her grandmother's hand and pulled her away.

With a laugh and a backward glance of apology towards Luke, Marnie followed Ellie. The bride and groom were not going far – home, to be exact – but the rituals had to be followed; so kisses were given, confetti (mainly rose petals) was thrown, tin cans bumped noisily behind the Land Rover (which had been cleaned up for the occasion) as it drove off. Gradually the guests dispersed.

CHAPTER TWENTY-FOUR

'So what are you going to do with the cottage now, Mother?' Jack asked Marnie, as they sat in the growing twilight.

It was their last night in Otterhaven all together as a family, Nick and Chloë having joined them for the farewell meal that was now over. The younger children were noisily getting into their pyjamas so that they could just be popped into bed when they were back at their B&B.

'I need to look for a small bureau,' Marnie replied. 'Rosewood, I thought. Then, come the autumn, I suppose there will be a lot of clearing up to do in the garden.'

'That's not what I meant at all. I mean, are you keeping it for rental, or are you going to sell it?'

'Why should I sell the cottage? I'd have nowhere to go.'

'You could buy another cottage,' suggested Ellie, who had been leaning against her father's chair. 'You can't have nowhere to live, Granny. Or you could come back to Australia and live with us again. We really do miss you.'

'That's a sweet thing to say, my darling,' said Marnie. 'Although I doubt if it's true, now that you're getting so big and have so many things to do. No, you misunderstand me. I am going to stay here, in Otterhaven, for a year or so.'

'Is that wise, Mother?' There was an edge to Jack's voice that was not lost on his sister, who had drifted through carrying a glass of water, followed by Nick who was carrying two chairs.

'Afraid the family wealth will be dissipated, Jack?'

'No, Chloë. Mother doesn't do dissipation.'

'Thank you, Jack,' muttered Marnie, thinking that there were times when dissipation definitely had its points.'By the way, my glass is empty, dear.'

Nick got up hastily and refilled his mother-in-law's glass with red wine. It was an interesting discovery, he thought, that there were hostile nuances in a family other than his own.

'Thank you.' Marnie smiled up at him.'I am certainly staying here until Chloë has had her baby. I think I shall be ready for some Aussie sun by February next year, though. Then I shall return to Otterhaven. Exactly what happens after that, or even when it happens, I haven't the least idea.'

It was with sadness that Marnie finally said goodbye to Ellie. She took her granddaughter to London where they booked into a hotel for a couple of nights, which Ellie thought was very grown up. They went to the Tower of London, did a trip on the London Eye and queued for ages for Madame Tussaud's, which Ellie said was 'Brill!'

Then they met up with Jack, whose conference had been a great success, for his paper had been well received and he had made some useful contacts. Marnie told him she was so proud of him and Jack was obviously touched. They said their farewells at Heathrow with every expression of fondness.

Marnie was well aware that Jack was still uneasy and that these feelings were unlikely to change completely. But Jack had at least been partly reconciled with his sister. It had pleased Marnie greatly to see his animosity become less obvious during the course of his visit. She was aware that this had more than a little to do with Chloë's choice of husband. Nick had a pleasing personality with the knack of getting on with people and he had certainly exercised this on his new brother-in-law to good effect. Jack was also impressed with Simon and the family's standing in the locality. Chloë and Nick's friendship with the owners of a castle, no less (however small that castle was), was not something to dismiss lightly. So however much Jack might disapprove of his mother's new lease of life, there was still affection and to spare.

Marnie stayed in London for another two nights, seeing an

exhibition at the Tate, visiting the V&A and going to the theatre on both evenings. She thought this was a thoroughly enjoyable aspect of British life she should cultivate, in a quiet way.

On her return to Otterhaven there was a message on her answer phone from Luke. She phoned him the next morning.

'Did you have a good time?' he asked.

'It was great. I wasn't so keen on eating alone, but the rest was splendid.' She told him what she had done.

'I am full of envy. It's such a long time since I did anything so cultured as visit galleries.'

'Did you never go up to London with Alison?'

'She hated crowds and galleries were never her thing. I can't remember the last time we went out together. As a couple, I mean. As opposed to a hospital appointment, or an occasional visit to her hairdresser.'

'That is so sad!' It was more than sad, Marnie thought.

'Yes. Well, I rang to ask you to dinner. You've just said you didn't care to eat out alone. Will you have dinner with me on Thursday?'

There had been a summer storm in the night. Marnie was woken shortly after two o'clock by a thunderclap crashing right over her head. It was followed by another, then another, with hardly a respite between them, the thunder interspersed with streaks of fork lightning that lit up her bedroom as though a bright search-light were playing on the windows. Storms did not scare her in the least, for she had been through far worse than this one in Australia. Indeed, she enjoyed their ferocity (provided she was safely indoors) though being woken up quite so abruptly had been momentarily alarming. It did not appear that this one was going to last for very long, however, for after that third clap the rumbles grew fainter and further apart.

Heavy rain began falling, the downpour lasting for perhaps fifteen minutes. As she drifted back to sleep, Marnie wondered how much damage had been done to her garden.

At first in the morning it did not seem that the storm had caused any harm at all, at least in Otterhaven, from what Marnie could see as she walked through the village to the general store.

'Nice drop of rain,' Mr Powell greeted her with, as she entered the store. 'We needed it, even if the farmers could have waited a week. Don't expect you seen much rain in Australia, Mrs Edgerton, it being such a hot country, like.'

'Good morning, Mr Powell. You know, we do get storms there. Very violent ones, but often the rain doesn't fall in the right place at the right time.'

'It's the same the whole world over.'

Mrs Powell entered the post office section of the shop from the back and her husband immediately ceased his small talk, just adding, 'Them raspberries is fresh in. Come from near Hereford, they do, just up the hill.'

Marnie bought the raspberries along with her milk and a loaf, and on impulse a pot of single cream. 'Do you ever sell crème fraîche, Mr Powell?'

'Don't get much call for that, Mrs Edgerton.'

Marnie sighed as she left the shop. There'd been yet another letter in the local paper the week before about the proposed closure of rural post offices. What village stores needed most was a more robust attitude to new lines, not the protest that there was no demand for them.

Back home, she put away her shopping and looked out of the kitchen window. It was then that she noticed there was something different about her garden. She went outside to see what it was. The grass had greened up overnight. The borders were fresh and the path looked as though it had been washed clean. Marnie stooped over a fuchsia bush which the rain had damaged and tenderly straightened the stems and readjusted the garden twine. Then she realized that a heavily laden branch of the old apple tree had snapped, presumably from a combination of the weight of the fruit, the wind, the rain and simple age.

The tree was an old-fashioned variety, tall, with substantial branches. This damaged branch had not broken off entirely. It swayed from side to side in the gentle breeze, hanging from its bark and a few fibres. Marnie could see that unless she removed it there was the distinct possibility that if the branch did fall it would land in the garden behind hers. As luck would have it, this was Vera Crawford's garden, for Church Lane lay behind the village shops. Both streets had gardens behind their houses. Moreover, Vera had a small glasshouse against her garden wall. It was right under Marnie's apple tree.

Afterwards Marnie admitted privately to Linda that if it had been anyone other than Vera who owned that particular garden, she would have got in touch to alert the owner of the danger and ask what was best to be done – perhaps who she could ask to do the job for her. But as the owner was Vera Crawford, Marnie decided it would be better if she coped herself. Immediately.

She considered the problem as she changed into her gardening clothes. She had found an old saw in the garden shed when she cleared it out after moving into the property. She had cleaned and oiled the saw and she had already used it on a couple of shrubs in the spring so she knew that it would be sharp enough to cut what was left of the apple branch.

Marnie had no garden ladder but she had bought a pair of kitchen steps to use when she was painting the spare bedroom and for when she was hanging curtains. The steps would come in handy now, she thought. She collected the steps, her thorn-proof gloves and the saw. Then she approached the tree once more.

Unfortunately, even once she was on the top step, she realized that the angle of the broken branch was such that she could not quite reach the point where she needed to sever it for it to fall into her garden. Marnie had not climbed a tree since she was a child. But Josh had, demonstrating on this very tree exactly how to use the bottom branches as a ladder, which action Gemma and Marnie had observed with considerable trepidation. Not that she intended to climb higher than the second branch, Marnie thought firmly.

She hauled herself, plus saw, into the tree. Once again, the optimum angle at which she could best wield the saw was higher than she had anticipated. She climbed up one more branch. A doddle now, she thought, triumphantly, thinking how resourceful she was. She began to attack the damaged branch.

The saw worked well enough – though it took rather more effort than she had expected for the teeth to cut through old wood. She landed the heavy branch with its complement of fruit almost exactly where she wanted it to fall, perhaps a little too near the steps, but not too near to present any obvious problem. Then she began to make her way back through the tree to the ground.

Marnie's descent was successful until she needed to climb from the bottom branch on to the kitchen steps. Hampered by her saw, and aware that the rain had made the bark slippery, she decided to drop the tool to the ground to free both her hands. But her aim was clumsy and the saw was deflected, which caused it to land on the protruding handle of the steps. In general, kitchen steps are not designed to cope with rain-soaked, uneven ground. Hit by the saw, the steps tottered, and fell to the ground on top of the branch.

Marnie swore. Though she was in good health and vigorous for her age, by now she was tired. Maybe it was sheer bad luck, maybe her concentration wandered for a vital second: it was probably a combination of both. As she moved, Marnie's Wellington boot slipped off the branch on which she was standing and the thin branch she had been grasping swayed. Her support lost, her balance gone, Marnie fell.

She did not bounce.

Marnie gradually became aware that she hurt. Everywhere. Stupid woman! she thought woozily.

She thought she heard the front doorbell. Was she expecting anyone? She couldn't remember. She thought she'd better get up and go and answer it. She tried to sit up, and moaned, and slid once more into unconsciousness.

Linda Griffiths went back down the garden path. Bother, she was thinking, as she closed the gate. She thought she had arranged to call around noon with that extra hank of wool Marnie needed to finish her cushion. Oh well. She'd put it through the letterbox so at least Marnie would have it. Maybe she'd phone at teatime to make sure she had delivered the correct colour.

Marnie moved her head, and pain shot through it. So it was possible to see stars when you hit your head, she thought whimsically. This was no joking matter, she thought, as she began to realize that she was lying in a very uncomfortable position. In the garden. Ah. The apple tree. Under the apple tree, to be precise. It still hurt her head to turn it, but she did, assessing where she was. She had fallen on top of the kitchen steps which themselves were lying across the branch of the apple tree that she had sawn off. With difficulty she extricated her left hand from the steps and felt her sore head. Her hand, which was badly bruised but not broken, came away sticky. With blood. At least she hadn't broken her wrist or either of her arms. The sun was low, and in her eyes. All things considered, it was definitely time she got out of this. She moved her body.

CHAPTER TWENTY-FIVE

'Did you say you was wanting eggs, Mrs Griffiths?' Mr Powell repeated in the general store.

'I beg your pardon? Ah. Eggs. Yes, I nearly forgot. Half-a-dozen, please, Mr Powell.'

'You seem a bit distracted, Mrs Griffiths, if you don't mind me saying it.'

'You haven't seen Mrs Edgerton today, have you?'

'She come into the shop early this morning, she did.'

'That one thinks we should be setting up as some sort of a deli,' sniffed Mrs Powell.

'At least she's thinking about us, dear. Unlike some,' retorted her husband, with a degree of courage his wife found disturbing.

'As if that matters,' snapped Mrs Powell. 'So why was you asking about that woman, Linda, my dear?'

'It's just that I thought she was expecting me to call this morning. I tried her doorbell only ten minutes ago. There wasn't any answer. I suppose she had to go out in a hurry.'

'Her car's in the lane,' offered Vera Crawford, who had passed by the houses in Church Lane not long before.

'I'll give her a ring when I get home.'

'I've always heard that Australians are noted for their casual attitude to the social niceties,' commented Vera snidely.

Linda shot her a glance of dislike. 'I've always found Marnie

meticulous. Besides, she wasn't born in Australia. I just hope . . .
Oh, never mind.'

When Marnie regained her senses the second time, the sun had
disappeared below the garden wall. The apple tree, itself in
shade, was casting long shadows across the lawn. Marnie
thought she heard the front doorbell again. Long insistent rings.
Once again it took her a minute or two to remember where she
was and what she was supposed to be doing.

'Help!' she called, realizing belatedly that getting herself out
of this mess was something she couldn't manage on her
own.'Help me . . .' She called for what seemed like a long time,
her voice becoming hoarser.

Then she stopped. No one was going to come to her rescue.
Why should they? She lived on her own. She was her own
mistress. If someone called and found the place unoccupied,
why should they worry?

'Help me . . .' she muttered, tears of frustration oozing from
her eyes.

Luke Firmer hesitated on the doorstep of 2 Church Lane for
several minutes. It had only been the day before that he had
asked Marnie to have dinner with him. They had arranged that
he would call for her sometime after seven and they would walk
around to The Otter for a meal. Marnie had been more than a
little dubious about the two of them eating together quite so
close to home.

'Won't people talk?' she had objected.

'People are talking about me already. And you've told me that
people have been talking about you since you arrived in
Otterhaven. The Otter does good food. I'd like to give you a
meal there. Be damned to everyone.'

So in the end she had agreed and Luke had said he'd book a
table for two. Now it appeared that Marnie wasn't at home. How
very strange. Of course, it was just possible that Marnie was in
the garden and hadn't heard him ring the bell. If the houses in
Church Lane had access to their back gardens other than

through their front doors, he would have gone round to the back to see if she was there. But there was no access and he didn't like to be seen peering through her window.

Luke disliked mobile phones. He shrugged, got into his car and went home. Once there he used his landline to phone Marnie. He allowed it to ring until he was automatically cut off. Something must have happened. Perhaps it was Chloë. Should he, perhaps, ring Marnie's daughter? Better not, he decided, upon reflection. He wouldn't want to worry Chloë unnecessarily, not in her condition. No doubt he'd get an explanation in the morning. In the meantime, he'd better cancel their table and raid his deep-freeze.

Some time later, as it grew quite dark, Marnie moved again. It hurt dreadfully as she attempted to straighten her limbs. 'Stupid woman,' she mumbled to herself. But somehow the sound of her own voice, shaky though it was, emboldened her. 'This is all your own fault. Fancy trying to tangle with steps and saws at your age!'

Bit by bit she managed to push herself away from the steps and gradually she extricated herself from the apple tree's branch. Though her head was throbbing badly, she was finally able to sit up. Her whole body was in pain. The left side of her face felt numb where it wasn't scratched and swollen and her mouth was sore from biting her tongue. Her left shoulder was stiff and her ribs felt bruised. Her left leg was definitely broken. She prodded it cautiously and was sure that she could feel bone protruding from her thigh. The rest of her leg also ached abominably. She tried putting weight on her right leg instead but that brought searing pain. . . .

Marnie spent a dreadful night lapsing in and out of consciousness. There was a moment when she was aware of something swooping low and swiftly over her head, followed by another. The shape was an inverted V; bat-shaped. An owl hooted in Vera's garden. The sense that she was not entirely alone, that the creatures of the night were occupied in their natural habits, comforted her.

Yet as time went by, the slightest movement was agonizing, and moreover, as the hours passed, she became extremely cold. Her teeth chattered and occasionally her shivering brought with it waves of yet more pain and with that, nausea. Daylight and the morning sun warmed her chilled body a little – but then she became aware of extreme thirst. She had to attract someone's notice.

She knew that unless she got help soon she could very well die for lack of attention. Somehow she had to call for help. Afterwards she thought it must have been delirium. She was not in the habit of addressing God. All the same, in the absence of human aid, it seemed entirely reasonable to call for supernatural assistance. Marnie gritted her teeth.'If you get me out of here,' she said aloud, 'I'll go to church regularly and sit on those damn cushions.'

Inch by agonizing inch, Marnie began to drag her body from under the apple tree towards the house.

Both Luke Firmer and Linda Griffiths called Marnie's landline around nine o'clock on the evening of her accident, each of them receiving no reply.

Luke came to the conclusion that, for what he maintained were absurd reasons, Marnie had definitely decided not to be seen with him in The Otter. He was inclined to be a little resentful that she had been unable to explain this simply to his face. It was not as if he were a total stranger. He'd thought they were becoming closer than that. If it had been Chloë who needed her mother, he was sure that Marnie would have found some time to let him know. This lack of contact must have only one explanation. Marnie Edgerton did not want to be seen with him in public in Otterhaven. Not only that, remembering Polly's attitude to Marnie, he thought that most probably Marnie was regretting that she had ever made contact with the Firmer family in the first place.

Not that he blamed her, of course. She'd had a rough ride in Otterhaven because of the village Mafia. It was, perhaps, understandable that the village gossips had rallied to the support of the person they perceived as the victim; in this instance his wife, Alison, even if this perception were downright unreasonable and unfair. But since when had reason and fairness had anything to do with group consciousness?

Luke decided that for the moment there was no future in any relationship with Marnie Edgerton. Which was a pity. She was kind and funny; she was good company and sympathetic. He liked her looks and her no-nonsense attitude. That time he'd kissed her was a moment of madness but a very enjoyable one, too. Closeness with a woman was something he'd not experienced for a long time. Even before Alison had become ill there had been distance between them, a lack of emotion stemming from a coolness that precluded all but the most essential of touches, like when she needed help with her clothes. For a long time Luke had felt he was no more than a dispassionate carer for his wife.

So maybe if he waited for a while – until Marnie saw fit to call him – she would reach the conclusion that she needed him as much as he was coming to understand he needed her.

He picked up the phone and called the Kent number. It was Lisa who answered.

'That invitation to stay with you for a weekend. I suppose I haven't left it too late to take you up on it? Only I . . .'

Whatever his daughter-in-law actually felt about the imminent arrival of the recently widowed Luke, Lisa said warmly:

'Of course we'd love to see you. Can you make it around teatime?'

So Luke packed a small bag, shut up the house and left Otterhaven for the solace of his family in Kent.

Linda Griffiths was inclined to be a little more charitably disposed towards Marnie. After all, Marnie had joined the stitching group as a volunteer. She hardly entered the church for services, so helping to make cushions for the comfort of the parishioners was an act of kindness. If she chose not to be available – even when she had said she would be – so be it.

Along with their aversion to mobile phones, both Linda and

Luke were of an age that felt it unnecessarily intrusive to make a telephone call after nine o'clock at night. Luke was waiting for Marnie to call him, however long that took. It was only Linda who tried to contact her friend after breakfast the following day.

Marnie was not at home, Linda decided. Marnie had been called away from Otterhaven. There was nothing more she could do.

By midday, Marnie had managed to drag her excruciatingly painful body from under the apple tree into the middle of the lawn but her state was no better. If anything, it was worse. The day was beautiful: a cloudless sky allowed a bright sun to shine, if not unmercifully, with an intensity that drove everything but the need for water out of Marnie's mind. Water that she could not reach because of the sheer agony involved.

'No sign of Marnie Edgerton, Linda?' Hetty Loveridge asked as they met for a stitching session.

'No. She seems to be away.'

'I heard that you were asking about her,' said Joan Graham. 'Strange she didn't tell you she was going away.'

Linda shrugged. 'No reason she should. Now, does anyone require any help?'

As they were packing up at the end of the morning, Hetty said to Linda: 'You're not worried about Marnie, are you?'

'I suppose not,' Linda sighed. 'It just seems a little out of character, that's all.'

Speaking to Mary Beresford around lunchtime, Hetty casually relayed Marnie's non-appearance to her friend. Mary, who had become fond of Marnie since she had come to know her better because of the wedding, decided to manufacture a visit to the general store after she had had her hair cut.

'Clive Makepeace and I were wondering if you would like a box of Worcesters, Mr Powell,' Mary said in her clear voice, to a full shop, the idea having come to her while her hair was being blow-dried. Selling through the village shop might bring more villagers to Ottergate Castle's own shop. It was certainly a marketing ploy worth a try.

'How much would you be wanting for them apples, Mrs Beresford?' asked Mr Powell cautiously. He rarely made any immediate decisions without consulting his wife first.

'I think I'd have to get you to talk to Clive. I was just making a general enquiry. They're looking very good and we have several old varieties for later on that you won't find in the super-markets.'

'Mebbe I'll give him a ring.'

'You do that. Has anyone seen Marnie Edgerton?' she asked then. 'Hetty Loveridge says she wasn't at the stitchers' group this morning. No?'

There was a general shaking of heads. Mary picked up a magazine, paid for it and left.

'I don't understand all this fuss about the non-appearance of that woman,' said Vera Crawford, who had entered in time to hear Mary Beresford's last question. 'Anyone would think she was of some importance in the village instead of being an inter-loper.'

'That's coming a bit strong, isn't it, Vera?' said Joan Graham, buying stamps from Mrs Powell. 'Marnie Edgerton's all right. She's ever so good with her needle, too.'

'She's an interloper who doesn't care about the village,' Vera insisted. 'She was at home yesterday morning. I saw her.'

'Did you, Vera?' Ginny Ingoldsby, buying milk, pricked up her ears.

'She was in her garden. I had to go upstairs to my store room which looks out at the back. I saw her examining her apple tree. It's very old and it got damaged in the storm. Personally I think it should have been cut down years ago. There's a dangerous branch that looks as though it might fall into my garden at any moment. It had better not do any harm to my greenhouse or I'll sue her.'

'Come, Vera. That's a bit strong, isn't it,' protested their vicar. 'I'm sure Marnie would do the right thing, if there was any damage.' She stressed the word 'if'.

'As to that . . .' Vera sounded a little abashed. 'We'll just have to see, won't we?'

CHAPTER TWENTY-SIX

It was late afternoon. Mrs Pritchard, who lived at 3 Church Lane, had occasion to go into her bathroom. She had opened the window wide after breakfast and now it needed closing. Casually she glanced outside, thinking that she ought to get someone to pick the plums before the wasps got at them. The only problem was finding a lad – or a man – who had the time and the energy to spare. Mrs Pritchard was an elderly widow who suffered from high blood pressure and indifferent eyesight. While she was happy to receive whatever pills the nice young doctor who held a surgery once a week in the village thought to prescribe, she disliked opticians, and she had an extreme aversion to any suggestion that she needed new lenses.

Her own garden gave her no qualms (though because of her eyesight and general debility it could have done with some attention). Although she wouldn't have admitted it, she very much admired the way in which Mrs Edgerton had tackled old Bert Wilson's neglected garden. There was a large terrace now (or did they call them patios?) and much less grass. She'd planted shrubs where Bert had grown vegetables. Bert would have turned in his grave if he'd died a younger man. As Mrs Pritchard pondered on the possibility of that, she screwed up her eyes behind her inadequate glasses and peered down into the garden next door. There was, she thought, something different about it today.

The cottages in Church Lane were numbered consecutively, being far older than the detached dwellings opposite. Mrs

Pritchard in No. 3, and Marnie Edgerton in No. 2, were still only on nodding terms. Sometimes Marnie would offer to fetch something from the shop for her neighbour, but Mrs Pritchard, who didn't want to be beholden to someone who wasn't that popular with the villagers, generally declined. Besides, Mr Powell was very obliging and delivered once a week.

Indeed, he had just arrived, she thought, as her doorbell rang. She closed the bathroom window and made a slow descent of her stairs.

Mr Powell waited patiently at the front door, a box of groceries at his feet. On Fridays he delivered to several elderly customers after Mrs Powell had closed the post office and he had cashed up and shut the shop. Mrs Pritchard's was his last call. He was looking forward to getting home for his tea. Val had promised him lamb chops, Welsh, of course. Some of his customers left their back doors open for him to put the grocery box inside if they knew they wouldn't be there to let him in. PC Watkins disapproved of that. He insisted that nowadays it wasn't safe for the vulnerable to keep their doors unlocked at any time. Personally Mr Powell didn't think much of the chances of young hooligans against some of the elderly in Otterhaven who weren't above keeping a walking stick by their doors as a precaution.

Unfortunately Mrs Pritchard, in Church Lane, didn't have a back door and while she was quite capable of seeing off a potential intruder, she also had a strong sense of self-preservation. He had a feeling of being observed through the spy hole in the door. There was the sound of the chain being taken off, the key was inserted and turned and the door opened.

'Hello, Mrs Pritchard. Keeping well, are you?' Mr Powell picked up the box of groceries and entered the house as Mrs Powell stood aside. He walked through the hall to the kitchen, where he put the box down on her kitchen table.

'Mustn't grumble, Mr Powell,' said Mrs Pritchard, proceeding to enumerate her current list of complaints.

'There's unlucky you are. Still, I suppose it could be worse.'

This produced reasons why anything worse would most

likely lead to her immediate demise.

'Yes, well, better go, Mrs P. My Val doesn't half grumble if I'm late for my tea.' He went towards the front door. Then he hovered.'Nothing you want doing?' he asked half-heartedly. Basically a good-natured man, he frequently did little jobs for his elderly customers, such as changing a lightbulb or taking a letter back to the post office for his wife to deal with.

Mrs Pritchard shook her head. Then, as Mr Powell began to walk down the garden path, she called after him:'You wouldn't take a look out of my bathroom window, would you, Mr Powell? It's just that there seems something a bit odd about Mrs Edgerton's garden.'

Mr Powell sighed. Silly old bag, he thought. If she had a new pair of glasses she could see for herself what was in the next door garden. Still, suddenly remembering that talk about Marnie Edgerton in the morning, he turned on his heel.'Suppose you show me,' he said.'It's probably that apple tree branch Vera Crawford was on about.'

If Marnie had succeeded in dragging herself just a few feet nearer the house, it is doubtful if Mr Pritchard would have seen her at all. What he saw was what looked like a heap of old clothes on the terrace. Then he thought he saw the heap stir. And now there was not the slightest breath of wind.

'Do you have a ladder, Mrs Pritchard?' he asked quietly, so as not to alarm the old lady.

Marnie, of course, was not aware of Mr Pritchard's exclamation of shock as he turned her over and saw the state she was in. She did not feel it when she was covered by an old blanket belonging to Mrs Pritchard, nor was she aware of a wait that seemed interminable to the man who had called the ambulance. Nor did she sense the frisson of interest in Church Lane as paramedics drew up in front of No. 2, the door of which had been opened by an agitated Mr Powell from the inside. In fact, it was not until the following morning that she came to in a hospital bed, to the purposeful atmosphere of an intensive care unit where she lay attached to various machines.

'Do you remember your name, love?' asked a male nurse, bending over her to do something to one of the lines that connected her with one of the machines.

'Marnie Edgerton,' answered Marnie, running her sore tongue over her dry lips. 'I'm thirsty.'

'Do you know what year it is?' The nurse moistened her lips with a tiny sip of water.

'It's 2008,' she said weakly.

He asked her various other questions but when a second nurse came and stood by her bed, he said:'She's either concussed or isn't interested in politics, Staff. Doesn't seem to know the name of the prime minister. She called him—'

'Hang on a bit, didn't someone say she's Australian? Sometimes I wonder about the questions we're supposed to ask. Marnie isn't concussed at all, are you, my love? How are you feeling?'

'Fine . . . Sore . . . Thirsty . . . Not very good, really.'

'Only to be expected, after that nasty fall.' She turned to leave.

'Please,' said Marnie weakly, 'how did I get here?'

'A neighbour found you, I think.'

A neighbour . . . She could puzzle that out later. But there was something she had to do; someone she knew she had to contact.

'Please could you let a friend know that I am here? It's important.'

She couldn't bear to allow Luke to think she had just forgotten about their dinner.

'Do you remember their number?'

Of course she did. 'It's very important. I wouldn't want him to think . . .' her voice tailed away.

The two nurses exchanged a glance. 'You just give me the number, my love, and I'll phone him straight away.'

Two days later, lying immobile in a four-bedded surgical ward, Marnie Edgerton was regaling Linda Griffiths with the sorry tale of her injuries. Chloë had already come and gone for the second time, Chloë having first called into the cottage in Church Lane to collect some essentials for her mother so that Marnie was at least out of the hospital gown she had been forced to wear.

'My left leg is broken in two places. That's why I've got the whole leg up to the groin in plaster,' Marnie said. 'My right ankle is also broken. My ribs are bruised. I think, if anything, the ribs are the most painful. I've strained a shoulder and I bit my tongue. I'm bruised all over. I'm a real mess, aren't I?'

'You've forgotten the black eye. I think you're lucky to be alive. Falling out of a tree . . .'

'At my age . . . Ouch. Don't make me laugh. It hurts.'

'Whatever were you doing, climbing a tree in the first place?'

Marnie explained why she had felt it was imperative to cut down the branch of the apple tree as soon as possible.

'Surely you could have found a man to do the job?'

'I know. I was just so worried that the branch would demolish Vera Crawford's greenhouse.'

Remembering that Vera had threatened to sue Marnie if her greenhouse were damaged, Linda conceded her friend had a point.

'Marnie, what are you going to do when they throw you out of hospital?' asked Linda abruptly.'They don't keep patients in any longer than they have to, nowadays. Besides . . .' She broke off that train of thought. 'Are you going to be able to stay with Chloë?'

Marnie grimaced. 'I know it would be the most sensible thing to do, but I don't relish it nor am I sure if it's even possible. She's so busy with their new project, and there's the baby, so at the moment she gets tired easily. Besides, I don't know where they'd put a bed, the house is so chaotic. What I'd like to do is go back home. Thank heavens I was talked into having that shower room downstairs. Putting a bed in the living-room wouldn't be too difficult as it's only me who'd be disrupted.'

'And you'd have the telly as well,' said Linda, grinning, who knew of Marnie's aversion to TVs in the bedroom.

'Um . . . Linda. I was supposed to be having dinner with Luke Firmer that evening. Goodness knows what he must be thinking of me when apparently I wasn't there when he called. I think I have a memory of the doorbell on a couple of occasions, but I'm not really sure if I dreamed it or not.'

'One of those bells would have been mine,' said Linda, aghast.'Good gracious, I suppose you'd already had the accident when I rang your bell. And I just walked away. How appalling!'

'What else could you have done? It's never even occurred to me before that having no access other than through the front door could be a hazard. Even if you'd peered through the window, you wouldn't have seen anything of the back garden. I daresay that was what Luke did.'

'What, peered through the window?'

'I don't think Luke Firmer is a window-peerer, if you see what I mean,' said Marnie. 'I expect he waited for a bit then went away.'

'Hasn't he been to see you yet?'

'I asked one of the nurses to phone him. There was no reply.'

'Leave it to me. I'll let him know what's happened.' Linda had more than a shrewd suspicion that the non-appearance of Luke Firmer was a source of dismay to her friend.

'Linda, how on earth am I going to manage, not being able to walk? The doctor says that my right leg might be in a walking plaster in six weeks or so. After a couple of months they may be able to give me a below-the-knee plaster for my left leg but it will probably be three months before I'm able to walk properly. Three months! I mean, I'll be wheelchair-bound for weeks. Think of the complications . . . you know . . .'

They regarded each other in consternation for a moment.

'Mm,' said Linda. 'I think I'd better think about this. I'm sure the hospital won't let you out of here until they are sure you can manage at home, one way or another. In the meantime, you're not to worry yourself about anything but getting better, because I don't think you are going to go anywhere for a week or so.'

A group of the village Mafia had gathered inside the general store. Naturally the only topic of conversation was the extraordinary accident suffered by Marnie Edgerton.

'You really are quite the hero, Mr Powell,' said Sandy Williams.'Just fancy what might have happened if you'd not climbed over Mrs Pritchard's wall and found poor Marnie lying on the ground.'

'It's lucky she wasn't killed,' said Jo Edwards, from Dollys, who was still smarting from the knowledge that Marnie Edgerton had chosen not to patronize her establishment for her wedding outfit, but who was willing to show magnanimity in the face of disaster.

'Two broken legs,' Mrs Powell added, with a degree of relish. 'There's nasty.'

'Mrs Pritchard deserves some of the praise, she do,' said Mr Powell, who had been enjoying star status ever since Marnie Edgerton had been rushed into hospital with all the ambulance sirens blaring.

'Noisy things, them ambulances,' muttered Mrs Powell, with a shudder. 'If that racket do be ringing in my head all the way to Abergavenny, I'm sure I'd have a heart attack before ever I'd got to the hospital.'

'Mrs Pritchard must have been very worried, to have taken you upstairs to her bathroom, Mr Powell,' said Sandy wickedly.

'If the silly . . . That is, if she'd have changed her glasses years ago, Mrs Pritchard might've seen Mrs Edgerton lying in her garden hours before,' commented Mrs Powell acerbically, who was unused to her husband receiving quite so much attention in the shop.

'Don't you think Mr Powell is a hero, Vera?' asked Joan Graham of the silent Vera who, apparently, was choosing a birthday card from the display next to the chocolate bars.

'Mm. Yes. I'll take this one, Mr Powell. I think the money's right.' And without another word, Vera Crawford left the shop.

The others exchanged glances. 'I wonder what's got into her?' Sandy said innocently.

CHAPTER TWENTY-SEVEN

An attack of conscience had stricken Vera Crawford the moment she heard of Marnie Edgerton's accident. (After also speculating what a woman of her age was doing up a tree.) Vera had seen for herself that the branch was dangerous. She'd also seen Marnie inspecting the damage and she knew very well that something had to be done about it to make it safe. Vera was also well aware that if the branch did damage her greenhouse it was very unlikely that she would do anything other than claim on her insurance for a new one. Moreover, although she was too busy to do anything about the branch at the moment when she realized what had happened in the storm, there had been no reason why she could not have phoned Marnie to offer sensible advice. That neighbourly act would have prevented the accident from happening at all.

So it was with considerable surprise that Marnie looked up from her book one afternoon to find that her visitor was Vera Crawford.

The two women regarded each other wordlessly.

'I've brought you some pomegranate juice,' said Vera, holding up a supermarket bag containing a small bottle.

'That's very kind of you,' said Marnie circumspectly, accepting the plastic bag from her visitor.

'I just happened to be passing.'

Abergavenny being at least twenty miles from Otterhaven, Marnie thought. 'I'm sure I shall enjoy it.'

'Pomegranate juice is supposed to be good for you.'

'I don't think I knew that. Thank you.'

'Yes. Well. I hope you'll be better soon. I can't stay.'

'No. As you see, it's likely to be a long haul. Still, all my own fault, as the doctors keep telling me.'

'Goodbye, then.' Vera turned to go.

'Vera!' Marnie said urgently, as her visitor moved away. 'Thank you for coming. It was good of you.'

A shrug, and Vera had gone.

Luke had spent the weekend after the accident enjoyably with Rupert and Lisa. They had taken him to a concert in Canterbury Cathedral on the Saturday evening and on Sunday the three had gone for a day's walk, which took in a local section of the coastal path.

Rupert had taken the manner of the death of his mother hard. He was still inclined to lay the entire blame on the staff of The Sycamores.'They had a duty of care,' he insisted, as they sat against a sheltered rock overlooking the sea for their picnic lunch.

'But unless a resident is literally behind bars, how can they guarantee that nothing untoward happens?' protested his father.

'Untoward, Dad! I think Mum committed suicide.'

'We don't actually know that, darling,' Lisa pointed out gently.'The coroner thought it was an accident.'

'Then it was an accident that shouldn't have happened,' snorted Rupert.

'At least your mother is at peace now,' said Luke.

'Always assuming you believe in an afterlife.'

'Rupert,' his father said helplessly, 'Alison did. I do. If that helps. Remember, she wasn't a very happy woman those last couple of years at home.'

'She seemed happy enough to me,' Alison's son said stubbornly.

'Of course she did. I made sure you and Lisa only came over when she was having one of her good periods. She loved you. She was always happy to see you.'

It took some digesting, this knowledge that the worst part of his mother's illness had been concealed from him, Luke could see that. Not for the first time he wondered if he had really done the right thing by his children. Yet Alison couldn't bear the thought that her children would ever see her diminished. Only Polly had inevitably discovered the truth about her dementia. For himself, Luke did not in the least want to know exactly how, or why, Alison had died.

'The personality change she suffered was so radical. Knowing what was happening to her must have been almost unbearable when she was rational. I'm glad it's over.'

Lisa understood, then, that a lot of Luke's mourning must already have occurred: the grief, the anger at what life had thrown at them; the guilt that he had not been at her side when his wife died. What was left was acceptance. Lisa was glad he had felt able to come and see them, even if the notice had been inconveniently short.

Luke was glad, too. It had been a therapeutic interval, though it was probably not one he would be repeating too frequently. After his visit he then drove home circuitously, on the way visiting an old friend who had given up his car the year before and who had not been able to attend Alison's funeral.

Thus it was five days after the accident before Linda was able to make contact with him.

'An accident! Are you telling me that Marnie was already lying under her apple tree with broken legs when I called for her and turned and walked away. Good grief!'

'You aren't going to blame yourself, I hope,' Linda said sharply.'I did that and it won't get any of us anywhere. Besides, you couldn't have done anything else.'

Well, of course he could, Luke reflected as he said tentatively: 'Do you think she would see me?'

'I think Marnie would be very glad if you visited her.'

'I'll go this afternoon.'

'In that case, would you take her a couple of books I've found for her? She much prefers those to magazines. Tell her I'll visit tomorrow.'

'What is she going to do? Where is she going to go, Linda?'

'I'm working on that. I think a few of us might meet for coffee one morning and discuss the matter. What do you think?'

Luke stood silently in the doorway of Marnie's ward. She was in a bed by the window, reading. He wondered if this was a good idea, after all. Then he saw her turn the last page of her book and he decided that he would have to fulfil Linda's commission. For a hospital patient who loved reading to be left without a book was cruel. He moved towards her.

Marnie looked up and beamed.

'I am so, so sorry,' Luke stood by her bed, looking very hang-dog. 'It was such a crass thing to do to imagine that you would just . . .'

'Stop right there,' Marnie said sternly.

'But I should never have left you.'

'You didn't leave me. You didn't know I was there to be left. Nothing was your fault. The only one to blame is me. After all, I'm the idiot who climbed that dratted tree in the first place.'

'I went away. I drove over to Canterbury to see Rupert and Lisa.'

'Did you have a good time?'

'What? Oh, yes. That's not important.'

'Of course it is. I'm very glad you had the opportunity to spend time with Rupert and Lisa. After all, you told me yourself you haven't seen much of your son in recent years.'

'Marnie, you have got yourself into a pickle. But you mustn't worry,' he said then, firmly.'Linda and I are going to sort something out.'

'What are you going to do?' she asked, intrigued.

'I don't know yet. But we'll definitely think of something.'

It was a small group that met in Linda Griffiths' sitting-room a week later. There was Mary Beresford, Ginny Ingoldsby, Daphne Jones, Chloë Hunter and Luke Firmer.

'Marnie thinks she may leave hospital next week,' said Linda.

'Even without a walking plaster?' exclaimed Daphne, whose mother-in-law had broken her leg in a fall the previous year and who considered herself an expert in the management of surgical patients.

'A bit of a tall order,' commented Luke dubiously.

'If there's a bed, Mum could go to the hospital in Monmouth until she has a walking plaster,' Chloë told them.'But I know she'd prefer to go straight home. You do realize that Nick and I would have her to stay, of course. But it just isn't practical with the cottage in the state it's in.'

'Better not, in your condition, dear,' agreed Linda.

'There'll be a nurse going to see Mum morning and evening,' said Chloë. 'I have to borrow a commode.'

'I expect she's been shown how to manoeuvre herself off the bed,' said Ginny. 'The bed?'

'Ian says that he and Clive will bring Marnie's bed downstairs,' said Mary.'Then there's the matter of her food.'

'I've already contacted The Otter,' said Luke unexpectedly.'The manager said he'd be happy to send one of his waiters round at lunchtime with a hot meal.'

'Bit pricey,' objected Linda.

'It needn't be every day,' said Luke. 'Not at the weekend, for instance. I can cope with lunch and suppers. But there's still breakfast.'

'What about Meals-on-Wheels?' suggested Daphne.

'I've checked,' said Ginny.'They could only manage twice a week for this area.'

'It sounds feeble,' said Chloë, 'but I still get morning sickness. I'll do all Mum's washing, naturally.'

'I'd be happy to go in and to give Marnie her breakfast,' said Linda.'I'd not be any good at lifting, though.'

'The nurse will manage that.'

'As I said, I'm good with suppers,' said Luke.'A sandwich, a small salad, a boiled egg. Alison and I ate our main meal at lunchtime, so we only needed something light in the evening.'

'Hetty said she'd be happy to help at the weekend,' said Mary.'I'll fit in wherever there's a gap.'

'I'll make a proper list,' said Linda.'See what it looks like on paper.'

'The only thing is, what is Marnie going to say?'

Marnie was inclined to be overwhelmed. Tears filled her eyes and threatened to spill down her cheeks when Linda gave her the 'Marnie Aid Rota'. She sniffed instead and groped for a tissue.

'This is so kind. Are you all sure you can cope?' she asked dubiously.'The hospital is talking about a private nursing home, since it doesn't look as though I can go to Monmouth. But the only room they can find is near Pontypool.'

'That's miles away!'

'It would be so good to be able to go home.'

'That's settled, then.'

Marnie had had an uncomfortable and extremely expensive three-minute conversation with Jack. Of course, the family had been full of sympathy when she had finally managed to call them, though even then Jack had been at pains to ensure his mother understood that it was totally out of the question for either him or Gemma to be able to fly over to nurse her.

'Mother, accidents at your age are a hazard to expect, if you live on your own. Mind you, I cannot imagine what possessed you to try to climb a tree, whatever the state of a particular branch.'

'I didn't try, Jack. I succeeded. I just slipped climbing back down,' Marnie said unwisely.

'Precisely. Well, you know what I think about that cottage of yours. Moreover, if you persist in remaining in that dreary country, away from your family, then all I can suggest is that you look for some sort of sheltered accommodation.'

'Sheltered . . .' Marnie was speechless.

The second time she managed to contact them – to tell them that she was having difficulty in finding somewhere to convalesce – she was able to e-mail them. Luke had brought in her laptop for this purpose. They had decided that he should take it home with him afterwards, bringing it back a couple of days later so that she could pick up any messages.

Jack was no more helpful over Marnie's convalescence, saying merely that if his sister could not cope with her, he did hope that a private nursing home would not prove too expensive.

It pleased Marnie enormously to be able to write back that her Otterhaven friends were rallying round to care for her and that she was looking forward to going home once she was strong enough.

Luke visited every other afternoon, taking Marnie new library books that she devoured voraciously. (She requested light reading only, saying that she didn't have the concentration for anything too serious.) He also took her soiled linen to Chloë, who visited every third day, occasionally coming with Nick, and who brought the clean laundry back.

Marnie enjoyed his visits. She also appreciated that he did not stay too long since she still tired easily.

'Luke is lovely,' she told Linda.'He's such a comfort. He always brings me exactly what I want and makes me feel that nothing is too much trouble. He also tells me precisely what I want to hear.'

'All the gossip?'

'Probably all that is fit for my ears,' she said, grinning. 'There is nothing worse than having a visitor sit silently beside you with nothing much to say, just imagining that their presence is enough to make you feel cherished,' she went on crossly.'Oh, God. That didn't come out quite as I meant it.'

Linda grinned.'I know. Anyway, I only stay for half an hour.'

'Joan Graham came to see me. She stayed for hours. Well, that's what it seemed like. I am so ungrateful!'

'You are getting better. When you come home, I have a project for you. Now don't look like that. I think it's something you will enjoy doing.'

'Then why do I have to wait?'

'Because I wouldn't want anything to happen to it while your back was turned,' said Linda darkly.

'This project wouldn't be more stitching?'

'Ginny and I were going through the church vestments the

other day. I've done my best over the years, but some of them are in a sorry state and it's too expensive to have them profession-ally restored. Ginny was saying wistfully that she wished she had a purple stole she could use for funerals instead of the old black one which is beginning to look rusty. In a rash moment I said I'd like to make one for her. I thought you'd like to help me embroider it.'

'I couldn't do a thing like that!' exclaimed Marnie.

'Oh yes, you could. Your stitching is very fine.'

'But I don't know the first thing about church stoles.'

'That's not important, because I do. I've already chosen the silk and I've brought some ideas for the design for you to look at. Once we've decided what to embroider, I'll buy the threads and get the material framed up. Then, when you're home there'll be something for you to do.'

'Slave-driver!' All the same, Marnie looked more cheerful than she had when Linda arrived.

CHAPTER TWENTY-EIGHT

The day came when the hospital considered Marnie sufficiently adept and strong enough to manage at home with all the help they were told was going to be provided for her. An ambulance drew up outside 2 Church Lane; Luke and Linda Griffiths opened the door to welcome Marnie and she was carried inside. There had been no possibility of anyone fetching her from Abergavenny in an ordinary car because of her full-length plaster.

Once inside, and with the minimum of fuss, she was deposited on her bed and propped up with pillows. The bed fitted across the room neatly; there was a table by the side of it, on which was a lamp, the TV remote control and a pile of books. There were vases of flowers round the room.

'Well!' Marnie beamed. 'Thank God for home comforts. Flowers, too. How lovely.'

'I simply cannot believe the ban on flowers in hospital really has anything to do with infection,' grumbled Linda, whose bunch of flowers for Marnie when she first visited had been banned. 'More likely to be that no one wants to change the water in the vases. I do hope we've got things right for you,' she added anxiously.'If, after a few days, you think it's all too much, I'm sure we could still find you a nursing-home bed.'

'This will do me just fine.'

Marnie sat in her wheelchair, her legs propped up in front of her, and watched as Luke carefully set a supper tray on the table by her side. Into her mind, unbidden, came the memory of that afternoon at The Sycamores when she had taken Alison into the garden and Alison had told her about the occasion when she couldn't remember her way home. That was when Alison had known there was something seriously wrong with her. But it was what Alison had said about going to The Sycamores that seemed the more significant. She had implied that she felt safer in the care home; safer than in her own home with her husband; with Luke.

'I've forgotten your glass,' he said, and went back into the kitchen.

Marnie carefully ran her needle into the backing fabric for the purple stole she had started embroidering and put aside her frame. She thought about Luke and her feelings for him that seemed to be growing stronger. She found him enormously attractive, both for his looks and for his personality. It was a very long time since she had experienced such sheer delight in a man's presence. Marnie knew that she had fallen out of love with Felix a long time before he left her. If she were honest, the fact of Felix's abandonment of her was a huge relief – though for many months the humiliation heaped on her by it was uppermost in her mind. Maybe, too, she did not want Jack to see exactly how she felt about his father.

'I've brought you a glass of the white wine you said you liked,' Luke said.

'Thank you. I hope you've poured one for yourself.'

There was a time when she was convinced that Luke had feelings for her, despite the fact that he was still married. Then, when Alison had drowned, he seemed to change. She had explained that to herself as the reaction of a good man to his appalling loss.

And now? Luke was the most assiduous of her volunteer carers. Nothing seemed too much trouble for him. She was still wheelchair-bound and so he fetched and carried and prepared simple meals for her, like the sardine sandwiches he had made tonight. He kept her company and she was extremely grateful to him. Although he did nothing for her of a personal nature, there had never been a moment when she felt intimidated by his presence. Nor was there anything in his demeanour to suggest that what he was doing for her was in any way a duty he would far rather hand over to someone else.

So should she be wary of him as his wife had been? She shook herself mentally. What Alison had said that afternoon at The Sycamores was the product of her poor, deranged mind; what the Alzheimer's had done to her. Of course Marnie had no reason on earth to doubt Luke's friendship or his caring nature. And if friendship were all there was to be between them? She would nurture that friendship for what it was, something very precious.

'Your good health,' she said, raising her glass to him.

'To your speedy recovery,' he said, toasting her in his turn.

'Dear Luke,' Linda said to Mary Beresford. 'He is so assiduous in his attentions to Marnie. Such a kind man. I believe he could not do more for her if they were married.'

'He is doing the bulk of the work. Hetty was saying the other day that she has only had to produce one supper since Marnie came home.' Mary looked at Linda quizzically. 'It's interesting, though. Have you noticed how men often gravitate towards women who exhibit the same traits as a former wife?'

Linda clasped her hands together ecstatically. 'Do you mean to suggest there might be a match between them? Wouldn't that be wonderful! So splendid for both.'

'How very Jane Austenish you sound.' Mary was amused. 'A match between them.'

'Just a minute, though. Were you suggesting that Marnie is the sort of woman who might have dementia in years to come?'

'Good heavens, no. I was merely thinking out loud that Luke must miss having to look after Alison. Her illness occupied him for such a long time. It gives him a new purpose, taking care of Marnie just at the moment. And, of course, it suits Marnie, too,' Mary finished.

'Still, I think they'd make a most compatible couple. But I wonder what Polly would have to say about it.'

*

Polly was not best pleased when she learned how much time her father was spending in Church Lane. She tackled him in a roundabout way.

'Isn't it about time the garden was put to bed?' she asked Luke. She had called in to have lunch with him, complaining mildly that she had seen very little of him since the funeral. 'Some of the beds are looking a bit unkempt.'

'Are they?' Luke peered through the kitchen window. 'I suppose you're right. Well, it was always your mother's province. I did my best when she more or less gave it all up but recently I've not had all that much time.'

'You wouldn't, with all your nursing duties,' she said drily.

Luke raised his eyebrows. 'Hardly nursing, dear,' he objected. 'I boil an egg, make the odd sandwich.'

'Visit regularly.'

'That, too. Marnie is good company. You know, you are perfectly right about the garden. Of course, the whole house is far too big for me now. Can't say I really enjoy rattling about in it on my own.'

There was a small pause. 'Would you ever consider living with Simon and me?'

'No.' Luke's denial was swift and uncompromising. 'Nor would I expect Simon to welcome me with open arms.'

'I'm sure he would,' Simon's wife said loyally. It had always lurked in the back of her mind; that problem of what would happen to the parent who was left behind. On the whole, though, Luke's coming to live with her had never really been an option.

'One of these days you and Simon will have a family. You won't want an aged parent then. As it happens, ever since your mother died, I have had the notion of selling and finding something smaller.'

Polly grimaced. 'I always thought I'd hate hearing you say that. You know, the family house and all that. Memories. But you are so isolated here, it might be a good idea. Where would you go? There aren't many good residential homes nearby. Except The Sycamores. And I wouldn't like to think of you there. Not after what happened to Mum.'

'Polly!' exclaimed her father.'Are you suggesting I'm in my dotage?'

'No, Dad. Certainly not.'

'Quite right. I have a good few years left of excellent living. I intend to enjoy them to the full. And that most definitely does not mean spending declining years in a residential home.'

'No. Sorry, Dad. I . . .'

'I think I shall see what there is on the market in Otterhaven itself.'

'Not in Church Lane?'

'Why do you dislike Marnie Edgerton so?'

Polly shook her head.'I don't know. I liked her very much when I first met her. Maybe it was stupid of me to blame her for Mum's deterioration.'

'It was. Alison's health was never going to improve. Marnie's visits had absolutely nothing to do with what happened in the end.'

It shook her, this sudden accusation of her father's. Polly had not imagined that her father had the slightest inkling that she thought Marnie Edgerton was a most dangerous woman. Dangerous? What did she mean by that? Well, naturally Polly knew exactly how she regarded Marnie Edgerton: as a woman who could very well supplant her in her father's affections. But her father was not yet seventy. He came from a line of long-lived men. In recent years he had had a raw deal from life in general. There was nothing wrong in wanting something better for the future. With a woman such as Marnie Edgerton? Should she, could she object?

Suddenly it seemed unimportant compared with what else was to come.

Once she was safely in her own kitchen, alone, Polly put her arms round her body, hugging herself protectively, the secret she had learned only the day before almost overwhelming her. The shifts in her family's circumstances were bewildering. First there was her mother's illness, then her mother's death. After that Nick had come back into their lives, a married Nick whose wife was pregnant with his child. Given his age, her father's signs of infatuation paled beside the prospect of the future generations. For at last she also was to have her own child.

Feuding families brought with them a hunger for power. In the case of the Hunters, if they continued to feud, the inevitable division of their family would bring about a loss of both prestige and wealth. There was no way she was going to stand aside and permit her and Simon's child to be outdone by Nick and Chloë and their offspring.

Yes, this was something that required thought and planning and a great deal of care. . . .

But first there were fences to mend. One afternoon a week or so later, when she had finished work and on a day when she knew Luke was otherwise occupied, Polly went to visit Marnie, walking in unannounced through the unlatched front door. 'I expect you are surprised to see me,' she said, as she entered the sitting-room.

'A little, but pleased all the same,' said Marnie. She now had one walking plaster and a supportive bandage on her right foot. Upstairs she used a stick and conveniently placed pieces of furniture, downstairs (she managed the stairs on her bottom) she used a walking frame and with those she could just about hobble from one room to another. 'Am I intended to feel pleased?'

Polly shrugged. 'I've come to apologise,' she said, awkwardly.

'Ah,' said Marnie, pointedly not asking for what. 'Do sit down.'

'You see,' said Polly, gracefully subsiding on to an easy chair, 'I do realize that you and my father have a relationship . . .'

'Hardly,' snapped Marnie, affronted.

'I mean, that you and he have become friends. And now that Chloë has married Nick, and Nick and Simon are working together, it seems absurd for us to be at loggerheads.'

'It does,' agreed Marnie seriously. There was a moment's pause. Marnie looked straight at Polly. 'Did you ever hurt your mother?'

Polly blinked. This was an attack that she had not expected. 'I take it you don't mean, did I say things that caused her anguish?' she answered guardedly.

'I mean physical abuse,' said Marnie, coming straight to the point. 'I know Alison was bruised because I saw the marks on her arms. I don't believe they were caused accidentally because she told me on one occasion that she felt safe at The Sycamores. That means to me that she didn't feel safe at home, where she had a right to feel protected. I also don't believe that Luke abused her. That leaves you. And I'm very much afraid that some people in the village also suspect abuse occurred but because Otterhaven is such a close community, no one will ever say anything. It saddens me that some of them inevitably blame Luke.'

Polly sighed. 'I never meant it to happen.'

'So, why did you do it? You, of all people, should know that there is a law now against abuse of the elderly.'

'I could deny everything, couldn't I? There's no evidence, except for a bruise you thought you saw.'

'If you want me to accept your apology for your behaviour to me, you have to be honest with me now.'

'Sometimes Mum couldn't sleep.' Polly began reluctantly, as if this were something she had never envisaged confessing. Gradually, though, what she had to say emerged more fluently. 'Mum had always had a sleeping problem and there were many occasions when we were young when she would get up at dawn and garden. She said she loved that time of day with everything quiet and still and fresh. After she stopped gardening, she began wandering in the night. It was incredibly wearing for Dad, caring for her in the day and lying awake at night, waiting for her to get up then having to persuade her to go back to bed. I started going over and sleeping at The Dingle every third night just so that he could get some rest.'

'But you were also doing a full day's work.'

'It's not an excuse.'

'No, it isn't, Polly, but it is a reason. What happened?'

'Mum could be very stubborn. She wouldn't go back to bed

unless I more or less dragged her. Sometimes – sometimes I was rougher than I should have been. I hated myself for it, but hurting her was often the only way I could get back to bed myself.'

'Oh, Polly. Why didn't you tell anyone?'

'Because I was ashamed. I didn't think Dad realized what was happening. He said nothing and Mum had always bruised easily. But once that incident with the china occurred, Dad admitted to the doctor that neither he nor I could cope any longer. That was when I knew he was being protective of me, too. So we found the room for her at The Sycamores. Did Mum really say she felt safer there?'

Marnie nodded. 'Alison said she liked the freedom to be bad. Polly, I know you blame yourself dreadfully now, and certainly what you did to Alison was wrong, but I think you should learn to accept what you did and eventually forgive yourself. I think a lot of people would have only sympathy for your situation. I do.'

'Marnie, do you know how very much I envy Chloë?'

'You envy my daughter?' That was the last thing Marnie expected to hear from Polly. 'Why is that?'

'Because you came all the way from Australia to be with her.'

'Polly, you do know that Chloë and I have had a very stormy relationship? We were estranged for years.'

'But you aren't any longer. I might have lived with both my parents during my teens, my mother was hardly there for me. And now she's dead. I don't have a second chance. Do you wonder why I'm consumed with envy?'

'I'd like to help,' said Marnie.'But I'm not sure what you would want from me.'

'Perhaps we could just start again?'

'I should think that would be a very good idea.'

CHAPTER TWENTY-NINE

It was late autumn. Marnie was being driven home from the hospital by Luke after her final plaster had been cut off.

It had been a dreadful fourteen weeks as she endured the immobility, the incapacity to do other than the most simple of things for herself, the periods of dreadful itching under those plasters that not even a knitting needle could ease; the sheer boredom. . . .

Well, actually this was not the case. Boredom had not really been an issue. The village Mafia had done a complete about face, visiting regularly, and not just to thrust a bunch of flowers into her hands (which she could do nothing with, anyway). They had come individually, bearing a meal, a library book. They stayed only so long as it took to do something useful, such as wield a duster, change her sheets, adjust the heating.

Ginny visited regularly to inspect the stole which was almost finished. It was worked in two halves on two frames, which were shared, and when it was finished the two halves would be joined to fit the nape of Ginny's neck, that seam being covered by a cross. Ginny and Linda had chosen a floral theme. There were sprigs of rosemary, thyme and sage on one side, with lilies and the dove of peace on the other. Linda was laying the gold and silver threads which outlined the flowers. These were being embroidered by Marnie, using glowing coloured silks.

There came a morning when Marnie set aside her frame and said tentatively to Ginny: 'Do you mind if I tell you something?'

'Go ahead,' answered Ginny, intrigued.

'It was while I was in the garden. You know, when I had my accident. I found myself making a bargain. I said that I'd sit on the cushions in church if God got me out of there.'

'Did you? I think that's a very human response, to call on God in a moment of crisis. On the other hand, I've never thought of God as a bargainer, myself. You could call it luck, coincidence if you will or, yes, even a small miracle that Mrs Pritchard enlisted the help of Mr Powell that day, without it being God's part of your bargain. Still,' and Ginny touched Marnie gently on her shoulder, 'you'd be very welcome if you came and sat on one of our beautiful cushions, for whatever the reason.'

Marnie sniffed. 'Thanks for not calling me mawkish.'

'My pleasure,' said the vicar gravely.

Chloë, near the end of her pregnancy, also came to visit her mother. She was beautiful, placid, yet full of an energy that Marnie did not remember having herself. There came an afternoon when Chloë arrived, breathless with an eagerness to impart unexpected news.

'You'll never guess!'

'An irritating introduction,' Marnie groaned.

'Polly's pregnant. Isn't it marvellous! And it happened naturally.'

Marnie was stunned. 'Does Luke know?'

'He does, as of this morning. Simon couldn't keep it to himself. He told Nick yesterday and I just had to go round to see Polly immediately. I know. You are thinking that going to see Polly wasn't a good idea. But actually it was just the right thing to do, seizing the moment like that. I thought, at first, that Polly was going to be cross with Simon for blabbing but, after all, the news is so stupendous she couldn't stay angry for long. There'll be six months between our babies, which will be so good for them when they're older, having a cousin of almost the same age.'

'And is Polly all right?' asked Marnie anxiously.

'She says she's feeling fine. Even her morning sickness has gone. The doctors are thrilled for her and Simon can't stop beaming. Anyway, she's telling Luke now, so perhaps you'd better pretend you haven't heard.'

'Oh, no I won't. I shall congratulate them all. Pass me my writing case. I'll send Polly a note straight away.'

But apart from the sheer relief now of getting rid of the dreadful weight on her legs, the excitement of the impending birth of her new grandchild, and her stitching project, Marnie was inclined to feel a little depressed. Very soon she would be able to cope without help. There would be no excuse for the villagers to call. She would discover if she had learnt anything about living on her own.

Yet there was another concern: Marnie knew that she could hardly expect Luke to continue to care for her as he had.

'What's up?' Luke demanded. He had got Marnie home. They had managed to walk up the garden path – with the help of a stick and his arm since her left leg was in dire need of physiotherapy. She was now sitting in a chair, drinking a cup of tea, but her face was a study in glumness.

'Nothing in the least,' she said, forcing a smile, which did not reach her eyes.

Luke had a shrewd idea what the matter was. 'Good,' he replied dismissively. 'Then you might be interested in my news.'

'What's that?' Even then, she could scarcely raise more than polite interest.

'I'm selling The Dingle. I had an offer at full asking price almost as soon as it went on the market.'

'You're going to move? Oh.' Marnie swallowed. 'Where – where are you thinking of moving to? You're not – not going to leave Otterhaven, are you?' He was going to move nearer Rupert and Lisa. He'd always said he liked his daughter-in-law very much. 'What about Polly?' she asked.

'Polly's fine.' He sounded mystified.

'No, I mean, I suppose you're going to live near Rupert? Won't you miss seeing Polly and the new baby?'

'I can't imagine what makes you think I'd leave Otterhaven. Especially now, with the baby coming.'

He was looking at her so fondly that Marnie's heart began to pound. 'So what are you going to do?' she asked slowly.

219

'You know the bungalow in the cul-de-sac opposite? The one at the end with only a small front garden and a sideways-on garage. It's just come on the market.'

'Has it? You forget. I've not been out recently.'

'Well, I've put in an offer.'

'A bungalow? You? Luke . . .'

'I'm fed up with old houses that need constant repair. I don't need a large garden.'

'They say that if you don't have a garden and you don't have stairs your knees go,' she said severely.

'Do they? Well, I intend to take up walking. It's such beautiful countryside around here and now I shall have the time. You may come with me, if you like,' he ended graciously. 'Once you feel up to it. We can start with short walks.'

'Thank you,' she said primly.

'Marnie, there are other reasons for my move. I want to be able to shut my house up and go away when I feel like it and not worry that when I come home I might find it burgled. I like the idea of being able to stroll to the church and the shops. I also like the idea of being close to my friends. Did you know that I've acquired a lot of friends since you came to Otterhaven, Marnie?'

'I can't imagine what that has to do with me,' she protested.

'Well, I suppose I mean that I've become involved with people in the village since your accident and they have become my friends.'

'Mm,' she said. 'I don't suppose I shall be seeing very much of you in future, then. What with all the work involved in your move and all that.'

He was looking at her closely. 'And how would you feel about that, Marnie, dear?'

She winced at the term of endearment. These past weeks had been very strange. In all that time, Luke had studiously kept his distance. Not by a look or a touch had he suggested there was – or could be – anything intimate between them. After those first few meetings when Luke had behaved so differently towards her, it was puzzling. To tell the truth, she had found it all incredibly frustrating!

220

'I don't know what you mean,' she answered, at last.

Luke, who was sitting on the other side of the fireplace, leant forward.'You do know that I've fallen in love with you, don't you?' He sounded diffident, painfully anxious that what he was trying to say would be acceptable to her.'I couldn't say it while you were so dependent on your friends. I was afraid you would think I was being opportunistic. It's nearly killed me.'

It was the last thing she expected. 'Luke, you hardly know me.' Marnie's voice was ragged. She cleared her throat.'This is too soon is such a cliché, but you don't truly know the real me, so how can you say that – that you've fallen in love with me?'

'I think I do know the real you, as you put it,' he said stubbornly. 'You are so lovely, you take my breath away every time I see you.'

'Lovely . . .' Again she croaked. 'I'm sixty-two, for heaven's sake.'

He shrugged dismissively. 'Lines, a few grey hairs . . .'

'A few rolls of fat.'

'I can't bear rake-thin women and, frankly, young ones terrify me.' He grinned.'I'm not exactly a pop idol myself. But that's not the point. You are gentle and kind. That business with Polly and her mother. . . . Yes, she told me about that. You coped so well. Marnie, you have the sense of humour I like. You are fun to be with, yet you have a quality of stillness that is peaceful and refreshing. You can be stubborn,' and he gestured towards her stick, 'but you are so brave. I can't imagine how not to love you and I'd like to spend the rest of my life – however much there is of it – with you.'

Marnie shook her head.'Are you sure you are not just saying this because you are lonely?' she suggested gently.

'Or that I'm looking for my own carer? That is a hazard anyone accepts at any stage of their lives, as I've proved. Or perhaps you mean, am I on the rebound from Alison? No, my dear. I loved Alison very much, you know. Once we were very happy. I mean, I was very happy, and I think – hope – she was equally so. But the woman Alison became was not the woman I married all those years ago. Long before we knew about the

221

dementia, she changed. Of course, now we know that it was the beginning of a long illness, but it was hard, seeing her become more and more introverted, less able to connect, either with me or with her children. Especially not with the outside world. Oh, I know we marry for better and for worse, but for it to last for such a long time . . .'

'It must have been very hard.'

'No,' he protested.'I don't want to you think that I stopped loving Alison immediately. I certainly didn't. What I'm trying to make you understand is that from being a passionately loving husband I became a carer. That alters your perspective. I cared for her. I cared deeply, but I was no longer in love with her. Does that make sense?'

'Of course it does. I understand completely. I also know that you've been a very lonely man for many years.'

'And now I've found you,' he said simply.

Marnie thought back to that time when Felix had left her. His decision to go had come as a total shock. Yet for all that she had had her children by her side (an obstreperous Chloë), a husband and a few friends (though not really anyone in whom she had ever confided), she had been a lonely woman. Later, once Felix and Chloë had gone, she had discovered that living with Jack and Gemma had not made for so much change. There were the grandchildren, but you couldn't confide in young children. It wasn't easy to confide in a son, or a daughter-in-law. And Gemma was a little too defensive of her position to become a confidante.

What would it be like to have a husband to love and to cher-ish, to love and to cherish her?

'It's too soon, Luke,' she repeated weakly.

'So, are you sending me away?'

'No!'

He grinned delightedly.'That came out very definitely, didn't it?'

'I suppose it did,' she agreed. Then she smiled.'It's far too soon to make definite plans to spend the rest of our lives together,' she said firmly.'We have a lot more finding out about each other to do first. We also have to reconcile our families to the idea.'

'Pooh to the families,' he declared.'What do you have in mind?' he asked wickedly.

'I might leave you to make the suggestions,' she answered meekly.'But I do have one. I told Jack that I would visit them in the New Year. Why don't we take an extended holiday? The timing would be fine because Chloë's baby will have arrived and Polly will only be in the middle of her pregnancy. We'll both be in need of a holiday by then and a few weeks together will give us the opportunity to discover whether we like the idea of prolonging the relationship.'

'So we do have a relationship?'

'Yes, Luke, my dear. I like the idea that we have something special between us, very much indeed.'

'Not quite enough to say that you love me?' he said wistfully.

Her heart lurched.'Luke, I never thought I'd feel this way again. Not after Felix. That was so horribly shocking. I can't tell you. Oh, I know we'd not been lovers for some years. I think I'd just accepted that that was what happened to people who'd been married for a long time. I had no idea that Felix felt differently. So although I was lonely when Felix left, I certainly had no intention of ever marrying again. Of sharing my life with another man. It all seemed too terrifying, too risky.'

'I can understand about the risk.'

'Maybe that's not what I mean, either. It's about being able to open up my life to another person.'

She held out her hand and he took it in both of his. 'I'd like to take things slowly.'

'But one day you might consider moving in with me?'

She thought of her beautiful old cottage that she had lovingly restored. She thought of the inconvenient stairs – and the old apple tree that might not recover from the storm damage. She weighed all this against the newish bungalow and the companionship of the man holding her hand, whose presence made her feel safe and whose appearance when he arrived made her feel young, and foolish, and romantically inclined.

223

'I think I'm going to have such fun finding out,' she said, with a sweet smile.

So this time he kissed her.

Vera Crawford had decided that she could not be the only one left in the village not to give Marnie Edgerton the support she still plainly required until she was properly on her feet again. Accordingly, she had made one of her fish pies for which she was well known and she was bringing it round to put in Marnie's fridge.

While she was unable to move out of her wheelchair, Marnie had left her front door open. Vera gave it a push, but this time it did not yield. Vera thought she would look through the window to see if Marnie were there or if she were still at the hospital having her plaster off.

She froze with her knuckles almost in contact with the glass.

Well, well, she thought. Now that really would make for an entertaining bit of gossip in the shop, Luke Firmer and Marnie Edgerton in each other's arms in the middle of the afternoon.

She put the fish pie on the doorstep and walked back down the garden path. But the smile on her face held not the least hint of malice, this time it was one of indulgence.